VIRAG
MODERN CL

Zora Neale Hurston (1891–1960) was born in Alabama but grew up in Eatonville, Florida, the first incorporated black town in America. At the age of twenty-six, claiming to be ten years younger – a fiction she maintained throughout her life – she got herself a high school education and went on to Howard University. Winning a scholarship to Barnard College in New York she discovered 'Harlem City' as she called it, and at the height of the Harlem Renaissance Zora Neale Hurston was the pre-eminent black woman writer in the United States. Her stories appeared in major magazines, she consulted on Hollywood screenplays, and she penned four novels, two books of folklore, an autobiography, essays, short stories and plays. By the late 1950s, however, Hurston was living in obscurity, working as a maid in a Florida hotel, and though she enjoyed some success during her lifetime, her greatest acclaim came posthumously. She is now recognised as one of the most influential African-American writers of the twentieth century. Nearly every black woman writer of significance – including Maya Angelou, Toni Morrison and Alice Walker – acknowledges Zora Neale Hurston as their literary foremother.

Zora Neale Hurston

THEIR EYES WERE WATCHING GOD

Introduced by Zadie Smith
and with an Afterword by
Sherley Anne Williams

VIRAGO

This edition published by Virago Press in 2018

Published by Virago Press in 1986
First published by J.B. Lippincott Company in 1937

This edition published by arrangement with Harper & Row Publishers, Inc., New York

1 3 5 7 9 10 8 6 4 2

A CIP catalogue record for this book
is available from the British Library.

ISBN 978-0-349-01033-5

Typeset in Goudy by M Rules
Printed and bound in Great Britain by
Clays Ltd, St Ives plc

Papers used by Virago are from well-managed forests
and other responsible sources.

MIX
Paper from
responsible sources
FSC
www.fsc.org FSC® C104740

Virago Press
An imprint of
Little, Brown Book Group
Carmelite House
50 Victoria Embankment
London EC4Y 0DZ

An Hachette UK Company
www.hachette.co.uk

www.virago.co.uk

To
Henry Allen Moe

INTRODUCTION

When I was fourteen I was given *Their Eyes Were Watching God* by my mother. I was reluctant to read it. I knew what she meant by giving it to me and I resented the inference. In the same spirit she had introduced me to *Wide Sargasso Sea* and *The Bluest Eye*, and I had not liked either of them (better to say, I had not *allowed* myself to like either of them). I preferred my own freely chosen, heterogeneous reading list. I flattered myself I ranged widely in my reading, never choosing books for genetic or socio-cultural reasons. Spotting *Their Eyes Were Watching God* unopened on my bedside table, my mother persisted:

'But you'll like it.'

'Why, because she's *black?*'

'No – because it's really good writing.'

I had my own ideas of 'good writing'. It was a category that did not include aphoristic or overtly 'lyrical' language, mythic imagery, accurately rendered 'folk speech' or the love tribulations of women. My literary defences were up in preparation for *Their Eyes Were Watching God*. Then I read the first page:

Ships at a distance have every man's wish on board. For some they come in with the tide. For others they sail forever on the horizon, never out of sight, never landing until the Watcher turns his eyes away in resignation, his dreams mocked to death by Time. That is the life of men.

Now, women forget all those things they don't want to remember, and remember everything they don't want to forget. The dream is the truth. Then they act and do things accordingly.

It was an aphorism, yet it had me pinned to the ground, unable to deny its strength. It capitalised Time (I was against the capitalisation of abstract nouns), but still I found myself melancholy for these nameless men and their inevitable losses. The second part, about women, struck home. It remains as accurate a description of my mother and me as I have ever read: *Then they act and do things accordingly*. Well, all right then. I relaxed in my chair a little and lay down my pencil. I inhaled that book. Three hours later I was finished and crying a lot, for reasons that both were, and were not, to do with the tragic finale.

I lost many literary battles the day I read *Their Eyes Were Watching God*. I had to concede that occasionally aphorisms have their power. I had to give up the idea that Keats had a monopoly on the lyrical:

She was stretched on her back beneath the pear tree soaking in the alto chant of the visiting bees, the gold of the sun and the panting breath of the breeze when the inaudible voice of it all came to her. She saw a dust-nearing bee sink into the sanctum of a bloom; the thousand sister-calyxes arch to meet the love embrace and the ecstatic shiver of the tree from root to tiniest branch creaming in every blossom and frothing with delight. So this was a marriage! She had been summoned to behold a revelation. Then Janie felt a pain remorseless sweet that left her limp and languid.[1]

I had to admit that mythic language is startling when it's good:

Death, that strange being with the huge square toes who lived way in the West. The great one who lived in the straight house like a platform without sides to it, and without a roof. What need has Death for a cover, and what winds can blow against him?

My resistance to dialogue (encouraged by Nabokov, whom I idolised) struggled and then tumbled before Hurston's ear for black colloquial speech. In the mouths of unlettered people she finds the bliss of quotidian metaphor:

'If God don't think no mo' 'bout 'em than Ah do, they's a lost ball in de high grass.'

Of wisdom lightly worn:

[1] But I still resist 'limp and languid'.

'To my thinkin' mourning oughtn't tuh last no longer'n grief.'

Her conversations reveal individual personalities, accurately, swiftly, as if they had no author at all:

'Where y'all come from in sich uh big haste?' Lee Coker asked.

'Middle Georgy,' Starks answered briskly. 'Joe Starks is mah name, from in and through Georgy.'

'You and yo' daughter goin' tuh join wid us in fellowship?' the other reclining figure asked. 'Mighty glad to have yuh. Hicks is the name. Guv'nor Amos Hicks from Buford, South Carolina. Free, single, disengaged.'

'I god, Ah ain't nowhere near old enough to have no grown daughter. This here is mah wife.'

Hicks sank back and lost interest at once.

'Where is de Mayor?' Starks persisted. 'Ah wants tuh talk wid *him*.'

'Youse uh mite too previous for dat,' Coker told him. 'Us ain't got none yit.'

Above all, I had to let go of my objection to the love tribulations of women. The story of Janie's progress through three marriages confronts the reader with the significant idea that the choice one makes between partners, between one man and another (or one woman and another) stretches far beyond romance. It is, in the end, the choice between values, possibilities, futures, hopes, arguments (shared concepts that fit the world as you experience it), languages (shared words that fit the world as you believe it to be) and lives. A world you share with Logan Killicks is evidently not the same world you will share with Vergible 'Tea Cake' Woods. In these two discrete worlds, you will not even think the same way; a mind trapped with Logan is freed with Tea Cake. But how can we talk of freedoms? In practical terms, a black woman in turn-of-the-century America, a woman like Janie, or like Hurston herself, had approximately the same civil liberties as a farm animal: 'De nigger woman is de mule uh de world.' So goes Janie's grandmother's famous line – it hurt my pride to read it. It hurts Janie, too; she rejects the realpolitik of her grandmother, embarking on an existential revenge which is of the imagination and impossible to restrict:

She knew that God tore down the old world every evening and built a new one by sun-up. It was wonderful to see it take form with the sun and emerge from the gray dust of its making. The familiar people and things had failed her so she hung over the gate and looked up the road towards way off.

That part of Janie that is looking for someone (or something) that 'spoke for far horizon' has its proud ancestors in Elizabeth Bennet, in Dorothea Brooke, in Jane Eyre, even – in a very debased form – in Emma Bovary. Since the beginning of fiction concerning the love tribulations of women (which is to say, since the beginning of fiction) the 'romantic quest' aspect of these fictions has been too often casually ridiculed:

xi

not long ago I sat down to dinner with an American woman who told me how disappointed she had been to finally read *Middlemarch* and find that it was, 'Just this long, whiny, trawling search for a man!' Those who read *Middlemarch* in that way will find little in *Their Eyes Were Watching God* to please them. It's about a girl who takes some time to find the man she really loves. It is about the discovery of self in and through another. It suggests that even the dark and terrible banality of racism can recede to a vanishing point when you understand, and are understood by, another human being. Goddamnit if it doesn't claim that love sets you free. These days 'self-actualisation' is the aim, and if you can't do it alone you are admitting a weakness. The potential rapture of human relationships to which Hurston gives unabashed expression, the profound 'self-crushing love' that Janie feels for Tea Cake, may, I suppose, look like the dull finale of a 'long, whiny, trawling search for a man'. For Tea Cake and Janie, though, the choice of each other is experienced not as desperation, but as discovery, and the need felt on both sides causes them joy, not shame. That Tea Cake would not be *our* choice, that we disapprove of him often, and despair of him occasionally, only lends power to the portrait. He seems to act with freedom, and Janie chooses him freely. We have no power; we only watch. Despite the novel's fairytale structure (as far as husbands go, third time's the charm), it is not a novel of wish-fulfilment, least of all the fulfilment of *our* wishes.[2] It is

2 Again, *Middlemarch* is an interesting comparison. Readers often prefer Lydgate and are disappointed at Dorothea's choice of Ladislaw.

odd to diagnose weakness where lovers themselves do not feel it.

After that first reading of the novel, I wept, and not only for Tea Cake, and not simply for the perfection of the writing, nor even the real loss I felt upon leaving the world contained in its pages. It meant something more than all that to me, something I could not, or would not, articulate. Later, I took it to the dinner table, still holding on to it, as we do sometimes with books we are not quite ready to relinquish.

'So?' my mother asked.

I told her it was basically sound.

At fourteen, I did Zora Neale Hurston a serious critical disservice. I feared my 'extra-literary' feelings for her. I wanted to be an objective aesthete and not a sentimental fool. I disliked the idea of 'identifying' with the fiction I read: I wanted to like Hurston because she represented 'good writing', not because she represented me. In the seventeen years since, Zora Neale Hurston has gone from being a well-kept, well-loved secret amongst black women of my mother's generation, to an entire literary industry – biographies[3] and films and Oprah and African-American literature departments all pay homage to her life[4] and work as avatars of black woman-ness. In the process, a different kind of critical disservice is being done to her; an overcompensation in the opposite direction. In *Their*

3 The (very good) biography is *Wrapped in Rainbows: The Life of Zora Neale Hurston* by Valerie Boyd. Also very good is *Zora Neale Hurston: A Life in Letters*, collected and edited by Carla Kaplan.
4 *Dust Tracks on a Road* is Hurston's autobiography.

Eyes Were Watching God, Janie is depressed by Joe Starks's determination to idolise her: he intends to put her on a lonely pedestal before the whole town and establish a symbol (The Mayor's Wife) in place of the woman she is. Something similar has been done to Hurston herself. She is like Janie, sat on her porch-pedestal ('Ah done nearly languished tuh death up dere'), far from the people and things she really cared about, representing only the ideas and beliefs of her admirers, distorted by their gaze. In the space of one volume of collected essays, we find a critic arguing that the negative criticism of Hurston's work represents an 'intellectual lynching' by black men, white men and white women; a critic dismissing Hurston's final work with the sentence, '*Seraph on the Suwanee* is not even about black people, which is no crime, but *is* about white people who are bores, which is'; and another explaining the 'one great flaw' in *Their Eyes Were Watching God*: Hurston's 'curious insistence' on having her main character's tale told in the omniscient third person instead of allowing Janie her 'voice outright'. We are in a critical world of some banality here, one in which most of our nineteenth-century heroines would be judged oppressed creatures, cruelly deprived of the therapeutic first-person voice. It is also a world in which what is called the 'Black Female Literary tradition' is beyond reproach:

Black women writers have consistently rejected the falsification of their Black female experience, thereby avoiding the negative stereotypes such falsification has often created in the white American female and Black male literary traditions. Unlike many of their Black male and white female peers, Black women writers have usually refused to dispense with whatever was clearly Black and/or female in their sensibilities in an effort to achieve the mythical 'neutral' voice of universal art.[5]

Gratifying as it would be to agree that black women writers 'have consistently rejected the falsification' of their experience, the honest reader knows that this is simply not the case. In place of negative falsification, we have nurtured, in the past thirty years, a new fetishisation. Black female protagonists are now too often unerringly strong and soulful; they are sexually voracious and unafraid; they take the unreal forms of earth mothers, African queens, divas, spirits of history; they process grandly through novels thick with a breed of greeting-card lyricism. They have little of the complexity, the flaws and uncertainties, depth and beauty of Janie Crawford and the novel she springs from. They are pressed into service as role models to patch over our psychic wounds; they are perfect[6]; they overcompensate. The truth is, black women writers, while writing many wonderful things[7], have been no more or less successful at avoiding the falsification of human

5 All the critical voices quoted above can be found in *Zora Neale Hurston's* Their Eyes Were Watching God: *Modern Critical Interpretations*, ed. Harold Bloom.
6 Hurston, by contrast, wanted her writing to demonstrate the fact that 'Negroes are no better nor no worse, and at times as boring as everybody else'.
7 Not least of which is Alice Walker's original introduction to *Their Eyes Were Watching God*. By championing the book she rescued Hurston from forty years of obscurity.

experience than any other group of writers. It is not the Black Female Literary Tradition that makes Hurston great. It is Hurston herself. Zora Neale Hurston – capable of expressing human vulnerability as well as its strength, lyrical without sentiment, romantic and yet rigorous, and one of the few truly eloquent writers of sex – is as exceptional amongst black women writers as Tolstoy is amongst white male writers.[8]

It is, however, true that Hurston rejected the 'neutral universal' for her novels – she wrote unapologetically in the black-inflected dialect in which she was raised. It took bravery to do that: the result was hostility and disinterest. In 1937, black readers were embarrassed by the unlettered nature of the dialogue and white readers preferred the exoticism of her anthropological writings. Who wanted to read about the poor Negroes one saw on the corner every day? Hurston's biographers make clear that no matter what positive spin she put on it, her life was horribly difficult: she finished life working as a cleaner, and died in obscurity. It is understandable that her reclaiming should be an emotive and personal journey for black readers and black critics. But still, one wants to make a neutral and solid case for her greatness, to say something more substantial than: 'She is my sister and I love her.' As a reader, I want to claim fellowship with 'good writing' without limits; to be able to say that Hurston is my sister and Baldwin is my brother, and so is Kafka my brother, and Nabokov, and Woolf my sister, and Eliot and Ozick. Like all readers, I want my

8 A footnote for the writers in the audience: *Their Eyes Were Watching God* was written in seven weeks.

limits to be drawn by my own sensibilities, not by my melanin count. These forms of criticism that make black women the privileged readers of a black woman writer go against Hurston's own grain. She saw things otherwise: 'When I set my hat at a certain angle and saunter down Seventh Avenue . . . the cosmic Zora emerges . . . How *can* anybody deny themselves the pleasure of my company? It's beyond me!'

This is exactly right. No one should deny themselves the pleasure of Zora – of whatever colour or background or gender. She's too delightful not to be shared. We all deserve to savour her neologisms ('sankled', 'monstropolous', 'rawbony') or to read of the effects of a bad marriage, sketched with tragic accuracy:

The years took all the fight out of Janie's face. For a while she thought it was gone from her soul. No matter what Jody did, she said nothing. She had learned how to talk some and leave some. She was a rut in the road. Plenty of life beneath the surface but it was kept beaten down by the wheels. Sometimes she stuck out into the future, imagining her life different from what it was. But mostly she lived between her hat and her heels, with her emotional disturbances like shade patterns in the woods – come and gone with the sun. She got nothing from Jody except what money could buy, and she was giving away what she didn't value.

The visual imagination on display in *Their Eyes Were Watching God* shares its clarity and iconicity with Christian story-telling – many scenes in the novel put one in mind of the bold-stroke illustrations in a children's bible: young Janie staring at a photograph, not understanding that the black girl in the crowd is her; Joe Starks atop a dead mule's distended belly, giving a speech; Tea Cake bitten high on his cheekbone by that rabid dog. I watched the TV footage of Hurricane Katrina with a strong sense of déjà vu, thinking of Hurston's flood rather than Noah's: 'Not the dead of sick and ailing with friends at the pillow and the feet . . . [but] the sodden and the bloated; the sudden dead, their eyes flung wide open in judgment . . .'

Above all, Hurston is essential universal reading because she is neither self-conscious nor restricted. Raised in the real Eatonville, Florida, an all-black town, this unique experience went some way to making Hurston the writer she was. She grew up a fully human being, unaware that she was meant to consider herself a minority, an other, an exotic, or something depleted in rights, talents, desires and expectations. As an adult, away from Eatonville, she found the world was determined to do its best to remind her of her supposed inferiority, but Hurston was already made, and the metaphysical confidence she claimed for her life ('I am not tragically colored') is present, with equal, refreshing force, in her fiction. She liked to yell 'Culllaaaah Struck!'[9] when she entered a fancy party – almost everybody was. But it is of fundamental significance to her writing that Hurston herself was not. 'Blackness', as she understood it and wrote about it, is as natural and inevitable

9 See chapter 16 for a sad portrayal of a truly colour-struck lady, Mrs Turner.

and complete to her as, say, 'Frenchness' is to Flaubert. It is also as complicated, as full of blessings and curses. One can be no more removed from it than from one's arm, but it is no more the total measure of one's being than an arm is. It begins a million of your songs – it ends none of them.

But still after all that there is something else to say – and the 'neutral universal' of literary criticism pens me in and makes it difficult. To write critically in English, even to write a little introduction, is to aspire to neutrality, to the high style of, say, Lionel Trilling or Edmund Wilson. In the high style, one's loves never seem partial or personal, or even like 'loves', because white novelists are not white novelists but simply 'novelists', and white characters are not white characters but simply 'human', and criticism of both is not partial or personal but a matter of aesthetics. Such critics will always sound like the neutral universal, and the black women who have championed *Their Eyes Were Watching God* in the past, and the one doing so now, will seem like black women talking about a black book. When I began this introduction, it felt important to distance myself from that idea. By doing so, I misrepresent a vital aspect of my response to this book, one that is entirely personal, as any response to a novel shall be. Fact is, I *am* a black woman[10], and a slither of this book goes straight in to my soul, I suspect, for that reason. And though it is, to me, a vulgar absurdity to say, 'Unless you are a black woman, you will never fully comprehend this novel', it is also disingenuous

10 I think this was the point my mother was trying to make.

to claim that many black women do not respond to this book in a particularly powerful manner that would seem 'extra-literary'. Those aspects of *Their Eyes Were Watching God* that plumb so profoundly the ancient build-up of cultural residue that is (for convenience sake) called 'Blackness'[11] are the parts that my own 'Blackness', as far as it goes, cannot help but respond to personally. At fourteen I couldn't find words (or words I liked) for the marvellous feeling of recognition that came with these characters who had my hair, my eyes, my skin, even the ancestors of the rhythm of my speech.[12] These forms of identification are so natural to white readers – (Of course Rabbit Angstrom is like me! Of course Madame Bovary is like me!) – that they believe themselves above personal identification, or at least that they are identifying only at the highest, metaphysical levels (His soul is like my soul. He is human; I am human). White readers often believe they are colour-blind.[13] I always thought I was a colour-blind reader – until I read this novel, and that ultimate cliché of black life that is inscribed in the word 'soulful' took on new weight and sense for me. But what does *soulful* even mean? The dictionary has it this way: 'expressing or appearing to express deep and often sorrowful feeling.' The culturally black meaning adds

11 As Kafka's *The Trial* plumbs that ancient build-up of cultural residue that is called 'Jewishness'.

12 Down on the muck, Janie and Tea Cake befriend the 'Saws', workers from the Caribbean.

13 Until they read books featuring non-white characters. I once overheard a young white man at a book festival say to his friend, 'Have you read the new Kureishi? Same old thing – loads of Indian people.' To which you want to reply, 'Have you read the new Franzen? Same old thing – loads of white people.'

several more shades of colour. First shade: *soulfulness* is sorrowful feeling transformed into something beautiful, creative and self-renewing, and – as it reaches a pitch – ecstatic. It is an alchemy of pain. In *Their Eyes Were Watching God*, when the townsfolk sing for the death of the mule, this is an example of *soulfulness*. Another shade: to be soulful is to follow and *fall in line* with a feeling, to go where it takes you and not to go against its grain.[14] When young Janie takes her lead from the blossoming tree and sits on her gate-post to kiss a passing boy, this is an example of *soulfulness*. A final shade: the word *soulful*, like its Jewish cousin, schmaltz[15], has its roots in the digestive tract. 'Soul food' is simple, flavoursome, hearty, unfussy, with spice. When Janie puts on her overalls and joyfully goes to work in the muck with Tea Cake, this is an example of *soulfulness*.[16]

This is a beautiful novel about soulfulness. That it should be so is a tribute to Hurston's skill. She makes 'culture' – that slow and particular[17] and artificial accretion of habit and circumstance – seem as natural and organic and beautiful as the sunrise. She makes 'black woman-ness' appear a real, tangible

14 At its most common and banal: catching a beat, following a rhythm.

15 In the *Oxford English Dictionary*: '**Schmaltz** n. informal. excessive sentimentality, esp. in music or movies. ORIGIN 1930s: from Yiddish *schmaltz*, from German *Schmalz* "dripping, lard."'

16 Of course, there are few things less soulful than attempting to define soulfulness.

17 In literary terms, we know that there is a tipping point in which the cultural particular – while becoming no less culturally particular – is accepted by readers as the neutral universal. The previously 'Jewish fiction' of Phillip Roth is now 'fiction'. We have moved from the particular complaints of Portnoy to the universal claims of Everyman.

quality, an essence I can almost believe I share, however improbably, with millions of complex individuals across centuries and continents and languages and religions . . .

Almost – but not quite. Better to say, when I'm reading this book, I believe it, with my whole soul. It allows me to say things I wouldn't normally. Things like: *She is my sister and I love her.*

Zadie Smith
Rome, June 2007

I

Ships at a distance have every man's wish on board. For some they come in with the tide. For others they sail forever on the horizon, never out of sight, never landing until the Watcher turns his eyes away in resignation, his dreams mocked to death by Time. That is the life of men.

Now, women forget all those things they don't want to remember, and remember everything they don't want to forget. The dream is the truth. Then they act and do things accordingly.

So the beginning of this was a woman and she had come back from burying the dead. Not the dead of sick and ailing with friends at the pillow and the feet. She had come back from the sodden and the bloated; the sudden dead, their eyes flung wide open in judgment.

The people all saw her come because it was sundown. The sun was gone, but he had left his footprints in the sky. It was the time for sitting on porches beside the road. It was the time to hear things and talk. These sitters had been tongueless, earless, eyeless conveniences all day long. Mules and other brutes had occupied their skins. But now, the sun and the bossman were gone, so the skins felt powerful and human. They became lords of sounds and lesser things. They passed nations through their mouths. They sat in judgment.

Seeing the woman as she was made them remember the envy they had stored up from other times. So they chewed up the back parts of their minds and swallowed with relish. They made burning statements with questions, and killing tools out of laughs. It was mass cruelty. A mood come alive. Words walking without masters; walking altogether like harmony in a song.

'What she doin' coming back here in dem overhalls? Can't she find no dress to put on?— Where's dat blue satin dress she left here in?— Where all dat money her husband took and died and left her?— What dat ole forty year ole 'oman doin' wid her hair swingin' down her back lak some young gal?— Where she left dat young lad of a boy she went off here wid?— Thought she was going to marry?— Where he left *her*?— What he done wid all her money?— Betcha he off wid some gal so young she ain't even got no hairs – why she don't stay in her class?—'

When she got to where they were she turned her face on the bander log and spoke. They scrambled a noisy 'good evenin'' and left their mouths setting open and their ears full of hope. Her speech was pleasant enough, but she kept walking straight on to her gate. The porch couldn't talk for looking.

The men noticed her firm buttocks like she had grape fruits

in her hip pockets; the great rope of black hair swinging to her waist and unraveling in the wind like a plume; then her pugnacious breasts trying to bore holes in her shirt. They, the men, were saving with the mind what they lost with the eye. The women took the faded shirt and muddy overalls and laid them away for remembrance. It was a weapon against her strength and if it turned out of no significance, still it was a hope that she might fall to their level some day.

But nobody moved, nobody spoke, nobody even thought to swallow spit until after her gate slammed behind her.

Pearl Stone opened her mouth and laughed real hard because she didn't know what else to do. She fell all over Mrs Sumpkins while she laughed. Mrs Sumpkins snorted violently and sucked her teeth.

'Humph! Y'all let her worry yuh. You ain't like me. Ah ain't got her to study 'bout. If she ain't got manners enough to stop and let folks know how she been makin' out, let her g'wan!'

'She ain't even worth talkin' after,' Lulu Moss drawled through her nose. 'She sits high, but she looks low. Dat's what Ah say 'bout dese ole women runnin' after young boys.'

Pheoby Watson hitched her rocking chair forward before she spoke. 'Well, nobody don't know if it's anything to tell or not. Me, Ah'm her best friend, and *Ah* don't know.'

'Maybe us don't know into things lak you do, but we all know how she went 'way from here and us sho seen her come back. 'Tain't no use in your tryin' to cloak no ole woman lak Janie Starks, Pheoby, friend or no friend.'

'At dat she ain't so ole as some of y'all dat's talking.'

'She's way past forty to my knowledge, Pheoby.'

'No more'n forty at de outside.'

'She's 'way too old for a boy like Tea Cake.'

'Tea Cake ain't been no boy for some time. He's round thirty his ownself.'

'Don't keer what it was, she could stop and say a few words with us. She act like we done done something to her,' Pearl Stone complained. 'She de one been doin' wrong.'

'You mean, you mad 'cause she didn't stop and tell us all her business. Anyhow, what you ever know her to do so bad as y'all make out? The worst thing Ah ever knowed her to do was taking a few years offa her age and dat ain't never harmed nobody. Y'all makes me tired. De way you talkin' you'd think de folks in dis town didn't do nothin' in de bed 'cept praise de Lawd. You have to 'scuse me, 'cause Ah'm bound to go take her some supper.' Pheoby stood up sharply.

'Don't mind us,' Lulu smiled, 'just go right ahead, us can mind yo' house for you till you git back. Mah supper is done. You bettah go see how she feel. You kin let de rest of us know.'

'Lawd,' Pearl agreed, 'Ah done scorched-up dat lil meat and bread too long to talk about. Ah kin stay 'way from home long as Ah please. Mah husband ain't fussy.'

'Oh, er, Pheoby, if youse ready to go, Ah could walk over dere wid you,' Mrs Sumpkins volunteered. 'It's sort of duskin' down dark. De booger man might ketch yuh.'

'Naw, Ah thank yuh. Nothin' couldn't ketch me dese few steps Ah'm goin'. Anyhow mah husband tell me say no first class booger would have me. If she got anything to tell yuh, you'll hear it.'

Pheoby hurried on off with a covered bowl in her hands.

4

She left the porch pelting her back with unasked questions. They hoped the answers were cruel and strange. When she arrived at the place, Pheoby Watson didn't go in by the front gate and down the palm walk to the front door. She walked around the fence corner and went in the intimate gate with her heaping plate of mulatto rice. Janie must be round that side.

She found her sitting on the steps of the back porch with the lamps all filled and the chimneys cleaned.

'Hello, Janie, how you comin'?'

'Aw, pretty good, Ah'm tryin' to soak some uh de tiredness and de dirt outa mah feet.' She laughed a little.

'Ah see you is. Gal, you sho looks *good*. You looks like youse yo' own daughter.' They both laughed. 'Even wid dem over-halls on, you shows yo' womanhood.'

'G'wan! G'wan! You must think Ah brought yuh somethin'. When Ah ain't brought home a thing but mahself.'

'Dat's a gracious plenty. Yo' friends wouldn't want nothin' better.'

'Ah takes dat flattery offa you, Pheoby, 'cause Ah know it's from de heart.' Janie extended her hand. 'Good Lawd, Pheoby! ain't you never goin' tuh gimme dat lil rations you brought me? Ah ain't had a thing on mah stomach today exceptin' mah hand.' They both laughed easily. 'Give it here and have a seat.'

'Ah knowed you'd be hongry. No time to be huntin' stove wood after dark. Mah mulatto rice ain't so good dis time. Not enough bacon grease, but Ah reckon it'll kill hongry.'

'Ah'll tell you in a minute,' Janie said, lifting the cover.

'Gal, it's *too* good! you switches a mean fanny round in a kitchen.'

'Aw, dat ain't much to eat, Janie. But Ah'm liable to have something sho nuff good tomorrow, 'cause you done come.'

Janie ate heartily and said nothing. The varicolored cloud dust that the sun had stirred up in the sky was settling by slow degrees.

'Here, Pheoby, take yo' ole plate. Ah ain't got a bit of use for a empty dish. Dat grub sho come in handy.'

Pheoby laughed at her friend's rough joke. 'Youse just as crazy as you ever was.'

'Hand me dat wash-rag on dat chair by you, honey. Lemme scrub mah feet.' She took the cloth and rubbed vigorously. Laughter came to her from the big road.

'Well, Ah see Mouth-Almighty is still sittin' in de same place. And Ah reckon they got *me* up in they mouth now.'

'Yes indeed. You know if you pass some people and don't speak tuh suit 'em dey got tuh go way back in yo' life and see whut you ever done. They know mo' 'bout yuh than you do yo' self. An envious heart makes a treacherous ear. They done "heard" 'bout you just what they hope done happened.'

'If God don't think no mo' 'bout 'em then Ah do, they's a lost ball in de high grass.'

'Ah hears what they say 'cause they just will collect round mah porch 'cause it's on de big road. Mah husband git so sick of 'em sometime he makes 'em all git for home.'

'Sam is right too. They just wearin' out yo' sittin' chairs.'

'Yeah, Sam say most of 'em goes to church so they'll be sure to rise in Judgment. Dat's de day dat every secret is s'posed to be made known. They wants to be there and hear it *all*.'

'Sam is *too* crazy! You can't stop laughin' when youse round him.'

'Uuh hunh. He says he aims to be there hisself so he can find out who stole his corn-cob pipe.'

'Pheoby, dat Sam of your'n just won't quit! Crazy thing!'

'Most of dese zigaboos is so het up over yo' business till they liable to hurry theyself to Judgment to find out about you if they don't soon know. You better make haste and tell 'em 'bout you and Tea Cake gittin' married, and if he taken all yo' money and went off wid some young gal, and where at he is now and where at is all yo' clothes dat you got to come back here in overhalls.'

'Ah don't mean to bother wid tellin' 'em nothin', Pheoby. 'Tain't worth de trouble. You can tell 'em what Ah say if you wants to. Dat's just de same as me 'cause mah tongue is in mah friend's mouf.'

'If you so desire Ah'll tell 'em what you tell me to tell 'em.'

'To start off wid, people like dem wastes up too much time puttin' they mouf on things they don't know nothin' about. Now they got to look into me loving Tea Cake and see whether it was done right or not! They don't know if life is a mess of corn-meal dumplings, and if love is a bed-quilt!'

'So long as they get a name to gnaw on they don't care whose it is, and what about, 'specially if they can make it sound like evil.'

'If they wants to see and know, why they don't come kiss and be kissed? Ah could then sit down and tell 'em things. Ah been a delegate to de big 'ssociation of life. Yessuh! De Grand Lodge, de big convention of livin' is just where Ah been dis year and a half y'all ain't seen me.'

They sat there in the fresh young darkness close together. Pheoby eager to feel and do through Janie, but hating to show her zest for fear it might be thought mere curiosity. Janie full of that oldest human longing – self revelation. Pheoby held her tongue for a long time, but she couldn't help moving her feet. So Janie spoke.

'They don't need to worry about me and my overhalls long as Ah still got nine hundred dollars in de bank. Tea Cake got me into wearing 'em – following behind him. Tea Cake ain't wasted up no money of mine, and he ain't left me for no young gal, neither. He give me every consolation in de world. He'd tell 'em so too, if he was here. If he wasn't gone.'

Pheoby dilated all over with eagerness, 'Tea Cake gone?'

'Yeah, Pheoby, Tea Cake is gone. And dat's de only reason you see me back here – cause Ah ain't got nothing to make me happy no more where Ah was at. Down in the Everglades there, down on the muck.'

'It's hard for me to understand what you mean, de way you tell it. And then again Ah'm hard of understandin' at times.'

'Naw, 'tain't nothin' lak you might think. So 'tain't no use in me telling you somethin' unless Ah give you de understandin' to go 'long wid it. Unless you see de fur, a mink skin ain't no different from a coon hide. Looka heah, Pheoby, is Sam waitin' on you for his supper?'

'It's all ready and waitin'. If he ain't got sense enough to eat it, dat's his hard luck.'

'Well then, we can set right where we is and talk. Ah got the house all opened up to let dis breeze get a little catchin'.

'Pheoby, we been kissin'-friends for twenty years, so Ah depend on you for a good thought. And Ah'm talking to you from dat standpoint.'

Time makes everything old so the kissing, young darkness became a monstropolous old thing while Janie talked.

2

Janie saw her life like a great tree in leaf with the things suffered, things enjoyed, things done and undone. Dawn and doom was in the branches.

'Ah know exactly what Ah got to tell yuh, but it's hard to know where to start at.

'Ah ain't never seen mah papa. And Ah didn't know 'im if Ah did. Mah mama neither. She was gone from round dere long before Ah wuz big enough tuh know. Mah grandma raised me. Mah grandma and de white folks she worked wid. She had a house out in de back-yard and dat's where Ah wuz born. They was quality white folks up dere in West Florida. Named Washburn. She had four gran'chillun on de place and all of us played together and dat's how come Ah never called mah Grandma nothin' but Nanny, 'cause dat's what everybody on de place called her. Nanny used to ketch us in our devilment and lick every youngun on de place and Mis' Washburn did de same. Ah reckon dey never hit us ah lick amiss 'cause dem three boys and us two girls wuz pretty aggravatin', Ah speck.

'Ah was wid dem white chillun so much till Ah didn't know Ah wuzn't white till Ah was round six years old. Wouldn't have found it out then, but a man come long takin' pictures and without askin' anybody, Shelby, dat was de oldest boy, he told him to take us. Round a week later de man brought de picture for Mis' Washburn to see and pay him which she did, then give us all a good lickin'.

'So when we looked at de picture and everybody got pointed out there wasn't nobody left except a real dark little girl with long hair standing by Eleanor. Dat's where Ah wuz s'posed to be, but Ah couldn't recognize dat dark chile as me. So Ah ast, "where is me? Ah don't see me."

'Everybody laughed, even Mr Washburn. Miss Nellie, de Mama of de chillun who come back home after her husband dead, she pointed to de dark one and said, "Dat's you, Alphabet, don't you know yo' ownself?"

'Dey all useter call me Alphabet 'cause so many people had done named me different names. Ah looked at de picture a long time and seen it was mah dress and mah hair so Ah said:

'"Aw, aw! Ah'm colored!"

'Den dey all laughed real hard. But before Ah seen de picture Ah thought Ah wuz just like de rest.

'Us lived dere havin' fun till de chillun at school got to teasin' me 'bout livin' in de white folks' back-yard. Dere wuz uh knotty head gal name Mayrella dat useter git mad every time she look at me. Mis' Washburn useter dress me up in all de clothes her gran'chillun didn't need no mo' which still wuz better'n whut de rest uh de colored chillun had. And then she useter put hair ribbon on mah head fuh me tuh wear. Dat useter rile Mayrella uh lot. So she would pick at me all de time and put some others up tuh do de same. They'd push me 'way from de ring plays and make out they couldn't play wid nobody dat lived on premises. Den they'd tell me not to be takin' on over mah looks 'cause they mama told 'em 'bout de hound dawgs huntin' mah papa all night long. 'Bout Mr Washburn and de sheriff puttin' de bloodhounds on de trail tuh ketch mah papa for whut he done tuh mah mama. Dey didn't tell about how he wuz seen tryin' tuh git in touch wid mah mama later on so he could marry her. Naw, dey didn't talk dat part of it atall. Dey made it sound real bad so as tuh crumple mah feathers. None of 'em didn't even remember whut his name wuz, but dey all knowed de bloodhound part by heart. Nanny didn't love tuh see me wid mah head hung down, so she figgered it would be mo' better fuh me if us had uh house. She got de land and everything and then Mis' Washburn helped out uh whole heap wid things.'

Pheoby's hungry listening helped Janie to tell her story. So she went on thinking back to her young years and explaining them to her friend in soft, easy phrases while all around the house, the night time put on flesh and blackness.

She thought awhile and decided that her conscious life had commenced at Nanny's gate. On a late afternoon Nanny had called her to come inside the house because she had spied Janie letting Johnny Taylor kiss her over the gatepost.

It was a spring afternoon in West Florida. Janie had spent most of the day under a blossoming pear tree in the back-yard. She had been spending every minute that she could steal from her chores under that tree for the last three days. That was to say, ever since the first tiny bloom had opened. It had called her to come and gaze on a mystery. From barren brown stems to glistening leaf-buds; from the leaf-buds to snowy virginity of bloom. It stirred her tremendously. How? Why? It was like a flute song forgotten in another existence and remembered again. What? How? Why? This singing she heard that had nothing to do with her ears. The rose of the world was breathing out smell. It followed her through all her waking moments and caressed her in her sleep. It connected itself with other vaguely felt matters that had struck her outside observation and buried themselves in her flesh. Now they emerged and quested about her consciousness.

She was stretched on her back beneath the pear tree soaking in the alto chant of the visiting bees, the gold of the sun and the panting breath of the breeze when the inaudible voice of it all came to her. She saw a dust-bearing bee sink into the sanctum of a bloom; the thousand sister-calyxes arch to meet the love embrace and the ecstatic shiver of the tree from root to tiniest branch creaming in every blossom and frothing with delight. So this was a marriage! She had been summoned to behold a revelation. Then Janie felt a pain remorseless sweet that left her limp and languid.

After a while she got up from where she was and went over the little garden field entire. She was seeking confirmation of the voice and vision, and everywhere she found and acknowledged answers. A personal answer for all other creations except herself. She felt an answer seeking her, but where? When? How? She found herself at the kitchen door and stumbled inside. In the air of the room were flies tumbling and singing, marrying and giving in marriage. When she reached the narrow hallway she was reminded that her grandmother was home with a sick headache. She was lying across the bed asleep so Janie tipped on out of the front door. Oh to be a pear tree – *any* tree in bloom! With kissing bees singing of the beginning of the world! She was sixteen. She had glossy leaves and bursting buds and she wanted to struggle with life but it seemed to elude her. Where were the singing bees for her? Nothing on the place nor in her grandma's house answered her. She searched as much of the world as she could from the top of the front steps and then went on down to the front gate and leaned over to gaze up and down the road. Looking, waiting, breathing short with impatience. Waiting for the world to be made.

Through pollinated air she saw a glorious being coming up the road. In her former blindness she had known him as shiftless Johnny Taylor, tall and lean. That was before the golden dust of pollen had beglamored his rags and her eyes.

In the last stages of Nanny's sleep, she dreamed of voices. Voices far-off but persistent, and gradually coming nearer. Janie's voice. Janie talking in whispery snatches with a male voice she couldn't quite place. That brought her wide awake. She bolted upright and peered out of the window and saw Johnny Taylor lacerating her Janie with a kiss.

'Janie!'

The old woman's voice was so lacking in command and reproof, so full of crumbling dissolution, – that Janie half believed that Nanny had not seen her. So she extended herself outside of her dream and went inside of the house. That was the end of her childhood.

Nanny's head and face looked like the standing roots of some old tree that had been torn away by storm. Foundation of ancient power that no longer mattered. The cooling palma christi leaves that Janie had bound about her grandma's head with a white rag had wilted down and become part and parcel of the woman. Her eyes didn't bore and pierce. They diffused and melted Janie, the room and the world into one comprehension.

'Janie, youse uh 'oman, now, so—'

'Naw, Nanny, naw Ah ain't no real 'oman yet.'

The thought was too new and heavy for Janie. She fought it away.

Nanny closed her eyes and nodded a slow, weary affirmation many times before she gave it voice.

'Yeah, Janie, youse got yo' womanhood on yuh. So Ah mout ez well tell yuh whut Ah been savin' up for uh spell. Ah wants to see you married right away.'

'Me, married? Naw, Nanny, no ma'am! Whut Ah know 'bout uh husband?'

'Whut Ah seen just now is plenty for me, honey, Ah don't want no trashy nigger, no breath-and-britches, lak Johnny Taylor usin' yo' body to wipe his foots on.'

Nanny's words made Janie's kiss across the gatepost seem like a manure pile after a rain.

'Look at me, Janie. Don't set dere wid yo' head hung down. Look at yo' ole grandma!' Her voice began snagging on the prongs of her feelings. 'Ah don't want to be talkin' to you lak dis. Fact is Ah done been on mah knees to mah Maker many's de time askin' *please* – for Him not to make de burden too heavy for me to bear.'

'Nanny, Ah just – Ah didn't mean nothin' bad.'

'Dat's what makes me skeered. You don't mean no harm. You don't even know where harm is at. Ah'm ole now. Ah can't be always guidin' yo' feet from harm and danger. Ah wants to see you married right away.'

'Who Ah'm goin' tuh marry off-hand lak dat? Ah don't know nobody.'

'De Lawd will provide. He know Ah done bore de burden in de heat uh de day. Somebody done spoke to me 'bout you long time ago. Ah ain't said nothin' 'cause dat wasn't de way Ah placed you. Ah wanted yuh to school out and pick from a higher bush and a sweeter berry. But dat ain't yo' idea, Ah see.'

'Nanny, who – who dat been askin' you for me?'

'Brother Logan Killicks. He's a good man, too.'

'Naw, Nanny, no ma'am! Is dat whut he been hangin' round here for? He look like some ole skull-head in de grave yard.'

The older woman sat bolt upright and put her feet to the floor, and thrust back the leaves from her face.

'So you don't want to marry off decent like, do yuh? You just wants to hug and kiss and feel around with first one man and then another, huh? You wants to make me suck de same sorrow yo' mama did, eh? Mah ole head ain't gray enough. Mah back ain't bowed enough to suit yuh!'

The vision of Logan Killicks was desecrating the pear tree, but Janie didn't know how to tell Nanny that. She merely hunched over and pouted at the floor.

'Janie.'

'Yes, ma'am.'

'You answer me when Ah speak. Don't you set dere poutin' wid me after all Ah done went through for you!'

She slapped the girl's face violently, and forced her head back so that their eyes met in struggle. With her hand uplifted for the second blow she saw the huge tear that welled up from Janie's heart and stood in each eye. She saw the terrible agony and the lips tightened down to hold back the cry and desisted. Instead she brushed back the heavy hair from Janie's face and stood there suffering and loving and weeping internally for both of them.

'Come to yo' Grandma, honey. Set in her lap lak yo' use tuh. Yo' Nanny wouldn't harm a hair uh yo' head. She don't want nobody else to do it neither if she kin help it. Honey, de white man is de ruler of everything as fur as Ah been able tuh find out. Maybe it's some place way off in de ocean where de black man is in power, but we don't know nothin' but what we see. So de white man throw down de load and tell de nigger man tuh pick it up. He pick it up because he have to, but he don't tote it. He hand it to his womenfolks. De nigger woman is de mule uh de world so fur as Ah can see. Ah been prayin' fuh it tuh be different wid you. Lawd, Lawd, Lawd!'

For a long time she sat rocking with the girl held tightly to her sunken breast. Janie's long legs dangled over one arm of the chair and the long braids of her hair swung low on the other side. Nanny half sung, half sobbed a running chant-prayer over the head of the weeping girl.

'Lawd have mercy! It was a long time on de way but Ah reckon it had to come. Oh Jesus! Do, Jesus! Ah done de best Ah could.'

Finally, they both grew calm.

'Janie, how long you been 'lowin' Johnny Taylor to kiss you?'

'Only dis one time, Nanny. Ah don't love him at all. Whut made me do it is – oh, Ah don't know.'

'Thank yuh, Massa Jesus.'

'Ah ain't gointuh do it no mo', Nanny. Please don't make me marry Mr Killicks.'

''Tain't Logan Killicks Ah wants you to have, baby, it's protection. Ah ain't gittin' ole, honey. Ah'm *done* ole. One mornin' soon, now, de angel wid de sword is gointuh stop by here. De day and de hour is hid from me, but it won't be long. Ah ast de Lawd when you was uh infant in mah arms to let me stay here till you got grown. He done spared me to see de day. Mah daily prayer now is tuh let dese golden moments rolls on a few days longer till Ah see you safe in life.'

'Lemme wait, Nanny, please, jus' a lil bit mo'.'

'Don't think Ah don't feel wid you, Janie, 'cause Ah do. Ah couldn't love yuh no more if Ah had uh felt yo' birth pains mahself. Fact uh de matter, Ah loves yuh a whole heap more'n Ah do yo' mama, de one Ah did birth. But you got to take in consideration you ain't no everyday chile like most of 'em. You ain't got no papa, you might jus' as well say no mama, for de good she do yuh. You ain't got nobody but me. And mah head is ole and tilted towards de grave. Neither can you stand alone by yo'self. De thought uh you bein' kicked around from pillar tuh post is uh hurtin' thing. Every tear you drop squeezes a cup uh blood outa mah heart. Ah got tuh try and do for you befo' mah head is cold.'

A sobbing sigh burst out of Janie. The old woman answered her with little soothing pats of the hand.

'You know, honey, us colored folks is branches without roots and that makes things come round in queer ways. You in particular. Ah was born back due in slavery so it wasn't for me to fulfill my dreams of whut a woman oughta be and to do. Dat's one of de hold-backs of slavery. But nothing can't stop you from wishin'. You can't beat nobody down so low till you can rob 'em of they will. Ah didn't want to be used for a work-ox and a brood-sow and Ah didn't want mah daughter used dat way neither. It sho wasn't mah will for things to happen lak they did. Ah even hated de way you was born. But, all de same Ah said thank God, Ah got another chance. Ah wanted to preach a great sermon about colored women sittin' on high, but they wasn't no pulpit for me. Freedom found me wid a baby daughter in mah arms, so Ah said Ah'd take a broom and a cook-pot and throw up a highway through de wilderness for her. She would expound what Ah felt. But somehow she got lost offa de highway and next thing Ah knowed here you was in de world. So whilst Ah was tendin' you of nights Ah said Ah'd save de text for you. Ah been waitin' a long time, Janie, but nothin' Ah been through ain't too much if you just take a stand on high ground lak Ah dreamed.'

Old Nanny sat there rocking Janie like an infant and thinking back and back. Mind-pictures brought feelings, and feelings dragged out dramas from the hollows of her heart.

'Dat mornin' on de big plantation close to Savannah, a rider come in a gallop tellin' 'bout Sherman takin' Atlanta. Marse Robert's son had done been kilt at Chickamauga. So he grabbed his gun and straddled his best horse and went off wid de rest of de gray-headed men and young boys to drive de Yankees back into Tennessee.

'They was all cheerin' and cryin' and shoutin' for de men dat was ridin' off. Ah couldn't see nothin' cause yo' mama wasn't but a week old, and Ah was flat uh mah back. But pretty soon he let on he forgot somethin' and run into mah cabin and made me let down mah hair for de last time. He sorta wropped his hand in it, pulled mah big toe, lak he always done, and was gone after de rest lak lightnin'. Ah heard 'em give one last whoop for him. Then de big house and de quarters got sober and silent.

'It was de cool of de evenin' when Mistis come walkin' in mah door. She throwed de door wide open and stood dere lookin' at me outa her eyes and her face. Look lak she been livin' through uh hundred years in January without one day of spring. She come stood over me in de bed.

'"Nanny, Ah come to see that baby uh yourn."

'Ah tried not to feel de breeze off her face, but it got so cold in dere dat Ah was freezin' to death under the kivvers. So Ah couldn't move right away lak Ah aimed to. But Ah knowed Ah had to make haste and do it.

'"You better git dat kivver offa dat youngun and dat quick!" she clashed at me. "Look lak you don't know who is Mistis on dis plantation, Madam. But Ah aims to show you."

'By dat time I had done managed tuh unkivver mah baby enough for her to see de head and face.

'"Nigger, whut's yo' baby doin' wid gray eyes and yaller hair?" She begin tuh slap mah jaws ever which a'way. Ah never felt the fust ones 'cause Ah wuz too busy gittin' de kivver back over mah chile. But dem last lick burnt me lak fire. Ah had too many feelin's tuh tell which one tuh follow so Ah didn't cry and Ah didn't do nothin' else. But then she kept on astin me how come mah baby look white. She asted me dat maybe twenty-five or thirty times, lak she got tuh sayin' dat and couldn't help herself. So Ah told her, "Ah don't know nothin' but what Ah'm told tuh do, 'cause Ah ain't nothin' but uh nigger and uh slave."

'Instead of pacifyin' her lak Ah thought, look lak she got madder. But Ah reckon she was tired and wore out 'cause she didn't hit me no more. She went to de foot of de bed and wiped her hands on her handksher. "Ah wouldn't dirty mah hands on yuh. But first thing in de mornin' de overseer will take you to de whippin' post and tie you down on yo' knees and cut de hide offa yo' yaller back. One hundred lashes wid a raw-hide on yo' bare back. Ah'll have you whipped till de blood run down to yo' heels! Ah mean to count de licks mah-self. And if it kills you Ah'll stand de loss. Anyhow, as soon as dat brat is a month old Ah'm going to sell it offa dis place."

'She flounced on off and left her wintertime wid me. Ah knowed mah body wasn't healed, but Ah couldn't consider dat. In de black dark Ah wrapped mah baby de best Ah knowed how and made it to de swamp by de river. Ah knowed de place was full uh moccasins and other bitin' snakes, but Ah was more skeered uh whut was behind me. Ah hide in dere day and night and suckled de baby every time she start to cry, for fear somebody might hear her and Ah'd git found. Ah ain't sayin' uh friend or two didn't feel mah care. And den de Good

Lawd seen to it dat Ah wasn't taken. Ah don't see how come mah milk didn't kill mah chile, wid me so skeered and worried all de time. De noise uh de owls skeered me; de limbs of dem cypress trees took to crawlin' and movin' round after dark, and two three times Ah heered panthers prowlin' round. But nothin' never hurt me 'cause de Lawd knowed how it was.

'Den, one night Ah heard de big guns boomin' lak thunder. It kept up all night long. And de next mornin' Ah could see uh big ship at a distance and a great stirrin' round. So Ah wrapped Leafy up in moss and fixed her good in a tree and picked mah way on down to de landin'. The men was all in blue, and Ah heard people say Sherman was comin' to meet de boats in Savannah, and all of us slaves was free. So Ah run got mah baby and got in quotation wid people and found a place Ah could stay.

'But it was a long time after dat befo' de Big Surrender at Richmond. Den de big bell ring in Atlanta and all de men in gray uniforms had to go to Moultrie, and bury their swords in de ground to show they was never to fight about slavery no mo'. So den we knowed we was free.

'Ah wouldn't marry nobody, though Ah could have uh heap uh times, cause Ah didn't want nobody mistreating mah baby. So Ah got with some good white people and come down here in West Florida to work and make de sun shine on both sides of de street for Leafy.

'Mah Madam help me wid her just lak she been doin' wid you. Ah put her in school when it got so it was a school to put her in. Ah was 'spectin' to make a school teacher outa her.

'But one day she didn't come home at de usual time and Ah

waited and waited, but she never come all dat night. Ah took a lantern and went round askin' everybody but nobody ain't seen her. De next mornin' she come crawlin' in on her hands and knees. A sight to see. Dat school teacher had done hid her in de woods all night long, and he had done raped mah baby and run on off just before day.

'She was only seventeen, and somethin' lak dat to happen! Lawd a'mussy! Look lak Ah kin see it all over agin. It was a long time before she was well, and by dat time we knowed you was on de way. And after you was born she took to drinkin' likker and stayin' out nights. Couldn't git her to stay here and nowhere else. Lawd knows where she is right now. She ain't dead, 'cause Ah'd know it by mah feelings, but sometimes Ah wish she was at rest.

'And, Janie, maybe it wasn't much, but Ah done de best Ah kin by you. Ah raked and scraped and bought dis lil piece uh land so you wouldn't have to stay in de white folks' yard and tuck yo' head befo' other chillun at school. Dat was all right when you was little. But when you got big enough to understand things, Ah wanted you to look upon yo'self. Ah don't want yo' feathers always crumpled by folks throwin' up things in yo' face. And Ah can't die easy thinkin' maybe de menfolks white or black is makin' a spit cup outa you: Have some sympathy fuh me. Put me down easy, Janie, Ah'm a cracked plate.'

3

There are years that ask questions and years that answer. Janie had had no chance to know things, so she had to ask. Did marriage end the cosmic loneliness of the unmated? Did marriage compel love like the sun the day?

In the few days to live before she went to Logan Killicks and his often-mentioned sixty acres, Janie asked inside of herself and out. She was back and forth to the pear tree continuously wondering and thinking. Finally out of Nanny's talk and her own conjectures she made a sort of comfort for herself. Yes, she would love Logan after they were married. She could see no way for it to come about, but Nanny and the old folks had said it, so it must be so. Husbands and wives always loved each other, and that was what marriage meant. It was just so. Janie felt glad of the thought, for then it wouldn't seem so destructive and mouldy. She wouldn't be lonely anymore.

Janie and Logan got married in Nanny's parlor of a Saturday evening with three cakes and big platters of fried rabbit and chicken. Everything to eat in abundance. Nanny and Mrs Washburn had seen to that. But nobody put anything on the seat of Logan's wagon to make it ride glorious on the way to his house. It was a lonesome place like a stump in the middle of the woods where nobody had ever been. The house was absent of flavor, too. But anyhow Janie went on inside to wait for love to begin. The new moon had been up and down three times before she got worried in mind. Then she went to see Nanny in Mrs Washburn's kitchen on the day for beaten biscuits.

Nanny beamed all out with gladness and made her come up to the bread board so she could kiss her.

'Lawd a'mussy, honey, Ah sho is glad tuh see mah chile! G'wan inside and let Mis' Washburn know youse heah. Umph! Umph! Umph! How is dat husband uh yourn?'

Janie didn't go in where Mrs Washburn was. She didn't say anything to match up with Nanny's gladness either. She just fell on a chair with her hips and sat there. Between the biscuits and her beaming pride Nanny didn't notice for a minute. But after a while she found the conversation getting lonesome so she looked up at Janie.

'Whut's de matter, sugar? You ain't none too spry dis mornin'.'

'Oh, nothin' much, Ah reckon. Ah come to get a lil information from you.'

The old woman looked amazed, then gave a big clatter of laughter. 'Don't tell me you done got knocked up already, less see – dis Saturday it's two month and two weeks.'

'No'm, Ah don't think so anyhow.' Janie blushed a little.

'You ain't got nothin' to be shamed of, honey, youse uh

25

married 'oman. You got yo' lawful husband same as Mis' Washburn or anybody else!'

'Ah'm all right dat way. Ah *know* 'tain't nothin' dere.'

'You and Logan been fussin'? Lawd, Ah know dat grass-gut, liver-lipted nigger ain't done took and beat mah baby already! Ah'll take a stick and salivate 'im!'

'No'm, he ain't even talked 'bout hittin' me. He says he never mean to lay de weight uh his hand on me in malice. He chops all de wood he think Ah wants and den he totes it inside de kitchin for me. Keeps both water buckets full.'

'Humph! don't 'spect all dat tuh keep up. He ain't kissin' yo' mouf when he carry on over yuh lak dat. He's kissin' yo' foot and 'tain't in uh man tuh kiss foot long. Mouf kissin' is on uh equal and dat's natural but when dey got to bow down tuh love, dey soon straightens up.'

'Yes'm.'

'Well, if he do all dat whut you come in heah wid uh face long as mah arm for?'

''Cause you told me Ah mus gointer love him, and, and Ah don't. Maybe if somebody was to tell me how, Ah could do it.'

'You come heah wid yo' mouf full uh foolishness on uh busy day. Heah you got uh prop tuh lean on all yo' bawn days, and big protection, and everybody got tuh tip dey hat tuh you and call you Mis' Killicks, and you come worryin' me 'bout love.'

'But Nanny, Ah wants to want him sometimes. Ah don't want him to do all de wantin'.'

'If you don't want him, you sho oughta. Heah you is wid de onliest organ in town, amongst colored folks, in yo' parlor. Got a house bought and paid for and sixty acres uh land right on de big road and . . . Lawd have mussy! Dat's de very prong all us black women gits hung on. Dis love! Dat's just whut's got us uh pullin' and uh haulin' and sweatin' and doin' from can't see in de mornin' till can't see at night. Dat's how come de ole folks say dat bein' uh fool don't kill nobody. It jus' makes you sweat. Ah betcha you wants some dressed up dude dat got to look at de sole of his shoe everytime he cross de street tuh see whether he got enough leather dere tuh make it across. You can buy and sell such as dem wid what you got. In fact you can buy 'em and give 'em away.'

'Ah ain't studyin' 'bout none of 'em. At de same time Ah ain't takin' dat ole land tuh heart neither. Ah could throw ten acres of it over de fence every day and never look back to see where it fell. Ah feel de same way 'bout Mr Killicks too. Some folks never was meant to be loved and he's one of 'em.'

'How come?'

''Cause Ah hates de way his head is so long one way and so flat on de sides and dat pone uh fat back uh his neck.'

'He never made his own head. You talk so silly.'

'Ah don't keer who made it, Ah don't like de job. His belly is too big too, now, and his toe-nails look lak mule foots. And 'tain't nothin' in de way of him washin' his feet every evenin' before he comes tuh bed. 'Tain't nothin' tuh hinder him 'cause Ah places de water for him. Ah'd ruther be shot wid tacks than tuh turn over in de bed and stir up de air whilst he is in dere. He don't even never mention nothin' pretty.'

She began to cry.

'Ah wants things sweet wid mah marriage lak when you sit under a pear tree and think. Ah . . .'

"Tain't no use in you cryin', Janie. Grandma done been long uh few roads herself. But folks is meant to cry 'bout somethin' or other. Better leave things de way dey is. Youse young yet. No tellin' whut mout happen befo' you die. Wait awhile, baby. Yo' mind will change.'

Nanny sent Janie along with a stern mien, but she dwindled all the rest of the day as she worked. And when she gained the privacy of her own little shack she stayed on her knees so long she forgot she was there herself. There is a basin in the mind where words float around on thought and thought on sound and sight. Then there is a depth of thought untouched by words, and deeper still a gulf of formless feelings untouched by thought. Nanny entered this infinity of conscious pain again on her old knees. Towards morning she muttered, 'Lawd, you know mah heart. Ah done de best Ah could do. De rest is left to you.' She scuffled up from her knees and fell heavily across the bed. A month later she was dead.

So Janie waited a bloom time, and a green time and an orange time. But when the pollen again gilded the sun and sifted down on the world she began to stand around the gate and expect things. What things? She didn't know exactly. Her breath was gusty and short. She knew things that nobody had ever told her. For instance, the words of the trees and the wind. She often spoke to falling seeds and said, 'Ah hope you fall on soft ground,' because she had heard seeds saying that to each other as they passed. She knew the world was a stallion rolling in the blue pasture of ether. She knew that God tore down the old world every evening and built a new one by sun-up. It was wonderful to see it take form with the sun and emerge from the gray dust of its making. The familiar people and things had failed her so she hung over the gate and looked up the road towards way off. She knew now that marriage did not make love. Janie's first dream was dead, so she became a woman.

4

Long before the year was up, Janie noticed that her husband had stopped talking in rhymes to her. He had ceased to wonder at her long black hair and finger it. Six months back he had told her, 'If Ah kin haul de wood heah and chop it fuh yuh, look lak you oughta be able tuh tote it inside. Mah fust wife never bothered me 'bout choppin' no wood nohow. She'd grab dat ax and sling chips lak uh man. You done been spoilt rotten.'

So Janie had told him, 'Ah'm just as stiff as you is stout. If you can stand not to chop and tote wood Ah reckon you can stand not to git no dinner. 'Scuse mah freezolity, Mist' Killicks, but Ah don't mean to chop de first chip.'

'Aw you know Ah'm gwine chop de wood fuh yuh. Even if you is stingy as you can be wid me. Yo' Grandma and me myself done spoilt yuh now, and Ah reckon Ah have tuh keep on wid it.'

One morning soon he called her out of the kitchen to the barn. He had the mule all saddled at the gate.

'Looka heah, LilBit, help me out some. Cut up dese seed taters fuh me. Ah got tuh go step off a piece.'

'Where you goin'?'

'Over tuh Lake City tuh see uh man about uh mule.'

'Whut you need two mules fuh? Lessen you aims to swap off dis one.'

'Naw, Ah needs two mules dis yeah. Taters is goin' tuh be taters in de fall. Bringin' big prices. Ah aims tuh run two plows, and dis man Ah'm talkin' 'bout is got uh mule all gentled up so even uh woman kin handle 'im.'

Logan held his wad of tobacco real still in his jaw like a thermometer of his feelings while he studied Janie's face and waited for her to say something.

'So Ah thought Ah mout as well go see.' He tagged on and swallowed to kill time but Janie said nothing except, 'Ah'll cut de p'taters fuh yuh. When yuh comin' back?'

'Don't know exactly. Round dust dark Ah reckon. It's uh sorta long trip – specially if Ah hafter lead one on de way back.'

When Janie had finished indoors she sat down in the barn with the potatoes. But springtime reached her in there so she moved everything to a place in the yard where she could see the road. The noon sun filtered through the leaves of the fine oak tree where she sat and made lacy patterns on the ground. She had been there a long time when she heard whistling coming down the road.

It was a cityfied, stylish dressed man with his hat set at an angle that didn't belong in these parts. His coat was over his arm, but he didn't need it to represent his clothes. The shirt with the silk sleeveholders was dazzling enough for the world. He whistled, mopped his face and walked like he knew where he was going. He was a seal-brown color but he acted like Mr Washburn or somebody like that to Janie. Where would such a man be coming from and where was he going? He didn't look her way nor no other way except straight ahead, so Janie ran to the pump and jerked the handle hard while she pumped. It made a loud noise and also made her heavy hair fall down. So he stopped and looked hard, and then he asked her for a cool drink of water.

Janie pumped it off until she got a good look at the man. He talked friendly while he drank.

Joe Starks was the name, yeah Joe Starks from in and through Georgy. Been workin' for white folks all his life. Saved up some money – round three hundred dollars, yes indeed, right here in his pocket. Kept hearin' 'bout them buildin' a new state down heah in Floridy and sort of wanted to come. But he was makin' money where he was. But when he heard all about 'em makin' a town all outa colored folks, he knowed dat was de place he wanted to be. He had always wanted to be a big voice, but de white folks had all de sayso where he come from and everywhere else, exceptin' dis place dat colored folks was buildin' theirselves. Dat was right too. De man dat built things oughta boss it. Let colored folks build things too if dey wants to crow over somethin'. He was glad he had his money all saved up. He meant to git dere whilst de town wuz yet a baby. He meant to buy in big. It had always been his wish and desire to be a big voice and he had to live nearly thirty years to find a chance. Where was Janie's papa and mama?

'Dey dead, Ah reckon. Ah wouldn't know 'bout 'em 'cause mah Grandma raised me. She dead too.'

'She dead too! Well, who's lookin' after a lil girlchile lak you?'

'Ah'm married.'

'You married? You ain't hardly old enough to be weaned. Ah betcha you still craves sugar-tits, doncher?'

'Yeah, and Ah makes and sucks 'em when de notion strikes me. Drinks sweeten' water too.'

'Ah loves dat mahself. Never specks to get too old to enjoy syrup sweeten' water when it's cools and nice.'

'Us got plenty syrup in de barn. Ribbon-cane syrup. If you so desires—'

'Where yo' husband at, Mis' er-er.'

'Mah name is Janie Mae Killicks since Ah got married. Useter be name Janie Mae Crawford. Mah husband is gone tuh buy a mule fuh me tuh plow. He left me cuttin' up seed p'taters.'

'You behind a plow! You ain't got no mo' business wid uh plow than uh hog is got wid uh holiday! You ain't got no business cuttin' up no seed p'taters neither. A pretty doll-baby lak you is made to sit on de front porch and rock and fan yo'self and eat p'taters dat other folks plant just special for you.'

Janie laughed and drew two quarts of syrup from the barrel and Joe Starks pumped the water bucket full of cool water. They sat under the tree and talked. He was going on down to the new part of Florida, but no harm to stop and chat. He later decided he needed a rest anyway. It would do him good to rest a week or two.

Every day after that they managed to meet in the scrub oaks across the road and talk about when he would be a big ruler of things with her reaping the benefits. Janie pulled back a long time because he did not represent sun-up and pollen and blooming trees, but he spoke for far horizon. He spoke for change and chance. Still she hung back. The memory of Nanny was still powerful and strong.

'Janie, if you think Ah aims to tole you off and make a dog outa you, youse wrong. Ah wants to make a wife outa you.'

'You mean dat, Joe?'

'De day you puts yo' hand in mine, Ah wouldn't let de sun go down on us single. Ah'm uh man wid principles. You ain't never knowed what it was to be treated lak a lady and Ah wants to be de one tuh show yuh. Call me Jody lak you do sometime.'

'Jody,' she smiled up at him, 'but s'posin'—'

'Leave de s'posin' and everything else to me. Ah'll be down dis road uh little after sun-up tomorrow mornin' to wait for you. You come go wid me. Den all de rest of yo' natural life you kin live lak you oughta. Kiss me and shake yo' head. When you do dat, yo' plentiful hair breaks lak day.'

Janie debated the matter that night in bed.

'Logan, you 'sleep?'

'If Ah wuz, you'd be done woke me up callin' me.'

'Ah wuz thinkin' real hard about us; about you and me.'

'It's about time. Youse powerful independent around here sometime considerin'.'

'Considerin' whut for instance?'

'Considerin' youse born in a carriage 'thout no top to it,

34

and yo' mama and you bein' born and raised in de white folks back-yard.'

'You didn't say all dat when you wuz begging Nanny for me to marry you.'

'Ah thought you would 'preciate good treatment. Thought Ah'd take and make somethin' outa yuh. You think youse white folks by de way you act.'

'S'posin' Ah wuz to run off and leave yuh sometime.'

There! Janie had put words to his held-in fears. She might run off sure enough. The thought put a terrible ache in Logan's body, but he thought it best to put on scorn.

'Ah'm gettin' sleepy, Janie. Let's don't talk no mo'. 'Tain't too many mens would trust yuh, knowin' yo' folks lak dey do.'

'Ah might take and find somebody dat did trust me and leave yuh.'

'Shucks! 'Tain't no mo' fools lak me. A whole lot of mens will grin in yo' face, but dey ain't gwine tuh work and feed yuh. You won't git far and you won't be long, when dat big gut reach over and grab dat little one, you'll be too glad to come back here.'

'You don't take nothin' to count but sow-belly and corn-bread.'

'Ah'm sleepy. Ah don't aim to worry mah gut into a fiddle-string wid no s'posin'.' He flopped over resentful in his agony and pretended sleep. He hoped that he had hurt her as she had hurt him.

Janie got up with him the next morning and had the breakfast halfway done when he bellowed from the barn.

'Janie!' Logan called harshly. 'Come help me move dis

manure pile befo' de sun gits hot. You don't take a bit of interest in dis place. 'Tain't no use in foolin' round in dat kitchen all day long.'

Janie walked to the door with the pan in her hand still stirring the cornmeal dough and looked towards the barn. The sun from ambush was threatening the world with red daggers, but the shadows were gray and solid-looking around the barn. Logan with his shovel looked like a black bear doing some clumsy dance on his hind legs.

'You don't need mah help out dere, Logan. Youse in yo' place and Ah'm in mine.'

'You ain't got no particular place. It's wherever Ah need yuh. Git uh move on yuh, and dat quick.'

'Mah mama didn't tell me Ah wuz born in no hurry. So whut business Ah got rushin' now? Anyhow dat ain't whut youse mad about. Youse mad 'cause Ah don't fall down and wash-up dese sixty acres uh ground yuh got. You ain't done me no favor by marryin' me. And if dat's what you call yo'self doin', Ah don't thank yuh for it. Youse mad 'cause Ah'm tellin' yuh whut you already knowed.'

Logan dropped his shovel and made two or three clumsy steps towards the house, then stopped abruptly.

'Don't you change too many words wid me dis mawnin', Janie, do Ah'll take and change ends wid yuh! Heah, Ah just as good as take you out de white folks' kitchen and set you down on yo' royal diasticutis and you take and low-rate me! Ah'll take holt uh dat ax and come in dere and kill yuh! You better dry up in dere! Ah'm too honest and hard-workin' for anybody in yo' family, dat's de reason you don't want me!' The last sentence was half a sob and half a cry. 'Ah guess some low-lifed nigger is grinnin' in yo' face and lyin' tuh yuh. God damn yo' hide!'

Janie turned from the door without answering, and stood still in the middle of the floor without knowing it. She turned wrongside out just standing there and feeling. When the throbbing calmed a little she gave Logan's speech a hard thought and placed it beside other things she had seen and heard. When she had finished with that she dumped the dough on the skillet and smoothed it over with her hand. She wasn't even angry. Logan was accusing her of her mama, her grandmama and her feelings, and she couldn't do a thing about any of it. The sow-belly in the pan needed turning. She flipped it over and shoved it back. A little cold water in the coffee pot to settle it. Turned the hoe-cake with a plate and then made a little laugh. What was she losing so much time for? A feeling of sudden newness and change came over her. Janie hurried out of the front gate and turned south. Even if Joe was not there waiting for her, the change was bound to do her good.

The morning road air was like a new dress. That made her feel the apron tied around her waist. She untied it and flung it on a low bush beside the road and walked on, picking flowers and making a bouquet. After that she came to where Joe Starks was waiting for her with a hired rig. He was very solemn and helped her to the seat beside him. With him on it, it sat like some high, ruling chair. From now on until death she was going to have flower dust and springtime sprinkled over everything. A bee for her bloom. Her old thoughts were going to come in handy now, but new words would have to be made and said to fit them.

'Green Cove Springs,' he told the driver. So they were married there before sundown, just like Joe had said. With new clothes of silk and wool.

They sat on the boarding house porch and saw the sun plunge into the same crack in the earth from which the night emerged.

5

On the train the next day, Joe didn't make many speeches with rhymes to her, but he bought her the best things the butcher had, like apples and a glass lantern full of candies. Mostly he talked about plans for the town when he got there. They were bound to need somebody like him. Janie took a lot of looks at him and she was proud of what she saw. Kind of portly like rich white folks. Strange trains, and people and places didn't scare him neither. Where they got off the train at Maitland he found a buggy to carry them over to the colored town right away.

It was early in the afternoon when they got there, so Joe said they must walk over the place and look around. They locked arms and strolled from end to end of the town. Joe noted the scant dozen of shamefaced houses scattered in the sand and palmetto roots and said, 'God, they call this a town? Why, 'tain't nothing but a raw place in de woods.'

'It is a whole heap littler than Ah thought.' Janie admitted her disappointment.

'Just like Ah thought,' Joe said. 'A whole heap uh talk and nobody doin' nothin'. I god, where's de Mayor?' He asked somebody. 'Ah want tuh speak wid de Mayor.'

Two men who were sitting on their shoulder-blades under a huge live oak tree almost sat upright at the tone of his voice. They stared at Joe's face, his clothes and his wife.

'Where y'all come from in sich uh big haste?' Lee Coker asked.

'Middle Georgy,' Starks answered briskly. 'Joe Starks is mah name, from in and through Georgy.'

'You and yo' daughter goin' tuh join wid us in fellowship?' the other reclining figure asked. 'Mighty glad tuh have yuh. Hicks is the name. Guv'nor Amos Hicks from Buford, South Carolina. Free, single, disengaged.'

'I god, Ah ain't nowhere near old enough to have no grown daughter. This here is mah wife.'

Hicks sank back and lost interest at once.

'Where is de Mayor?' Starks persisted. 'Ah wants tuh talk wid *him*.'

'Youse uh mite too previous for dat,' Coker told him. 'Us ain't got none yit.'

'Ain't got no Mayor! Well, who tells y'all what to do?'

'Nobody. Everybody's grown. And then agin, Ah reckon us just ain't thought about it. Ah know Ah ain't.'

'Ah did think about it one day,' Hicks said dreamily, 'but then Ah forgot it and ain't thought about it since then.'

'No wonder things ain't no better,' Joe commented. 'Ah'm buyin' in here, and buyin' in big. Soon's we find some place to sleep tonight us menfolks got to call people together and form a committee. Then we can get things movin' round here.'

'Ah kin point yuh where yuh kin sleep,' Hicks offered. 'Man got his house done built and his wife ain't come yet.'

Starks and Janie moved on off in the direction indicated with Hicks and Coker boring into their backs with looks.

'Dat man talks like a section foreman,' Coker commented. 'He's mighty compellment.'

'Shucks!' said Hicks. 'Mah britches is just as long as his. But dat wife uh hisn! Ah'm uh son of uh Combunction if Ah don't go tuh Georgy and git me one just like her.'

'Whut wid?'

'Wid mah talk, man.'

'It takes money tuh feed pretty women. Dey gits uh lavish uh talk.'

'Not lak mine. Dey loves to hear me talk because dey can't understand it. Mah co-talkin' is too deep. Too much co to it.'

'Umph!'

'You don't believe me, do yuh? You don't know de women Ah kin git to mah command.'

'Umph!'

'You ain't never seen me when Ah'm out pleasurin' and givin' pleasure.'

'Umph!'

'It's uh good thing he married her befo' she seen me. Ah kin be some trouble when Ah take uh notion.'

'Umph!'

'Ah'm uh bitch's baby round lady people.'

'Ah's much ruther see all dat than to hear 'bout it. Come on less go see whut he gointuh do 'bout dis town.'

They got up and sauntered over to where Starks was living

for the present. Already the town had found the strangers. Joe was on the porch talking to a small group of men. Janie could be seen through the bedroom window getting settled. Joe had rented the house for a month. The men were all around him, and he was talking to them by asking questions.

'Whut is de real name of de place?'

'Some say West Maitland and some say Eatonville. Dat's 'cause Cap'n Eaton give us some land along wid Mr Laurence. But Cap'n Eaton give de first piece.'

'How much did they give?'

'Oh 'bout fifty acres.'

'How much is y'all got now?'

'Oh 'bout de same.'

'Dat ain't near enough. Who owns de land joining on to whut yuh got?'

'Cap'n Eaton.'

'Where *is* dis Cap'n Eaton?'

'Over dere in Maitland, 'ceptin' when he go visitin' or somethin'.'

'Lemme speak to mah wife a minute and Ah'm goin' see de man. You cannot have no town without some land to build it on. Y'all ain't got enough here to cuss a cat on without gittin' yo' mouf full of hair.'

'He ain't got no mo' land tuh give away. Yuh needs plenty money if yuh wants any mo'.'

'Ah specks to pay him.'

The idea was funny to them and they wanted to laugh. They tried hard to hold it in, but enough incredulous laughter burst out of their eyes and leaked from the corners of their mouths to inform anyone of their thoughts. So Joe walked off abruptly. Most of them went along to show him the way and to be there when his bluff was called.

Hicks didn't go far. He turned back to the house as soon as he felt he wouldn't be missed from the crowd and mounted the porch.

'Evenin', Miz Starks.'

'Good evenin'.'

'You reckon you gointuh like round here?'

'Ah reckon so.'

'Anything *Ah* kin do tuh help out, why you kin call on me.'

'Much obliged.'

There was a long dead pause. Janie was not jumping at her chance like she ought to. Look like she didn't hardly know he was there. She needed waking up.

'Folks must be mighty close-mouthed where you come from.'

'Dat's right. But it must be different at yo' home.'

He was a long time thinking but finally he saw and stumbled down the steps with a surly "Bye."

'Good bye.'

That night Coker asked him about it.

'Ah saw yuh when yuh ducked back tuh Starks' house. Well, how didju make out?'

'Who, me? Ah ain't been near de place, man. Ah been down tuh de lake tryin' tuh ketch me uh fish.'

'Umph!'

'Dat 'oman ain't so awfully pretty nohow when yuh take de second look at her. Ah had to sorta pass by de house on de way back and seen her good. 'Tain't nothin' to her 'ceptin' dat long hair.'

'Umph!'

'And anyhow, Ah done took uhlikin' tuh de man. Ah wouldn't harm him at all. She ain't half ez pretty ez uh gal Ah run off and left up in South Cal'lina.'

'Hicks, Ah'd git mad and say you wuz lyin' if Ah didn't know yuh so good. You just talkin' to consolate yo'self by word of mouth. You got uh willin' mind, but youse too light behind. A whole heap uh men seen de same thing you seen but they got better sense than you. You oughta know you can't take no 'oman lak dat from no man lak him. A man dat ups and buys two hundred acres uh land at one whack and pays cash for it.'

'Naw! He didn't buy it sho nuff?'

'He sho did. Come off wid de papers in his pocket. He done called a meetin' on his porch tomorrow. Ain't never seen no sich uh colored man befo' in all mah bawn days. He's gointuh put up uh store and git uh post office from de Goven'ment.'

That irritated Hicks and he didn't know why. He was the average mortal. It troubled him to get used to the world one way and then suddenly have it turn different. He wasn't ready to think of colored people in post offices yet. He laughed boisterously.

'Y'all let dat stray darky tell y'all any ole lie! Uh colored man sittin' up in uh post office!' He made an obscene sound.

'He's liable tuh do it too, Hicks. Ah hope so anyhow. Us colored folks is too envious of one 'nother. Dat's how come us don't git no further than us do. Us talks about de white man keepin' us down! Shucks! He don't have tuh. Us keeps our own selves down.'

'Now who said Ah didn't want de man tuh git us uh post office? He kin be de king uh Jerusalem fuh all Ah keer. Still and all, 'tain't no use in telling lies just 'cause uh heap uh folks don't know no better. Yo' common sense oughta tell yuh de white folks ain't goin' tuh 'low him tuh run no post office.'

'Dat we don't know, Hicks. He say he kin and Ah b'lieve he know whut he's talkin' 'bout. Ah reckon if colored folks got they own town they kin have post offices and whatsoever they please, regardless. And then agin, Ah don't speck de white folks way off yonder give uh damn. Less us wait and see.'

'Oh, Ah'm waitin' all right. Specks tuh keep on waitin' till hell freeze over.'

'Aw, git reconciled! Dat woman don't want you. You got tuh learn dat all de women in de world ain't been brought up on no teppentine still, and no saw-mill camp. There's some women dat jus' ain't for you tuh broach. You can't git *her* wid no fish sandwich.'

They argued a bit more then went on to the house where Joe was and found him in his shirt-sleeves, standing with his legs wide apart, asking questions and smoking a cigar.

'Where's de closest saw-mill?' He was asking Tony Taylor.

''Bout seben miles goin' t'wards Apopka,' Tony told him. 'Thinkin' 'bout buildin' right away?'

'I god, yeah. But not de house Ah specks tuh live in. Dat kin wait till Ah make up mah mind where Ah wants it located. Ah figgers we all needs uh store in uh big hurry.'

'Uh store?' Tony shouted in surprise.

45

'Yeah, uh store right heah in town wid everything in it you needs. 'Tain't uh bit uh use in everybody proagin' way over tuh Maitland tuh buy uh little meal and flour when they could git it right heah.'

'Dat would be kinda nice, Brother Starks, since you mention it.'

'I god, course it would! And then agin uh store is good in other ways. Ah got tuh have a place tuh be at when folks comes tuh buy land. And furthermo' everything is got tuh have uh center and uh heart tuh it, and uh town ain't no different from nowhere else. It would be natural fuh de store tuh be meetin' place fuh de town.'

'Dat sho is de truth, now.'

'Oh, we'll have dis town all fixed up tereckly. Don't miss bein' at de meetin' tuhmorrow.'

Just about time for the committee meeting called to meet on his porch next day, the first wagon load of lumber drove up and Jody went to show them where to put it. Told Janie to hold the committee there until he got back, he didn't want to miss them, but he meant to count every foot of that lumber before it touched the ground. He could have saved his breath and Janie could have kept right on with what she was doing. In the first place everybody was late in coming; then the next thing as soon as they heard where Jody was, they kept right on up there where the new lumber was rattling off the wagon and being piled under the big live oak tree. So that's where the meeting was held with Tony Taylor acting as chairman and Jody doing all the talking. A day was named for roads and they all agreed to bring axes and things like that and chop out two roads running each way. That applied to everybody except Tony and Coker. They could carpenter, so Jody hired them to go to work on his store bright and soon the next morning. Jody himself would be busy driving around from town to town telling people about Eatonville and drumming up citizens to move there.

Janie was astonished to see the money Jody had spent for the land come back to him so fast. Ten new families bought lots and moved to town in six weeks. It all looked too big and rushing for her to keep track of. Before the store had a complete roof, Jody had canned goods piled on the floor and was selling so much he didn't have time to go off on his talking tours. She had her first taste of presiding over it the day it was complete and finished. Jody told her to dress up and stand in the store all that evening. Everybody was coming sort of fixed up, and he didn't mean for nobody else's wife to rank with her. She must look on herself as the bell-cow, the other women were the gang. So she put on one of her bought dresses and went up the new-cut road all dressed in wine-colored red. Her silken ruffles rustled and muttered about her. The other women had on percale and calico with here and there a head-rag among the older ones.

Nobody was buying anything that night. They didn't come there for that. They had come to make a welcome. So Joe knocked in the head of a barrel of soda crackers and cut some cheese.

'Everybody come right forward and make merry. I god, it's mah treat.' Jody gave one of his big heh heh laughs and stood back. Janie dipped up the lemonade like he told her. A big tin cup full for everybody. Tony Taylor felt so good when it was all gone that he felt to make a speech.

'Ladies and gent'men, we'se come tuhgether and gethered heah tuh welcome tuh our midst one who has seen fit tuh cast in his lot amongst us. He didn't just come hisself neither. He have seen fit tuh bring his, er, er, de light uh his home, dat is his wife amongst us also. She couldn't look no mo' better and no nobler if she wuz de queen uh England. It's uh pledger fuh her tuh be heah amongst us. Brother Starks, we welcomes you and all dat you have seen fit tuh bring amongst us – yo' beloved wife, yo' store, yo' land—'

A big-mouthed burst of laughter cut him short.

'Dat'll do, Tony,' Lige Moss yelled out. 'Mist' Starks is uh smart man, we'se all willin' tuh acknowledge tuh dat, but de day he comes waggin' down de road wid two hund'ed acres uf land over his shoulder, Ah wants tuh be dere tuh see it.'

Another big blow-out of a laugh. Tony was a little peeved at having the one speech of his lifetime ruined like that.

'All y'all know whut wuz meant. Ah don't see how come—'

''Cause you jump up tuh make speeches and don't know how,' Lige said.

'Ah wuz speakin' jus' all right befo' you stuck yo' bill in.'

'Naw, you wuzn't, Tony. Youse way outa jurisdiction. You can't welcome uh man and his wife 'thout you make comparison about Isaac and Rebecca at de well, else it don't show de love between 'em if you don't.'

Everybody agreed that that was right. It was sort of pitiful for Tony not to know he couldn't make a speech without saying that. Some tittered at his ignorance. So Tony said testily, 'If all them dat's gointuh cut de monkey is done cut it and through wid, we'll thank Brother Starks fuh a respond.'

So Joe Starks and his cigar took the center of the floor.

'Ah thanks you all for yo' kind welcome and for extendin' tuh me de right hand uh fellowship. Ah kin see dat dis town is full uh union and love. Ah means tuh put mah hands tuh de plow heah, and strain every nerve tuh make dis our town de metropolis uh de state. So maybe Ah better tell yuh in case you don't know dat if we expect tuh move on, us got tuh incorporate lak every other town. Us got tuh incorporate, and us got tuh have uh mayor, if things is tuh be done and done right. Ah welcome you all on behalf uh me and mah wife tuh dis store and tuh de other things tuh come. Amen.'

Tony led the loud hand-clapping and was out in the center of the floor when it stopped.

'Brothers and sisters, since us can't never expect tuh better our choice, Ah move dat we make Brother Starks our Mayor until we kin see further.'

'Second dat motion!!!' It was everybody talking at once, so it was no need of putting it to a vote.

'And now we'll listen tuh uh few words uh encouragement from Mrs Mayor Starks.'

The burst of applause was cut short by Joe taking the floor himself.

'Thank yuh fuh yo' compliments, but mah wife don't know nothin' 'bout no speech-makin'. Ah never married her for nothin' lak dat. She's uh woman and her place is in de home.'

Janie made her face laugh after a short pause, but it wasn't too easy. She had never thought of making a speech, and

49

didn't know if she cared to make one at all. It must have been the way Joe spoke out without giving her a chance to say anything one way or another that took the bloom off of things. But anyway, she went down the road behind him that night feeling cold. He strode along invested with his new dignity, thought and planned out loud, unconscious of her thoughts.

'De mayor of uh town lak dis can't lay round home too much. De place needs buildin' up. Janie, Ah'll git hold uh somebody tuh help out in de store and you kin look after things whilst Ah drum up things otherwise.'

'Oh Jody, Ah can't do nothin' wid no store lessen youse there. Ah could maybe come in and help you when things git rushed, but—'

'I god, Ah don't see how come yuh can't. 'Tain't nothin' atall tuh hinder yuh if yuh got uh thimble full uh sense. You got tuh. Ah got too much else on mah hands as Mayor. Dis town needs some light right now.'

'Unh hunh, it *is* uh little dark right long heah.'

''Course it is. 'Tain't no use in scufflin' over all dese stumps and roots in de dark. Ah'll call uh meetin' bout de dark and de roots right away. Ah'll sit on dis case first thing.'

The very next day with money out of his own pocket he sent off to Sears, Roebuck and Company for the street lamp and told the town to meet the following Thursday night to vote on it. Nobody had ever thought of street lamps and some of them said it was a useless notion. They went so far as to vote against it, but the majority ruled.

But the whole town got vain over it after it came. That was because the Mayor didn't just take it out of the crate and stick it up on a post. He unwrapped it and had it wiped off carefully and put it up on a showcase for a week for everybody to see. Then he set a time for the lighting and sent word all around Orange County for one and all to come to the lamp-lighting. He sent men out to the swamp to cut the finest and the straightest cypress post they could find, and kept on sending them back to hunt another one until they found one that pleased him. He had talked to the people already about the hospitality of the occasion.

'Y'all know we can't invite people to our town just dry long so. I god, naw. We got tuh feed 'em something, and 'tain't nothin' people laks better'n barbecue. Ah'll give one whole hawg mah ownself. Seem lak all de rest uh y'all put tuhgether oughta be able tuh scrape up two mo'. Tell yo' womenfolks tuh do 'round 'bout some pies and cakes and sweet p'tater pone.'

That's the way it went, too. The women got together the sweets and the men looked after the meats. The day before the lighting, they dug a big hole in back of the store and filled it full of oak wood and burned it down to a glowing bed of coals. It took them the whole night to barbecue the three hogs. Hambo and Pearson had full charge while the others helped out with turning the meat now and then while Hambo swabbed it all over with the sauce. In between times they told stories, laughed and told more stories and sung songs. They cut all sorts of capers and whiffed the meat as it slowly came to perfection with the seasoning penetrating to the bone. The younger boys had to rig up the saw-horses with boards for the women to use as tables. Then it was after sun-up and everybody not needed went home to rest up for the feast.

By five o'clock the town was full of every kind of a vehicle and swarming with people. They wanted to see that lamp lit at dusk. Near the time, Joe assembled everybody in the street before the store and made a speech.

'Folkses, de sun is goin' down. De Sun-maker brings it up in de mornin', and de Sun-maker sends it tuh bed at night. Us poor weak humans can't do nothin' tuh hurry it up nor to slow it down. All we can do, if we want any light after de settin' or befo' de risin', is tuh make some light ourselves. So dat's how come lamps was made. Dis evenin' we'se all assembled heah tuh light uh lamp. Dis occasion is something for us all tuh remember tuh our dyin' day. De first street lamp in uh colored town. Lift yo' eyes and gaze on it. And when Ah touch de match tuh dat lamp-wick let de light penetrate inside of yuh, and let it shine, let it shine, let it shine. Brother Davis, lead us in a word uh prayer. Ask uh blessin' on dis town in uh most particular manner.'

While Davis chanted a traditional prayer-poem with his own variations, Joe mounted the box that had been placed for the purpose and opened the brazen door of the lamp. As the word Amen was said, he touched the lighted match to the wick, and Mrs Bogle's alto burst out in:

We'll walk in de light, de beautiful light
Come where the dew drops of mercy shine bright
Shine all around us by day and by night
Jesus, the light of the world.

They, all of them, all of the people took it up and sung it over and over until it was wrung dry, and no further innovations of tone and tempo were conceivable. Then they hushed and ate barbecue.

When it was all over that night in bed Jody asked Janie, 'Well, honey, how yuh lak bein' Mrs Mayor?'

'It's all right Ah reckon, but don't yuh think it keeps us in uh kinda strain?'

'Strain? You mean de cookin' and waitin' on folks?'

'Naw, Jody, it jus' looks lak it keeps us in some way we ain't natural wid one 'nother. You'se always off talkin' and fixin' things, and Ah feels lak Ah'm jus' markin' time. Hope it soon gits over.'

'Over, Janie? I god, Ah ain't even started good. Ah told you in de very first beginnin' dat Ah aimed tuh be uh big voice. You oughta be glad, 'cause dat makes uh big woman outa you.'

A feeling of coldness and fear took hold of her. She felt far away from things and lonely.

Janie soon began to feel the impact of awe and envy against her sensibilities. The wife of the Mayor was not just another woman as she had supposed. She slept with authority and so she was part of it in the town mind. She couldn't get but so close to most of them in spirit. It was especially noticeable after Joe had forced through a town ditch to drain the street in front of the store. They had murmured hotly about slavery being over, but every man filled his assignment.

There was something about Joe Starks that cowed the town. It was not because of physical fear. He was no fist fighter. His bulk was not even imposing as men go. Neither was it because he was more literate than the rest. Something else made men give way before him. He had a bow-down command in his face, and every step he took made the thing more tangible.

Take for instance that new house of his. It had two stories with porches, with bannisters and such things. The rest of the town looked like servant's quarters surrounding the 'big house.' And different from everybody else in the town he put off moving in until it had been painted, in and out. And look at the way he painted it – a gloaty, sparkly white. The kind of promenading white that the houses of Bishop Whipple, W. B. Jackson and the Vanderpools wore. It made the village feel funny talking to him – just like he was anybody else. Then there was the matter of the spittoons. No sooner was he all set as the Mayor – post master – landlord – storekeeper, than he bought a desk like Mr Hill or Mr Galloway over in Maitland with one of those swing-around chairs to it. What with him biting down on cigars and saving his breath on talk and swinging round in that chair, it weakened people. And then he spit in that gold-looking vase that anybody else would have been glad to put on their front-room table. Said it was a spittoon just like his used-to-be bossman used to have in his bank up there in Atlanta. Didn't have to get up and go to the door every time he had to spit. Didn't spit on his floor neither. Had that golded-up spitting pot right handy. But he went further than that. He bought a little lady-size spitting pot for Janie to spit in. Had it right in the parlor with little sprigs of flowers painted all around the sides. It took people by surprise because most of the women dipped snuff and of course had a spit-cup in the house. But how could they know up-to-date folks was spitting in flowery little things like that? It sort of made the rest of them feel that they had been taken advantage of. Like things had been kept from them. Maybe more things in the world besides spitting pots had been hid from them, when they wasn't told no better than to spit in tomato cans. It was bad enough for white people, but when one of your own color could be so different it put you on a wonder. It was like seeing your sister turn into a 'gator. A familiar strangeness. You keep seeing your sister in the 'gator and the 'gator in your sister, and you'd rather not. There was no doubt that the town respected him and even admired him in a way. But any man who walks in the way of power and property is bound to meet hate. So when speakers stood up when the occasion demanded and said 'Our beloved Mayor,' it was one of those statements that everybody says but nobody actually believes like 'God is everywhere.' It was just a handle to wind up the tongue with. As time went on and the benefits he had conferred upon the town receded in time they sat on his store porch while he was busy inside and discussed him. Like one day after he caught Henry Pitts with a wagon load of his ribbon cane and took the cane away from Pitts and made him leave town. Some of them thought Starks ought not to have done that. He had so much cane and everything else. But they didn't say that while Joe Starks was on the porch. When the mail came from Maitland and he went inside to sort it out everybody had their say.

Sim Jones started off as soon as he was sure that Starks couldn't hear him.

'It's uh sin and uh shame runnin' dat po' man way from here lak dat. Colored folks oughtn't tuh be so hard on one 'nother.'

'Ah don't see it dat way atall,' Sam Watson said shortly. 'Let colored folks learn to work for what dey git lak everybody else. Nobody ain't stopped Pitts from plantin' de cane he wanted tuh. Starks give him uh job, what mo' do he want?'

'Ah know dat too,' Jones said, 'but, Sam, Joe Starks is too exact wid folks. All he got he done made it offa de rest of us. He didn't have all dat when he come here.'

'Yeah, but none uh all dis you see and you'se settin' on wasn't here neither, when he come. Give de devil his due.'

'But now, Sam, you know dat all he do is big-belly round and tell other folks what tuh do. He loves obedience out of everybody under de sound of his voice.'

'You kin feel a switch in his hand when he's talkin' to yuh,' Oscar Scott complained. 'Dat chastisin' feelin' he totes sorter gives yuh de protolapsis uh de cutinary linin'.'

'He's uh whirlwind among breezes,' Jeff Bruce threw in.

'Speakin' of winds, he's de wind and we'se de grass. We bend which ever way he blows,' Sam Watson agreed, 'but at dat us needs him. De town wouldn't be nothin' if it wasn't for him. He can't help bein' sorta bossy. Some folks needs thrones, and ruling-chairs and crowns tuh make they influence felt. He don't. He's got uh throne in de seat of his pants.'

'Whut Ah don't lak 'bout de man is, he talks tuh unlettered folks wid books in his jaws,' Hicks complained. 'Showin' off his learnin'. To look at me you wouldn't think it, but Ah got uh brother pastorin' up round Ocala dat got good learnin'. If he wuz here, Joe Starks wouldn't make no fool outa him lak he do de rest uh y'all.'

'Ah often wonder how dat lil wife uh hisn makes out wid

him, 'cause he's uh man dat changes everything, but nothin' don't change him.'

'You know many's de time Ah done thought about dat mahself. He gits on her ever now and then when she make little mistakes round de store.'

'Whut make her keep her head tied up lak some ole 'oman round de store? Nobody couldn't *git* me tuh tie no rag on mah head if Ah had hair lak dat.'

'Maybe he make her do it. Maybe he skeered some de rest of us mens might touch it round dat store. It sho is uh hidden mystery tuh me.'

'She sho don't talk much. De way he rears and pitches in de store sometimes when she make uh mistake is sort of ungodly, but she don't seem to mind at all. Reckon dey understand one 'nother.'

The town had a basketful of feelings good and bad about Joe's positions and possessions, but none had the temerity to challenge him. They bowed down to him rather, because he was all of these things, and then again he was all of these things because the town bowed down.

6

Every morning the world flung itself over and exposed the town to the sun. So Janie had another day. And every day had a store in it, except Sundays. The store itself was a pleasant place if only she didn't have to sell things. When the people sat around on the porch and passed around the pictures of their thoughts for the others to look at and see, it was nice. The fact that the thought pictures were always crayon enlargements of life made it even nicer to listen to.

Take for instance the case of Matt Bonner's yellow mule. They had him up for conversation every day the Lord sent. Most especial if Matt was there himself to listen. Sam and Lige and Walter were the ringleaders of the mule-talkers. The others threw in whatever they could chance upon, but it seemed as if Sam and Lige and Walter could hear and see more about that mule than the whole county put together. All they needed was to see Matt's long spare shape coming down the street and by the time he got to the porch they were ready for him.

'Hello, Matt.'

'Evenin', Sam.'

'Mighty glad you come 'long right now, Matt. Me and some others wuz jus' about tuh come hunt yuh.'

'Whut for, Sam?'

'Mighty serious matter, man. Serious!!'

'Yeah man,' Lige would cut in, dolefully. 'It needs yo' strict attention. You ought not tuh lose no time.'

'Whut is it then? You oughta hurry up and tell me.'

'Reckon we better not tell yuh heah at de store. It's too fur off tuh do any good. We better all walk on down by Lake Sabelia.'

'Whut's wrong, man? Ah ain't after none uh y'alls foolishness now.'

'Dat mule uh yourn, Matt. You better go see 'bout him. He's bad off.'

'Where 'bouts? Did he wade in de lake and uh alligator ketch him?'

'Worser'n dat. De womenfolks got yo' mule. When Ah come round de lake 'bout noontime mah wife and some others had 'im flat on de ground usin' his sides fuh uh wash board.'

The great clap of laughter that they have been holding in, bursts out. Sam never cracks a smile. 'Yeah, Matt, dat mule so skinny till de women is usin' his rib bones fuh uh rub-board, and hangin' things out on his hock-bones tuh dry.'

Matt realizes that they have tricked him again and the laughter makes him mad and when he gets mad he stammers.

'You'se uh stinkin' lie, Sam, and yo' feet ain't mates. Y-y-y-you!'

'Aw, man, 'tain't no use in you gittin' mad. Yuh know yuh don't feed de mule. How he gointuh git fat?'

'Ah-ah-ah d-d-does feed 'im! Ah g-g-gived 'im uh full cup uh cawn every feedin'.'

'Lige knows all about dat cup uh cawn. He hid round yo' barn and watched yuh. 'Tain't no feed cup you measures dat cawn outa. It's uh tea cup.'

'Ah does feed 'im. He's jus' too mean tuh git fat. He stay poor and rawbony jus' fuh spite. Skeered he'll hafta work some.'

'Yeah, you feeds 'im. Feeds 'im offa "come up" and seasons it wid raw-hide.'

'Does feed de ornery varmint! Don't keer whut Ah do Ah can't git long wid 'im. He fights every inch in front uh de plow, and even lay back his ears tuh kick and bite when Ah go in de stall tuh feed 'im.'

'Git reconciled, Matt,' Lige soothed. 'Us all knows he's mean. Ah seen 'im when he took after one uh dem Roberts chillun in de street and woulda caught 'im and maybe trompled 'im tuh death if de wind hadn't of changed all of a sudden. Yuh see de youngun wuz tryin' tuh make it tuh de fence uh Starks' onion patch and de mule wuz dead in behind 'im and gainin' on 'im every jump, when all of a sudden de wind changed and blowed de mule way off his course, him bein' so poor and everything, and before de ornery varmint could tack, de youngun had done got over de fence.' The porch laughed and Matt got mad again.

'Maybe de mule takes out after everybody,' Sam said, "'cause he thinks everybody he hear comin' is Matt Bonner comin' tuh work 'im on uh empty stomach.'

'Aw, naw, aw, naw. You stop dat right now,' Walter objected. 'Dat mule don't think Ah look lak no Matt Bonner. He ain't dat dumb. If Ah thought he didn't know no better Ah'd have mah picture took and give it tuh dat mule so's he could learn better. Ah ain't gointuh 'low 'im tuh hold nothin' lak dat against me.'

Matt struggled to say something but his tongue failed him so he jumped down off the porch and walked away as mad as he could be. But that never halted the mule talk. There would be more stories about how poor the brute was; his age; his evil disposition and his latest caper. Everybody indulged in mule talk. He was next to the Mayor in prominence, and made better talking.

Janie loved the conversation and sometimes she thought up good stories on the mule, but Joe had forbidden her to indulge. He didn't want her talking after such trashy people. 'You'se Mrs Mayor Starks, Janie. I god, Ah can't see what uh woman uh yo' sability would want tuh be treasurin' all dat gum-grease from folks dat don't even own de house dey sleep in. 'Tain't no earthly use. They's jus' some puny humans playin' round de toes uh Time.'

Janie noted that while he didn't talk the mule himself, he sat and laughed at it. Laughed his big heh, heh laugh too. But then when Lige or Sam or Walter or some of the other big pic-ture talkers were using a side of the world for a canvas, Joe would hustle her off inside the store to sell something. Look like he took pleasure in doing it. Why couldn't he go himself sometimes? She had come to hate the inside of that store anyway. That Post Office too. People always coming and asking for mail at the wrong time. Just when she was trying to count up something or write in an account book. Get her so hackled she'd make the wrong change for stamps. Then too, she couldn't read everybody's writing. Some folks wrote so funny and spelt things different from what she knew about. As a rule, Joe put up the mail himself, but sometimes when he was off she had to do it herself and it always ended up in a fuss.

The store itself kept her with a sick headache. The labor of getting things down off of a shelf or out of a barrel was nothing. And so long as people wanted only a can of tomatoes or a pound of rice it was all right. But supposing they went on and said a pound and a half of bacon and a half pound of lard? The whole thing changed from a little walking and stretching to a mathematical dilemma. Or maybe cheese was thirty-seven cents a pound and somebody came and asked for a dime's worth. She went through many silent rebellions over things like that. Such a waste of life and time. But Joe kept saying that she could do it if she wanted to and he wanted her to use her privileges. That was the rock she was battered against.

This business of the head-rag irked her endlessly. But Jody was set on it. Her hair was NOT going to show in the store. It didn't seem sensible at all. That was because Joe never told Janie how jealous he was. He never told her how often he had seen the other men figuratively wallowing in it as she went about things in the store. And one night he had caught Walter standing behind Janie and brushing the back of his hand back and forth across the loose end of her braid ever so lightly so as to enjoy the feel of it without Janie knowing what he was doing. Joe was at the back of the store and Walter didn't see him. He felt like rushing forth with the meat knife and chopping off the offending hand. That night he ordered Janie to tie up her hair around the store. That was all. She was there in the store for *him* to look at, not those others. But he never said things like that. It just wasn't in him. Take the matter of the yellow mule, for instance.

Late one afternoon Matt came from the west with a halter in his hand. 'Been huntin' fuh mah mule. Anybody seen 'im?' he asked.

'Seen 'im soon dis mornin' over behind de school-house,' Lum said. "Bout ten o'clock or so. He musta been out all night tuh be way over dere dat early.'

'He wuz,' Matt answered. 'Seen 'im last night but Ah couldn't ketch 'im. Ah'm 'bliged tuh git 'im in tuhnight 'cause Ah got some plowin' fuh tuhmorrow. Done promised tuh plow Thompson's grove.'

'Reckon you'll ever git through de job wid dat mule-frame?' Lige asked.

'Aw dat mule is plenty strong. Jus' evil and don't want tuh be led.'

'Dat's right. Dey tell me he brought you heah tuh dis town. Say you started tuh Miccanopy but de mule had better sense and brung yuh on heah.'

'It's uh l-l-lie! Ah set out fuh dis town when Ah left West Floridy.'

'You mean tuh tell me you rode dat mule all de way from West Floridy down heah?'

'Sho he did, Lige. But he didn't mean tuh. He wuz satisfied

up dere, but de mule wuzn't. So one mornin' he got straddle uh de mule and he took and brought 'im on off. Mule had sense. Folks up dat way don't eat biscuit bread but once uh week.'

There was always a little seriousness behind the teasing of Matt, so when he got huffed and walked on off nobody minded. He was known to buy side-meat by the slice. Carried home little bags of meal and flour in his hand. He didn't seem to mind too much so long as it didn't cost him anything.

About half an hour after he left they heard the braying of the mule at the edge of the woods. He was coming past the store very soon.

'Less ketch Matt's mule fuh 'im and have some fun.'

'Now, Lum, you know dat mule ain't aimin' tuh let hisself be caught. Less watch *you* do it.'

When the mule was in front of the store, Lum went out and tackled him. The brute jerked up his head, laid back his ears and rushed to the attack. Lum had to run for safety. Five or six more men left the porch and surrounded the fractious beast, goosing him in the sides and making him show his temper. But he had more spirit left than body. He was soon panting and heaving from the effort of spinning his old carcass about. Everybody was having fun at the mule-baiting. All but Janie.

She snatched her head away from the spectacle and began muttering to herself. 'They oughta be shamed uh theyselves! Teasin' dat poor brute beast lak they is! Done been worked tuh death; done had his disposition ruint wid mistreatment, and now they got tuh finish devilin' 'im tuh death. Wisht Ah had mah way wid 'em all.'

She walked away from the porch and found something to busy herself with in the back of the store so she did not hear Jody when he stopped laughing. She didn't know that he had heard her, but she did hear him yell out, 'Lum, I god, dat's enough! Y'all done had yo' fun now. Stop yo' foolishness and go tell Matt Bonner Ah wants tuh have uh talk wid him right away.'

Janie came back out front and sat down. She didn't say anything and neither did Joe. But after a while he looked down at his feet and said, 'Janie, Ah reckon you better go fetch me dem old black gaiters. Dese tan shoes sets mah feet on fire. Plenty room in 'em, but they hurts regardless.'

She got up without a word and went off for the shoes. A little war of defense for helpless things was going on inside her. People ought to have some regard for helpless things. She wanted to fight about it. 'But Ah hates disagreement and confusion, so Ah better not talk. It makes it hard tuh git along.' She didn't hurry back. She fumbled around long enough to get her face straight. When she got back, Joe was talking with Matt.

'Fifteen dollars? I god you'se as crazy as uh betsy bug! Five dollars.'

'L-l-less we strack uh compermise, Brother Mayor. Less m-make it ten.'

'Five dollars.' Joe rolled his cigar in his mouth and rolled his eyes away indifferently.

'If dat mule is wuth somethin' tuh *you* Brother Mayor, he's wuth mo' tuh me. More special when Ah got uh job uh work tuhmorrow.'

'Five dollars.'

'All right, Brother Mayor. If you wants tuh rob uh poor man lak me uh everything he got tuh make uh livin' wid, Ah'll take de five dollars. Dat mule been wid me twenty-three years. It's mighty hard.'

Mayor Starks deliberately changed his shoes before he reached into his pocket for the money. By that time Matt was wringing and twisting like a hen on a hot brick. But as soon as his hand closed on the money his face broke into a grin.

'Beatyuh tradin' dat time, Starks! Dat mule is liable tuh be dead befo' de week is out. You won't git no work outa him.'

'Didn't buy 'im fuh no work. I god, Ah bought dat varmint tuh let 'im rest. You didn't have gumption enough tuh do it.'

A respectful silence fell on the place. Sam looked at Joe and said, 'Dat's uh new idea 'bout varmints, Mayor Starks. But Ah laks it mah ownself. It's uh noble thing you done.' Everybody agreed with that.

Janie stood still while they all made comments. When it was all done she stood in front of Joe and said, 'Jody, dat wuz uh mighty fine thing fuh you tuh do. 'Tain't everybody would have thought of it, 'cause it ain't no everyday thought. Freein' dat mule makes uh mighty big man outa you. Something like George Washington and Lincoln. Abraham Lincoln, he had de whole United States tuh rule so he freed de Negroes. You got uh town so you freed uh mule. You have tuh have power tuh free things and dat makes you lak uh king uh something.'

Hambo said, 'Yo' wife is uh born orator, Starks. Us never knowed dat befo'. She put jus' de right words tuh our thoughts.'

Joe bit down hard on his cigar and beamed all around, but

he never said a word. The town talked it for three days and said that's just what they would have done if they had been rich men like Joe Starks. Anyhow a free mule in town was something new to talk about. Starks piled fodder under the big tree near the porch and the mule was usually around the store like the other citizens. Nearly everybody took the habit of fetching along a handful of fodder to throw on the pile. He almost got fat and they took a great pride in him. New lies sprung up about his free-mule doings. How he pushed open Lindsay's kitchen door and slept in the place one night and fought until they made coffee for his breakfast; how he stuck his head in the Pearsons' window while the family was at the table and Mrs Pearson mistook him for Rev. Pearson and handed him a plate; he ran Mrs Tully off of the croquet ground for having such an ugly shape; he ran and caught up with Becky Anderson on the way to Maitland so as to keep his head out of the sun under her umbrella; he got tired of listening to Redmond's long-winded prayer, and went inside the Baptist church and broke up the meeting. He did everything but let himself be bridled and visit Matt Bonner.

But way after awhile he died. Lum found him under the big tree on his rawbony back with all four feet up in the air. That wasn't natural and it didn't look right, but Sam said it would have been more unnatural for him to have laid down on his side and died like any other beast. He had seen Death coming and had stood his ground and fought it like a natural man. He had fought it to the last breath. Naturally he didn't have time to straighten himself out. Death had to take him like it found him.

When the news got around, it was like the end of a war or something like that. Everybody that could knocked off from work to stand around and talk. But finally there was nothing to do but drag him out like all other dead brutes. Drag him out to the edge of the hammock which was far enough off to satisfy sanitary conditions in the town. The rest was up to the buzzards. Everybody was going to the dragging-out. The news had got Mayor Starks out of bed before time. His pair of gray horses was out under the tree and the men were fooling with the gear when Janie arrived at the store with Joe's breakast.

'I god, Lum, you fasten up dis store good befo' you leave, you hear me?' He was eating fast and talking with one eye out of the door on the operations.

'Whut you tellin' 'im tuh fasten up for, Jody?' Janie asked surprised.

''Cause it won't be nobody heah tuh look after de store. Ah'm goin' tuh de draggin'-out mahself.'

''Tain't nothin' so important Ah got tuh do tuhday, Jody. How come Ah can't go long wid you tuh de draggin'-out?'

Joe was struck speechless for a minute. 'Why, Janie! You wouldn't be seen at uh draggin'-out, wouldja? Wid any and everybody in uh passle pushin' and shovin' wid they no-manners selves? Naw, naw!'

'You would be dere wid me, wouldn't yuh?'

'Dat's right, but Ah'm uh man even if Ah is de Mayor. But de mayor's wife is somethin' different again. Anyhow they's liable tuh need me tuh say uh few words over de carcass, dis bein' uh special case. But *you* ain't goin' off in all dat mess uh commonness. Ah'm surprised at yuh fuh askin'.'

He wiped his lips of ham gravy and put on his hat. 'Shet de door behind yuh, Janie. Lum is too busy wid de hawses.'

After more shouting of advice and orders and useless comments, the town escorted the carcass off. No, the carcass moved off with the town, and left Janie standing in the doorway.

Out in the swamp they made great ceremony over the mule. They mocked everything human in death. Starks led off with a great eulogy on our departed citizen, our most distinguished citizen and the grief he left behind him, and the people loved the speech. It made him more solid than building the schoolhouse had done. He stood on the distended belly of the mule for a platform and made gestures. When he stepped down, they hoisted Sam up and he talked about the mule as a school teacher first. Then he set his hat like John Pearson and imitated his preaching. He spoke of the joys of mule-heaven to which the dear brother had departed this valley of sorrow; the mule-angels flying around; the miles of green corn and cool water, a pasture of pure bran with a river of molasses running through it; and most glorious of all, *No* Matt Bonner with plow lines and halters to come in and corrupt. Up there, mule-angels would have people to ride on and from his place beside the glittering throne, the dear departed brother would look down into hell and see the devil plowing Matt Bonner all day long in a hell-hot sun and laying the rawhide to his back.

With that the sisters got mock-happy and shouted and had to be held up by the menfolks. Everybody enjoyed themselves to the highest and then finally the mule was left to the already impatient buzzards. They were holding a great flying-meet way up over the heads of the mourners and some of the nearby trees were already peopled with the stoop-shouldered forms.

As soon as the crowd was out of sight they closed in in circles. The near ones got nearer and the far ones got near. A circle, a swoop and a hop with spread-out wings. Close in, close in till some of the more hungry or daring perched on the carcass. They wanted to begin, but the Parson wasn't there, so a messenger was sent to the ruler in a tree where he sat.

The flock had to wait the white-headed leader, but it was hard. They jostled each other and pecked at heads in hungry irritation. Some walked up and down the beast from head to tail, tail to head. The Parson sat motionless in a dead pine tree about two miles off. He had scented the matter as quickly as any of the rest, but decorum demanded that he sit oblivious until he was notified. Then he took off with ponderous flight and circled and lowered, circled and lowered until the others danced in joy and hunger at his approach.

He finally lit on the ground and walked around the body to see if it were really dead. Peered into its nose and mouth. Examined it well from end to end and leaped upon it and bowed, and the others danced a response. That being over, he balanced and asked:

'What killed this man?'

The chorus answered, 'Bare, bare fat.'

'What killed this man?'

'Bare, bare fat.'

'What killed this man?'

'Bare, bare fat.'

'Who'll stand his funeral?'

'We!!!!!'

'Well, all right now.'

So he picked out the eyes in the ceremonial way and the feast went on. The yaller mule was gone from the town except for the porch talk, and for the children visiting his bleaching bones now and then in the spirit of adventure.

Joe returned to the store full of pleasure and good humor but he didn't want Janie to notice it because he saw that she was sullen and he resented that. She had no right to be, the way he thought things out. She wasn't even appreciative of his efforts and she had plenty cause to be. Here he was just pouring honor all over her; building a high chair for her to sit in and overlook the world and she here pouting over it! Not that he wanted anybody else, but just too many women would be glad to be in her place. He ought to box her jaws! But he didn't feel like fighting today, so he made an attack upon her position backhand.

'Ah had tuh laugh at de people out dere in de woods dis mornin', Janie. You can't help but laugh at de capers they cuts. But all the same, Ah wish mah people would git mo' business in 'em and not spend so much time on foolishness.'

'Everybody can't be lak you, Jody. Somebody is bound tuh want tuh laugh and play.'

'Who don't love tuh laugh and play?'

'You make out like you don't, anyhow.'

'I god, Ah don't make out no such uh lie! But it's uh time fuh all things. But it's awful tuh see so many people don't want nothin' but uh full belly and uh place tuh lay down and sleep afterwards. It makes me sad sometimes and then agin it makes me mad. They say things sometimes that tickles me nearly tuh death, but Ah won't laugh jus' tuh dis-incourage 'em.' Janie took the easy way away from a fuss. She didn't change her mind but she agreed with her mouth. Her heart said, 'Even so, but you don't have to cry about it.'

But sometimes Sam Watson and Lige Moss forced a belly laugh out of Joe himself with their eternal arguments. It never ended because there was no end to reach. It was a contest in hyperbole and carried on for no other reason.

Maybe Sam would be sitting on the porch when Lige walked up. If nobody was there to speak of, nothing happened. But if the town was there like on Saturday night, Lige would come up with a very grave air. Couldn't even pass the time of day, for being so busy thinking. Then when he was asked what was the matter in order to start him off, he'd say, 'Dis question done 'bout drove me crazy. And Sam, he know so much into things, Ah wants some information on de subject.'

Walter Thomas was due to speak up and egg the matter on. 'Yeah, Sam always got more information than he know what to do wid. He's bound to tell yuh whatever it is you wants tuh know.'

Sam begins an elaborate show of avoiding the struggle. That draws everybody on the porch into it.

'How come you want me *tuh* tell yuh? You always claim God done met you round de cornder and talked His inside business wid yuh. 'Tain't no use in you askin' *me* nothin'. Ah'm questionizin' *you*.'

'How you gointuh do dat, Sam, when Ah arrived dis conversation mahself? Ah'm askin' *you*.'

'Askin' me what? You ain't told me de subjick yit.'

'Don't aim tuh tell yuh! Ah aims tuh keep yuh in de dark all de time. If you'se smart lak you let on you is, you kin find out.'

'Yuh skeered to lemme know whut it is, 'cause yuh know Ah'll tear it tuh pieces. You got to have a subjick tuh talk from, do yuh can't talk. If uh man ain't got no bounds, he ain't got no place tuh stop.'

By this time, they are the center of the world.

'Well all right then. Since you own up you ain't smart enough tuh find out whut Ah'm talkin' 'bout, Ah'll tell you. Whut is it dat keeps uh man from gettin' burnt on uh red-hot stove – caution or nature?'

'Shucks! Ah thought you had somethin' hard tuh ast me. Walter kin tell yuh dat.'

'If de conversation is too deep for yuh, how come yuh don't tell me so, and hush up? Walter can't tell me nothin' uh de kind. Ah'm uh educated man, Ah keeps mah arrangements in mah hands, and if it kept me up all night long studyin' 'bout it, Walter ain't liable tuh be no help to me. Ah needs uh man lak you.'

'And then again, Lige, Ah'm gointuh tell yuh. Ah'm gointuh run dis conversation from uh gnat heel to uh lice. It's nature dat keeps uh man off of uh red-hot stove.'

'Uuh huuh! Ah knowed you would going tuh crawl up in dat holler! But Ah aims tuh smoke yuh right out. 'Tain't no nature at all, it's caution, Sam.'

''Tain't no sich uh thing! Nature tells yuh not tuh fool wid no red-hot stove, and you don't do it neither.'

'Listen, Sam, if it was nature, nobody wouldn't have tuh look out for babies touchin' stoves, would they? 'Cause dey just naturally wouldn't touch it. But dey sho will. So it's caution.'

'Naw it ain't, it's nature, cause nature makes caution. It's de strongest thing dat God ever made, now. Fact is it's de onliest thing God ever made. He made nature and nature made everything else.'

'Naw nature didn't neither. A whole heap of things ain't even been made yit.'

'Tell me somethin' you know of dat nature ain't made.'

'She ain't made it so you kin ride uh butt-headed cow and hold on tuh de horns.'

'Yeah, but dat ain't yo' point.'

'Yeah it is too.'

'Naw it ain't neither.'

'Well what *is* mah point?'

'You ain't got none, so far.'

'Yeah he is too,' Walter cut in, 'de red-hot stove is his point.'

'He know mighty much, but he ain't proved it yit.'

'Sam, Ah say it's caution, not nature dat keeps folks off uh red-hot stove.'

'How is de son gointuh be before his paw? Nature is de first of everything. Ever since self was self, nature been keepin' folks off of red-hot stoves. Dat caution you talkin' 'bout ain't nothin' but uh humbug. He's uh inseck dat nothin' he got belongs to him. He got eyes, lak somethin' else; wings lak somethin' else – everything! Even his hum is de sound of somebody else.'

'Man, whut you talkin' 'bout? Caution is de greatest thing in de world. If it wasn't for caution—'

'Show me somethin' dat caution ever made! Look whut nature took and done. Nature got so high in uh black hen she got tuh lay uh white egg. Now you tell me, how come, whut got intuh man dat he got tuh have hair round his mouth? Nature!'

'Dat ain't—'

The porch was boiling now. Starks left the store to Hezekiah Potts, the delivery boy, and come took a seat in his high chair.

'Look at dat great big ole scoundrel-beast up dere at Hall's fillin' station – uh great big old scoundrel. He eats up all de folks outa de house and den eat de house.'

'Aw 'tain't no sich a varmint nowhere dat kin eat no house! Dat's uh lie. Ah wuz dere yiste'ddy and Ah ain't seen nothin' lak dat. Where is he?'

'Ah didn't see him but Ah reckon he is in de back-yard some place. But dey got his picture out front dere. They was nailin' it up when Ah come pass dere dis evenin'.'

'Well all right now, if he eats up houses how come he don't eat up de fillin' station?'

'Dat's 'cause dey got him tied up so he can't. Dey got uh great big picture tellin' how many gallons of dat Sinclair high-compression gas he drink at one time and how he's more'n uh million years old.'

''Tain't *nothin'* no million years old!'

'De picture is right up dere where anybody kin see it. Dey can't make de picture till dey see de thing, kin dey?'

'How dey goin' to tell he's uh million years old? Nobody wasn't born dat fur back.'

'By de rings on his tail Ah reckon. Man, dese white folks got ways for tellin' anything dey wants tuh know.'

'Well, where he been at all dis time, then?'

'Dey caught him over dere in Egypt. Seem lak he used tuh hang round dere and eat up dem Pharaohs' tombstones. Dey got de picture of him doin' it. Nature is high in uh varmint lak dat. Nature and salt. Dat's whut makes up strong man lak Big John de Conquer. He was uh man wid salt in him. He could give uh flavor to *anything*.'

'Yeah, but he was uh man dat wuz more'n man. 'Tain't no mo' lak him. He wouldn't dig potatoes, and he wouldn't rake hay: He wouldn't take a whipping, and he wouldn't run away.'

'Oh yeah, somebody else could if dey tried hard enough. Me mahself, Ah got salt in *me*. If Ah like man flesh, Ah could eat some man every day, some of 'em is so trashy they'd let me eat 'em.'

'Lawd, Ah loves to talk about Big John. Less we tell lies on Ole John.'

But here come Bootsie, and Teadi and Big 'oman down the street making out they are pretty by the way they walk. They have got that fresh, new taste about them like young mustard greens in the spring, and the young men on the porch are just bound to tell them about it and buy them some treats.

'Heah come mah order right now,' Charlie Jones announces

and scrambles off the porch to meet them. But he has plenty of competition. A pushing, shoving show of gallantry. They all beg the girls to just buy anything they can think of. Please let them pay for it. Joe is begged to wrap up all the candy in the store and order more. All the peanuts and soda water – everything!

'Gal, Ah'm crazy 'bout you,' Charlie goes on to the entertainment of everybody. 'Ah'll do anything in the world except work for you and give you mah money.'

The girls and everybody else help laugh. They know it's not courtship. It's acting-out courtship and everybody is in the play. The three girls hold the center of the stage till Daisy Blunt comes walking down the street in the moonlight.

Daisy is walking a drum tune. You can almost hear it by looking at the way she walks. She is black and she knows that white clothes look good on her, so she wears them for dress up. She's got those big black eyes with plenty shiny white in them that makes them shine like brand new money and she knows what God gave women eyelashes for, too. Her hair is not what you might call straight. It's negro hair, but it's got a kind of white flavor. Like the piece of string out of a ham. It's not ham at all, but it's been around ham and got the flavor. It was spread down thick and heavy over her shoulders and looked just right under a big white hat.

'Lawd, Lawd, Lawd,' that same Charlie Jones exclaims rushing over to Daisy. 'It must be uh recess in heben if St Peter is lettin' his angels out lak dis. You got three men already layin' at de point uh death 'bout yuh, and heah's uhnother fool dat's willin' tuh make time on yo' gang.'

All the rest of the single men have crowded around Daisy by this time. She is parading and blushing at the same time.

'If you know anybody dat's 'bout tuh die 'bout me, yuh know more'n Ah do,' Daisy bridled. 'Wisht Ah knowed who it is.'

'Now, Daisy, *you* know Jim, and Dave and Lum is 'bout tuh kill one 'nother 'bout you. Don't stand up here and tell dat big ole got-dat-wrong.'

'Dey a mighty hush-mouf about it if dey is. Dey ain't never told me nothin'.'

'Unhunh, you talked too fast. Heah, Jim and Dave is right upon de porch and Lum is inside de store.'

A big burst of laughter at Daisy's discomfiture. The boys had to act out their rivalry too. Only this time, everybody knew they meant some of it. But all the same the porch enjoyed the play and helped out whenever extras were needed.

David said, 'Jim don't love Daisy. He don't love yuh lak Ah do.'

Jim bellowed indignantly, 'Who don't love Daisy? Ah know you ain't talkin' 'bout me.'

Dave: 'Well all right, less prove dis thing right now. We'll prove right now who love dis gal de best. How much time is you willin' tuh make fuh Daisy?'

Jim: 'Twenty yeahs!'

Dave: 'See? Ah told yuh dat nigger didn't love yuh. Me, Ah'll beg de Judge tuh hang me, and wouldn't take nothin' less than life.'

There was a big long laugh from the porch. Then Jim had to demand a test.

'Dave, how much would you be willin' tuh do for Daisy if she was to turn fool enough tuh marry yuh.'

'Me and Daisy done talked dat over, but if you just got tuh know, Ah'd buy Daisy uh passenger train and give it tuh her.'

'Humph! Is dat all? Ah'd buy her uh steamship and then Ah'd hire some mens tuh run it fur her.'

'Daisy, don't let Jim fool you wid his talk. He don't aim tuh do nothin' fuh yuh. Uh lil ole steamship! Daisy, Ah'll take uh job cleanin' out de Atlantic Ocean fuh you any time you say you so desire.' There was a great laugh and then they hushed to listen.

'Daisy,' Jim began, 'you know mah heart and all de ranges uh mah mind. And you know if Ah wuz ridin' up in uh earoplane way up in de sky and Ah looked down and seen you walkin' and knowed you'd have tuh walk ten miles tuh git home, Ah'd step backward offa dat earoplane just to walk home wid you.'

There was one of those big blow-out laughs and Janie was wallowing in it. Then Jody ruined it all for her.

Mrs Bogle came walking down the street towards the porch. Mrs Bogle who was many times a grandmother, but had a blushing air of coquetry about her that cloaked her sunken cheeks. You saw a fluttering fan before her face and magnolia blooms and sleepy lakes under the moonlight when she walked. There was no obvious reason for it, it was just so. Her first husband had been a coachman but 'studied jury' to win her. He had finally become a preacher to hold her till his death. Her second husband worked in Fohnes orange grove – but tried to preach when he caught her eye. He never got any further than a class leader, but that was something to offer her. It proved his love and pride. She was a wind on the ocean. She moved men, but the helm determined the port. Now, this night she mounted the steps and the men noticed her until she passed inside the door.

'I god, Janie,' Starks said impatiently, 'why don't you go on and see whut Mrs Bogle want? Whut you waitin' on?'

Janie wanted to hear the rest of the play-acting and how it ended, but she got up sullenly and went inside. She came back to the porch with her bristles sticking out all over her and with dissatisfaction written all over her face. Joe saw it and lifted his own hackles a bit.

Jim Weston had secretly borrowed a dime and soon he was loudly beseeching Daisy to have a treat on him. Finally she consented to take a pickled pig foot on him. Janie was getting up a large order when they came in, so Lum waited on them. That is, he went back to the keg but came back without the pig foot.

'Mist' Starks, de pig feets is all gone!' he called out.

'Aw naw dey ain't, Lum. Ah bought uh whole new kag of 'em wid dat last order from Jacksonville. It come in yistiddy.'

Joe came and helped Lum look but he couldn't find the new keg either, so he went to the nail over his desk that he used for a file to search for the order.

'Janie, where's dat last bill uh ladin'?'

'It's right dere on de nail, ain't it?'

'Naw it ain't neither. You ain't put it where Ah told yuh tuh. If you'd git yo' mind out de streets and keep it on yo' business maybe you could git somethin' straight sometimes.'

'Aw, look around dere, Jody. Dat bill ain't apt tuh be gone off nowheres. If it ain't hangin' on de nail, it's on yo' desk. You bound tuh find it if you look.'

'Wid you heah, Ah oughtn't tuh hafta do all dat lookin' and searchin'. Ah done told you time and time agin tuh stick all dem papers on dat nail! All you got tuh do is mind me. How come you can't do lak Ah tell yuh?'

'You sho loves to tell me whut to do, but Ah can't tell you nothin' Ah see!'

'Dat's 'cause you need tellin',' he rejoined hotly. 'It would be pitiful if Ah didn't. Somebody got to think for women and chillun and chickens and cows. I god, they sho don't think none theirselves.'

'Ah knows uh few things, and womenfolks thinks sometimes too!'

'Aw naw they don't. They just think they's thinkin'. When Ah see one thing Ah understands ten. You see ten things and don't understand one.'

Times and scenes like that put Janie to thinking about the inside state of her marriage. Time came when she fought back with her tongue as best she could, but it didn't do her any good. It just made Joe do more. He wanted her submission and he'd keep on fighting until he felt he had it.

So gradually, she pressed her teeth together and learned to hush. The spirit of the marriage left the bedroom and took to living in the parlor. It was there to shake hands whenever company came to visit, but it never went back inside the bedroom again. So she put something in there to represent the spirit like a Virgin Mary image in a church. The bed was no longer a daisy-field for her and Joe to play in. It was a place where she went and laid down when she was sleepy and tired.

She wasn't petal-open anymore with him. She was twenty-four and seven years married when she knew. She found that out one day when he slapped her face in the kitchen. It happened over one of those dinners that chasten all women sometimes. They plan and they fix and they do, and then some kitchen-dwelling fiend slips a scrochy, soggy, tasteless mess into their pots and pans. Janie was a good cook, and Joe had looked forward to his dinner as a refuge from other things. So when the bread didn't rise, and the fish wasn't quite done at the bone, and the rice was scorched, he slapped Janie until she had a ringing sound in her ears and told her about her brains before he stalked on back to the store.

Janie stood where he left her for unmeasured time and thought. She stood there until something fell off the shelf inside her. Then she went inside there to see what it was. It was her image of Jody tumbled down and shattered. But looking at it she saw that it never was the flesh and blood figure of her dreams. Just something she had grabbed up to drape her dreams over. In a way she turned her back upon the image where it lay and looked further. She had no more blossomy openings dusting pollen over her man, neither any glistening young fruit where the petals used to be. She found that she had a host of thoughts she had never expressed to him, and numerous emotions she had never let Jody know about. Things packed up and put away in parts of her heart where he could never find them. She was saving up feelings for some man she had never seen. She had an inside and an outside now and suddenly she knew how not to mix them.

She bathed and put on a fresh dress and head kerchief and went on to the store before Jody had time to send for her. That was a bow to the outside of things.

Jody was on the porch and the porch was full of Eatonville as usual at this time of the day. He was baiting Mrs Tony Robbins as he always did when she came to the store. Janie could see Jody watching her out of the corner of his eye while he joked roughly with Mrs Robbins. He wanted to be friendly with her again. His big, big laugh was as much for her as for the baiting. He was longing for peace but on his own terms.

'I god, Mrs Robbins, whut make you come heah and worry me when you see Ah'm readin' mah newspaper?' Mayor Starks lowered the paper in pretended annoyance.

Mrs Robbins struck her pity-pose and assumed the voice.

''Cause Ah'm hongry, Mist' Starks. 'Deed Ah is. Me and mah chillun is hongry. Tony don't fee-eed me!'

This was what the porch was waiting for. They burst into a laugh.

'Mrs Robbins, how can you make out you'se hongry when Tony comes in here every Satitday and buys groceries lak a man? Three weeks' shame on yuh!'

'If he buy all dat you talkin' 'bout, Mist' Starks, God knows whut he do wid it. He sho don't bring it home, and me and mah po' chillun is *so* hongry! Mist' Starks, please gimme uh lil piece uh meat fur me and mah chillun.'

'Ah know you don't need it, but come on inside. You ain't goin' tuh lemme read till Ah give it to yuh.'

Mrs Tony's ecstasy was divine. 'Thank you, Mist' Starks. You'se noble! You'se du most gentlemanfied man Ah ever did see. You'se uh king!'

The salt pork box was in the back of the store and during the walk Mrs Tony was so eager she sometimes stepped on Joe's heels, sometimes she was a little before him. Something like a hungry cat when somebody approaches her pan with meat. Running a little, caressing a little and all the time making little urging-on cries.

'Yes, indeedy, Mist' Starks, you'se noble. You got sympathy for me and mah po' chillun. Tony don't give us nothin' tuh eat and we'se *so* hungry. Tony don't fee-eed me!'

This brought them to the meat box. Joe took up the big meat knife and selected a piece of side meat to cut. Mrs Tony was all but dancing around him.

'Dat's right, Mist' Starks! Gimme uh lil piece 'bout dis wide.' She indicated as wide as her wrist and hand. 'Me and mah chillun is *so* hongry!'

Starks hardly looked at her measurements. He had seen them too often. He marked off a piece much smaller and sunk the blade in. Mrs Tony all but fell to the floor in her agony.

'Lawd a'mussy! Mist' Starks, you ain't gointuh gimme dat lil tee-ninchy piece fuh me and all mah chillun, is yuh? Lawd, we'se *so* hongry!'

Starks cut right on and reached for a piece of wrapping paper. Mrs Tony leaped away from the proffered cut of meat as if it were a rattlesnake.

'Ah wouldn't tetch it! Dat lil eyeful uh bacon for me and all

84

mah chillun! Lawd, some folks is got everything and they's so gripin' and so mean!'

Starks made as if to throw the meat back in the box and close it. Mrs Tony swooped like lightning and seized it, and started towards the door.

'Some folks ain't got no heart in dey bosom. They's willin' tuh see uh po' woman and her helpless chillun starve tuh death. God's gointuh put 'em under arrest, some uh dese days, wid dey stingy gripin' ways.'

She stepped from the store porch and marched off in high dudgeon! Some laughed and some got mad.

'If dat wuz *mah* wife,' said Walter Thomas, 'Ah'd kill her cemetery dead.'

'More special after Ah done bought her everything mah wages kin stand, lak Tony do,' Coker said. 'In de fust place Ah never would spend on *no* woman whut Tony spend on *her*.'

Starks came back and took his seat. He had to stop and add the meat to Tony's account.

'Well, Tony tells me tuh humor her along. He moved here from up de State hopin' tuh change her, but it ain't. He say he can't bear tuh leave her and he hate to kill her, so 'tain't nothin' tuh do but put up wid her.'

'Dat's 'cause Tony love her too good,' said Coker. 'Ah could break her if she wuz mine. Ah'd break her or kill her. Makin' uh fool outa me in front of everybody.'

'Tony won't never hit her. He says beatin' women is just like steppin' on baby chickens. He claims 'tain't no place on uh woman tuh hit,' Joe Lindsay said with scornful disapproval, 'but Ah'd kill uh baby just born dis mawnin' fuh uh thing lak dat. 'Tain't nothin' but low-down spitefulness 'ginst her husband make her do it.'

'Dat's de God's truth,' Jim Stone agreed. 'Dat's de very reason.'

Janie did what she had never done before, that is, thrust herself into the conversation.

'Sometimes God gits familiar wid us womenfolks too and talks His inside business. He told me how surprised He was 'bout y'all turning out so smart after Him makin' yuh different; and how surprised y'all is goin' tuh be if you ever find out you don't know half as much 'bout us as you think you do. It's so easy to make yo'self out God Almighty when you ain't got nothin' tuh strain against but women and chickens.'

'You gettin' too moufy, Janie,' Starks told her. 'Go fetch me de checker-board *and* de checkers. Sam Watson, you'se mah fish.'

7

The years took all the fight out of Janie's face. For a while she thought it was gone from her soul. No matter what Jody did, she said nothing. She had learned how to talk some and leave some. She was a rut in the road. Plenty of life beneath the surface but it was kept beaten down by the wheels. Sometimes she stuck out into the future, imagining her life different from what it was. But mostly she lived between her hat and her heels, with her emotional disturbances like shade patterns in the woods – come and gone with the sun. She got nothing from Jody except what money could buy, and she was giving away what she didn't value.

Now and again she thought of a country road at sun-up and considered flight. To where? To what? Then too she considered thirty-five is twice seventeen and nothing was the same at all.

'Maybe he ain't nothin',' she cautioned herself, 'but he is something in my mouth. He's got tuh be else Ah ain't got nothin' tuh live for. Ah'll lie and say he is. If Ah don't, life won't be nothin' but uh store and uh house.'

She didn't read books so she didn't know that she was the world and the heavens boiled down to a drop. Man attempting to climb to painless heights from his dung hill.

Then one day she sat and watched the shadow of herself going about tending store and prostrating itself before Jody, while all the time she herself sat under a shady tree with the wind blowing through her hair and her clothes. Somebody near about making summertime out of lonesomeness.

This was the first time it happened, but after a while it got so common she ceased to be surprised. It was like a drug. In a way it was good because it reconciled her to things. She got so she received all things with the stolidness of the earth which soaks up urine and perfume with the same indifference.

One day she noticed that Joe didn't sit down. He just stood in front of a chair and fell in it. That made her look at him all over. Joe wasn't so young as he used to be. There was already something dead about him. He didn't rear back in his knees any longer. He squatted over his ankles when he walked. That stillness at the back of his neck. His prosperous-looking belly that used to thrust out so pugnaciously and intimidate folks, sagged like a load suspended from his loins. It didn't seem to be a part of him anymore. Eyes a little absent too.

Jody must have noticed it too. Maybe, he had seen it long before Janie did, and had been fearing for her to see. Because he began to talk about her age all the time, as if he didn't want her to stay young while he grew old. It was always 'You oughta throw somethin' over yo' shoulders befo' you go outside. You ain't no young pullet no mo'. You'se uh ole hen now.' One day he called her off the croquet grounds. 'Dat's somethin' for de young folks, Janie, you out dere jumpin' round and won't be able tuh git out de bed tuhmorrer.' If he thought to deceive her, he was wrong. For the first time she could see a man's head naked of its skull. Saw the cunning thoughts race in and out through the caves and promontories of his mind long before they darted out of the tunnel of his mouth. She saw he was hurting inside so she let it pass without talking. She just measured out a little time for him and set it aside to wait.

It got to be terrible in the store. The more his back ached and his muscle dissolved into fat and the fat melted off his bones, the more fractious he became with Janie. Especially in the store. The more people in there the more ridicule he poured over her body to point attention away from his own. So one day Steve Mixon wanted some chewing tobacco and Janie cut it wrong. She hated that tobacco knife anyway. It worked very stiff. She fumbled with the thing and cut way away from the mark. Mixon didn't mind. He held it up for a joke to tease Janie a little.

'Looka heah, Brother Mayor, whut yo' wife done took and done.' It was cut comical, so everybody laughed at it. 'Uh woman and uh knife – no kind of uh knife, don't b'long tuhgether.' There was some more good-natured laughter at the expense of women.

Jody didn't laugh. He hurried across from the post office side and took the plug of tobacco away from Mixon and cut it again. Cut it exactly on the mark and glared at Janie.

'I god amighty! A woman stay round uh store till she get old as Methusalem and still can't cut a little thing like a plug of tobacco! Don't stand dere rollin' yo' pop eyes at me wid yo' rump hangin' nearly to yo' knees!'

A big laugh started off in the store but people got to thinking

89

and stopped. It was funny if you looked at it right quick, but it got pitiful if you thought about it awhile. It was like somebody snatched off part of a woman's clothes while she wasn't looking and the streets were crowded. Then too, Janie took the middle of the floor to talk right into Jody's face, and that was something that hadn't been done before.

'Stop mixin' up mah doings wid mah looks, Jody. When you git through tellin' me how tuh cut uh plug uh tobacco, then you kin tell me whether mah behind is on straight or not.'

'Wha – whut's dat you say, Janie? You must be out yo' head.'

'Naw, Ah ain't outa mah head neither.'

'You must be. Talkin' any such language as dat.'

'You de one started talkin' under people's clothes. Not me.'

'Whut's de matter wid you, nohow? You ain't no young girl to be gettin' all insulted 'bout yo' looks. You ain't no young courtin' gal. You'se uh ole woman, nearly forty.'

'Yeah, Ah'm nearly forty and you'se already fifty. How come you can't talk about dat sometimes instead of always pointin' at me?'

'T'ain't no use in gettin' all mad, Janie, 'cause Ah mention you ain't no young gal no mo'. Nobody in heah ain't lookin' for no wife outa yuh. Old as you is.'

'Naw, Ah ain't no young gal no mo' but den Ah ain't no old woman neither. Ah reckon Ah looks mah age too. But Ah'm uh woman every inch of me, and Ah know it. Dat's uh whole lot more'n *you* kin say. You big-bellies round here and put out a lot of brag, but 'tain't nothin' to it but yo' big voice. Humph! Talkin' 'bout *me* lookin' old! When you pull down yo' britches, you look lak de change uh life.'

'Great God from Zion!' Sam Watson gasped. 'Y'all really playin' de dozens tuhnight.'

'Wha – whut's dat you said?' Joe challenged, hoping his ears had fooled him.

'You heard her, you ain't blind,' Walter taunted.

'Ah ruther be shot with tacks than tuh hear dat 'bout mahself,' Lige Moss commiserated.

Then Joe Starks realized all the meanings and his vanity bled like a flood. Janie had robbed him of his illusion of irresistible maleness that all men cherish, which was terrible. The thing that Saul's daughter had done to David. But Janie had done worse, she had cast down his empty armor before men and they had laughed, would keep on laughing. When he paraded his possessions hereafter, they would not consider the two together. They'd look with envy at the things and pity the man that owned them. When he sat in judgment it would be the same. Good-for-nothing's like Dave and Lum and Jim wouldn't change place with him. For what can excuse a man in the eyes of other men for lack of strength? Raggedy-behind squirts of sixteen and seventeen would be giving him their merciless pity out of their eyes while their mouths said something humble. There was nothing to do in life anymore. Ambition was useless. And the cruel deceit of Janie! Making all that show of humbleness and scorning him all the time! Laughing at him, and now putting the town up to do the same. Joe Starks didn't know the words for all this, but he knew the feeling. So he struck Janie with all his might and drove her from the store.

8

After that night Jody moved his things and slept in a room downstairs. He didn't really hate Janie, but he wanted her to think so. He had crawled off to lick his wounds. They didn't talk too much around the store either. Anybody that didn't know would have thought that things had blown over, it looked so quiet and peaceful around. But the stillness was the sleep of swords. So new thoughts had to be thought and new words said. She didn't want to live like that. Why must Joe be so mad with her for making him look small when he did it to her all the time? Had been doing it for years. Well, if she must eat out of a long-handled spoon, she must. Jody might get over his mad spell any time at all and begin to act like somebody towards her.

Then too she noticed how baggy Joe was getting all over. Like bags hanging from an ironing board. A little sack hung from the corners of his eyes and rested on his cheek-bones; a loose-filled bag of feathers hung from his ears and rested on his neck beneath his chin. A sack of flabby something hung from his loins and rested on his thighs when he sat down. But even these things were running down like candle grease as time moved on.

He made new alliances too. People he never bothered with one way or another now seemed to have his ear. He had always been scornful of root-doctors and all their kind, but now she saw a faker from over around Altamonte Springs, hanging around the place almost daily. Always talking in low tones when she came near, or hushed altogether. She didn't know that he was driven by a desperate hope to appear the old-time body in her sight. She was sorry about the root-doctor because she feared that Joe was depending on the scoundrel to make him well when what he needed was a doctor, and a good one. She was worried about his not eating his meals, till she found out he was having old lady Davis to cook for him. She knew that she was a much better cook than the old woman, and cleaner about the kitchen. So she bought a beef-bone and made him some soup.

'Naw, thank you,' he told her shortly. 'Ah'm havin' uh hard enough time tuh try and git well as it is.'

She was stunned at first and hurt afterwards. So she went straight to her bosom friend, Pheoby Watson, and told her about it.

'Ah'd ruther be dead than for Jody tuh think Ah'd hurt him,' she sobbed to Pheoby. 'It ain't always been too pleasant, 'cause you know how Joe worships de works of his own hands, but God in heben knows Ah wouldn't do one thing tuh hurt nobody. It's too underhand and mean.'

'Janie, Ah thought maybe de thing would die down and you

never would know nothin' 'bout it, but it's been singin' round here ever since de big fuss in de store dat Joe was "fixed" and you wuz de one dat did it.'

'Pheoby, for de longest time, Ah been feelin' dat somethin' set for still-bait, but dis is – is – oh Pheoby! Whut *kin* I do?'

'You can't do nothin' but make out you don't know it. It's too late fuh y'all tuh be splittin' up and gittin' divorce. Just g'wan back home and set down on yo' royal diasticutis and say nothin'. Nobody don't b'lieve it nohow.'

'Tuh think Ah been wid Jody twenty yeahs and Ah just now got tuh bear de name uh poisonin' him! It's 'bout to kill me, Pheoby. Sorrow dogged by sorrow is in mah heart.'

'Dat's lie dat trashy nigger dat calls hisself uh two-headed doctor brought tuh 'im in order tuh git in wid Jody. He seen he wuz sick – everybody been knowin' dat for de last longest, and den Ah reckon he heard y'all wuz kind of at variance, so dat wuz his chance. Last summer dat multiplied cockroach wuz round heah tryin' tuh sell gophers!'

'Pheoby, Ah don't even b'lieve Jody b'lieve dat lie. He ain't never took no stock in de mess. He just make out he b'lieve it tuh hurt me. Ah'm stone dead from standin' still and tryin' tuh smile.'

She cried often in the weeks that followed. Joe got too weak to look after things and took to his bed. But he relentlessly refused to admit her to his sick-room. People came and went in the house. This one and that one came into her house with covered plates of broth and other sick-room dishes without taking the least notice of her as Joe's wife. People who never had known what it was to enter the gate of the Mayor's yard unless it were to do some menial job now paraded in and out as his confidants. They came to the store and ostentatiously looked over whatever she was doing and went back to report to him at the house. Said things like 'Mr Starks need *somebody* tuh sorta look out for 'im till he kin git on his feet again and look for hisself.'

But Jody was never to get on his feet again. Janie had Sam Watson to bring her the news from the sick-room, and when he told her how things were, she had him bring a doctor from Orlando without giving Joe a chance to refuse, and without saying she sent for him.

'Just a matter of time,' the doctor told her. 'When a man's kidneys stop working altogether, there is no way for him to live. He needed medical attention two years ago. Too late now.'

So Janie began to think of Death. Death, that strange being with the huge square toes who lived way in the West. The great one who lived in the straight house like a platform without sides to it, and without a roof. What need has Death for a cover, and what winds can blow against him? He stands in his high house that overlooks the world. Stands watchful and motionless all day with his sword drawn back, waiting for the messenger to bid him come. Been standing there before there was a where or a when or a then. She was liable to find a feather from his wings lying in her yard any day now. She was sad and afraid too. Poor Jody! He ought not to have to wrassle in there by himself. She sent Sam in to suggest a visit, but Jody said No. These medical doctors wuz all right with the Godly sick, but they didn't know a thing about a case like his. He'd

95

be all right just as soon as the two-headed man found what had been buried against him. He wasn't going to die at all. That was what he thought. But Sam told her different, so she knew. And then if he hadn't, the next morning she was bound to know, for people began to gather in the big yard under the palm and chinaberry trees. People who would not have dared to foot the place before crept in and did not come to the house. Just squatted under the trees and waited. Rumor, that wingless bird, had shadowed over the town.

She got up that morning with the firm determination to go on in there and have a good talk with Jody. But she sat a long time with the walls creeping in on her. Four walls squeezing her breath out. Fear lest he depart while she sat trembling upstairs nerved her and she was inside the room before she caught her breath. She didn't make the cheerful, casual start that she had thought out. Something stood like an oxen's foot on her tongue, and then too, Jody, no Joe, gave her a ferocious look. A look with all the unthinkable coldness of outer space. She must talk to a man who was ten immensities away.

He was lying on his side facing the door like he was expecting somebody or something. A sort of changing look on his face. Weak-looking but sharp-pointed about the eyes. Through the thin counterpane she could see what was left of his belly huddled before him on the bed like some helpless thing seeking shelter.

The half-washed bedclothes hurt her pride for Jody. He had always been so clean.

'Whut you doin' in heah, Janie?'

'Come tuh see 'bout you and how you wuz makin' out.'

He gave a deep-growling sound like a hog dying down in the swamp and trying to drive off disturbance. 'Ah come in heah tuh git shet uh you but look lak 'tain't doin' me no good. G'wan out. Ah needs tuh rest.'

'Naw, Jody, Ah come in heah tuh talk widja and Ah'm gointuh do it too. It's for both of our sakes Ah'm talkin'.'

He gave another ground grumble and eased over on his back.

'Jody, maybe Ah ain't been sich uh good wife tuh you, but Jody—'

'Dat's 'cause you ain't got de right feelin' for nobody. You oughter have some sympathy 'bout yo'self. You ain't no hog.'

'But, Jody, Ah meant tuh be awful nice.'

'Much as Ah done fuh yuh. Holdin' me up tuh scorn. No sympathy!'

'Naw, Jody, it wasn't because Ah didn't have no sympathy. Ah had uh lavish uh dat. Ah just didn't never git no chance tuh use none of it. You wouldn't let me.'

'Dat's right, blame everything on me. Ah wouldn't let you show no feelin'! When, Janie, dat's all Ah ever wanted or desired. Now you come blamin' me!'

''Tain't dat, Jody. Ah ain't here tuh blame nobody. Ah'm just tryin' tuh make you know what kinda person Ah is befo' it's too late.'

'Too late?' he whispered.

His eyes buckled in a vacant-mouthed terror and she saw the awful surprise in his face and answered it.

'Yeah, Jody, don't keer whut dat multiplied cockroach told yuh tuh git yo' money, you got tuh die, and yuh can't live.'

A deep sob came out of Jody's weak frame. It was like beating a bass drum in a hen-house. Then it rose high like pulling in a trombone.

'Janie! Janie! don't tell me Ah got tuh die, and Ah ain't used tuh thinkin' 'bout it.'

"Tain't really no need of you dying, Jody, if you had of – de doctor – but it don't do no good bringin' dat up now. Dat's just whut Ah wants tuh say, Jody. You wouldn't listen. You done lived wid me for twenty years and you don't half know me atall. And you could have but you was so busy worshippin' de works of yo' own hands, and cuffin' folks around in their minds till you didn't see uh whole heap uh things yuh could have.'

'Leave heah, Janie. Don't come heah—'

'Ah knowed you wasn't gointuh lissen tuh me. You changes everything but nothin' don't change you – not even death. But Ah ain't goin' outa here and Ah ain't gointuh hush. Naw, you gointuh listen tuh me one time befo' you die. Have yo' way all yo' life, trample and mash down and then die ruther than tuh let yo'self heah 'bout it. Listen, Jody, you ain't de Jody ah run off down de road wid. You'se whut's left after he died. Ah run off tuh keep house wid you in uh wonderful way. But you wasn't satisfied wid me de way Ah was. Naw! Mah own mind had tuh be squeezed and crowded out tuh make room for yours in me.'

'Shut up! Ah wish thunder and lightnin' would kill yuh!'

'Ah know it. And now you got tuh die tuh find out dat you got tuh pacify somebody besides yo'self if you wants any love and any sympathy in dis world. You ain't tried tuh pacify *nobody* but yo'self. Too busy listening tuh yo' own big voice.'

'All dis tearin' down talk!' Jody whispered with sweat globules forming all over his face and arms. 'Git outa heah!'

'All dis bowin' down, all dis obedience under yo' voice – dat ain't whut Ah rushed off down de road tuh find out about you.'

A sound of strife in Jody's throat, but his eyes stared unwillingly into a corner of the room so Janie knew the futile fight was not with her. The icy sword of the square-toed one had cut off his breath and left his hands in a pose of agonizing protest. Janie gave them peace on his breast, then she studied his dead face for a long time.

'Dis sittin' in de rulin' chair is been hard on Jody,' she muttered out loud. She was full of pity for the first time in years. Jody had been hard on her and others, but life had mishandled him too. Poor Joe! Maybe if she had known some other way to try, she might have made his face different. But what that other way could be, she had no idea. She thought back and forth about what had happened in the making of a voice out of a man. Then thought about herself. Years ago, she had told her girl self to wait for her in the looking glass. It had been a long time since she had remembered. Perhaps she'd better look. She went over to the dresser and looked hard at her skin and features. The young girl was gone, but a handsome woman had taken her place. She tore off the kerchief from her head and let down her plentiful hair. The weight, the length, the glory was there. She took careful stock of herself, then combed her hair and tied it back up again. Then she starched and ironed her face, forming it into just what people wanted to see, and opened up the window and cried, 'Come heah people! Jody is dead. Mah husband is gone from me.'

9

Joe's funeral was the finest thing Orange County had ever seen with Negro eyes. The motor hearse, the Cadillac and Buick carriages; Dr Henderson there in his Lincoln; the hosts from far and wide. Then again the gold and red and purple, the gloat and glamor of the secret orders, each with its insinuations of power and glory undreamed of by the uninitiated. People on farm horses and mules; babies riding astride of brothers' and sisters' backs. The Elks band ranked at the church door and playing 'Safe in the Arms of Jesus' with such a dominant drum rhythm that it could be stepped off smartly by the long line as it filed inside. The Little Emperor of the cross-roads was leaving Orange County as he had come – with the out-stretched hand of power.

Janie starched and ironed her face and came set in the funeral behind her veil. It was like a wall of stone and steel. The funeral was going on outside. All things concerning death and burial were said and done. Finish. End. Nevermore. Darkness. Deep hole. Dissolution. Eternity. Weeping and wailing outside.

Inside the expensive black folds were resurrection and life. She did not reach outside for anything, nor did the things of death reach inside to disturb her calm. She sent her face to Joe's funeral, and herself went rollicking with the springtime across the world. After a while the people finished their celebration and Janie went on home.

Before she slept that night she burnt up every one of her head rags and went about the house next morning with her hair in one thick braid swinging well below her waist. That was the only change people saw in her. She kept the store in the same way except of evenings she sat on the porch and listened and sent Hezekiah in to wait on late custom. She saw no reason to rush at changing things around. She would have the rest of her life to do as she pleased.

Most of the day she was at the store, but at night she was there in the big house and sometimes it creaked and cried all night under the weight of lonesomeness. Then she'd lie awake in bed asking lonesomeness some questions. She asked if she wanted to leave and go back where she had come from and try to find her mother. Maybe tend her grandmother's grave. Sort of look over the old stamping ground generally. Digging around inside of herself like that she found that she had no interest in that seldom-seen mother at all. She hated her grandmother and had hidden it from herself all these years under a cloak of pity. She had been getting ready for her great journey to the horizons in search of *people*; it was important to all the world that she should find them and they find her. But she had been whipped like a cur dog, and run off down a back road after *things*. It was all according to the way you see things.

Some people could look at a mud-puddle and see an ocean with ships. But Nanny belonged to that other kind that loved to deal in scraps. Here Nanny had taken the biggest thing God ever made, the horizon – for no matter how far a person can go the horizon is still way beyond you – and pinched it in to such a little bit of a thing that she could tie it about her granddaughter's neck tight enough to choke her. She hated the old woman who had twisted her so in the name of love. Most humans didn't love one another nohow, and this mislove was so strong that even common blood couldn't overcome it all the time. She had found a jewel down inside herself and she had wanted to walk where people could see her and gleam it around. But she had been set in the market-place to sell. Been set for still-bait. When God had made The Man, he made him out of stuff that sung all the time and glittered all over. Then after that some angels got jealous and chopped him into millions of pieces, but still he glittered and hummed. So they beat him down to nothing but sparks but each little spark had a shine and a song. So they covered each one over with mud. And the lonesomeness in the sparks make them hunt for one another, but the mud is deaf and dumb. Like all the other tumbling mud-balls, Janie had tried to show her shine.

Janie found out very soon that her widowhood and property was a great challenge in South Florida. Before Jody had been dead a month, she noticed how often men who had never been intimates of Joe, drove considerable distances to ask after her welfare and offer their services as advisor.

'Uh woman by herself is uh pitiful thing,' she was told over and again. 'Dey needs aid and assistance. God never meant 'em tuh try tuh stand by theirselves. You ain't been used tuh knockin' round and doin' fuh yo'self, Mis' Starks. You been well taken keer of, you needs uh man.'

Janie laughed at all these well-wishers because she knew that they knew plenty of women alone; that she was not the first one they had ever seen. But most of the others were poor. Besides she liked being lonesome for a change. This freedom feeling was fine. These men didn't represent a thing she wanted to know about. She had already experienced them through Logan and Joe. She felt like slapping some of them for sitting around grinning at her like a pack of chessy cats, trying to make out they looked like love.

Ike Green sat on her case seriously one evening on the store porch when he was lucky enough to catch her alone.

'You wants be keerful 'bout who you marry, Mis' Starks. Dese strange men runnin' heah tryin' tuh take advantage of yo' condition.'

'Marry!' Janie almost screamed. 'Joe ain't had time tuh git cold yet. Ah ain't even give marryin' de first thought.'

'But you will. You'se too young uh 'oman tuh stay single, and you'se too pretty for de mens tuh leave yuh alone. You'se bound tuh marry.'

'Ah hope not. Ah mean, at dis present time it don't come befo' me. Joe ain't been dead two months. Ain't got settled down in his grave.'

'Dat's whut you say now, but two months mo' and you'll sing another tune. Den you want tuh be keerful. Womenfolks is easy taken advantage of. You know what tuh let none uh dese stray niggers dat's settin' round heah git de inside track on yuh. They's jes lak uh pack uh hawgs, when dey see uh full trough. Whut yuh needs is uh man dat yuh done lived uhround and know all about tuh sort of manage yo' things fuh yuh and ginerally do round.'

Janie jumped upon her feet. 'Lawd, Ike Green, you'se uh case! Dis subjick you bringin' up ain't fit tuh be talked about at all. Lemme go inside and help Hezekiah weigh up dat barrel uh sugar dat just come in.' She rushed on inside the store and whispered to Hezekiah, 'Ah'm gone tuh de house. Lemme know when dat ole pee-de-bed is gone and Ah'll be right back.'

Six months of wearing black passed and not one suitor had ever gained the house porch. Janie talked and laughed in the store at times, but never seemed to want to go further. She was happy except for the store. She knew by her head that she was absolute owner, but it always seemed to her that she was still clerking for Joe and that soon he would come in and find something wrong that she had done. She almost apologized to the tenants the first time she collected the rents. Felt like a usurper. But she hid that feeling by sending Hezekiah who was the best imitation of Joe that his seventeen years could make. He had even taken to smoking, and smoking cigars, since Joe's death and tried to bite 'em tight in one side of his mouth like Joe. Every chance he got he was reared back in Joe's swivel chair trying to thrust out his lean belly into a paunch. She'd laugh quietly at his no-harm posing and pretend she didn't see it. One day as she came in the back door of the store she heard him bawling at Tripp Crawford, 'Naw indeed, we can't do nothin' uh de kind! I god, you ain't paid for dem last rations you done et up. I god, you won't git no mo' outa dis store than you got money tuh pay for. I god, dis ain't Gimme, Florida, dis is Eatonville.' Another time she overheard him using Joe's favorite expression for pointing out the differences between himself and the careless-living, mouthy town. 'Ah'm an educated man, Ah keep mah arrangements in mah hands.' She laughed outright at that. His acting didn't hurt nobody and she wouldn't know what to do without him. He sensed that and came to treat her like baby-sister, as if to say 'You poor little thing, give it to big brother. He'll fix it for you.' His sense of ownership made him honest too, except for an occasional jaw-breaker, or a packet of sen-sen. The sen-sen was to let on to the other boys and the pullet-size girls that he had a liquor breath to cover. This business of managing stores and women store-owners was trying on a man's nerves. He needed a drink of liquor now and then to keep up.

When Janie emerged into her mourning white, she had hosts of admirers in and out of town. Everything open and frank. Men of property too among the crowd, but nobody seemed to get any further than the store. She was always too busy to take them to the house to entertain. They were all so respectful and stiff with her, that she might have been the Empress of Japan. They felt that it was not fitting to mention desire to the widow of Joseph Starks. You spoke of honor and respect. And all that they said and did was refracted by her inattention and shot off towards the rim-bones of nothing. She and Pheoby Watson visited back and forth and once in awhile sat around the lakes and fished. She was just basking in freedom for the most part without the need for thought. A Sanford undertaker was pressing his cause through Pheoby, and Janie was listening pleasantly but undisturbed. It might be nice to marry him, at that. No hurry. Such things take time to think about, or rather she pretended to Pheoby that that was what she was doing.

"Tain't dat Ah worries over Joe's death, Pheoby. Ah jus' loves dis freedom.'

'Sh-sh-sh! Don't let nobody hear you say dat, Janie. Folks will say you ain't sorry he's gone.'

'Let 'em say whut dey wants tuh, Pheoby. To my thinkin' mourning oughtn't tuh last no longer'n grief.'

10

One day Hezekiah asked off from work to go off with the ball team. Janie told him not to hurry back. She could close up the store herself this once. He cautioned her about the catches on the windows and doors and swaggered off to Winter Park.

Business was dull all day, because numbers of people had gone to the game. She decided to close early, because it was hardly worth the trouble of keeping open on an afternoon like this. She had set six o'clock as her limit.

At five-thirty a tall man came into the place. Janie was leaning on the counter making aimless pencil marks on a piece of wrapping paper. She knew she didn't know his name, but he looked familiar.

'Good evenin', Mis' Starks,' he said with a sly grin as if they had a good joke together. She was in favor of the story that was making him laugh before she even heard it.

'Good evenin',' she answered pleasantly. 'You got all de advantage 'cause Ah don't know yo' name.'

'People wouldn't know me lak dey would *you*.'

'Ah guess standin' in uh store do make uh person git tuh be known in de vicinity. Look lak Ah seen you somewhere.'

'Oh, Ah don't live no further than Orlandah. Ah'm easy tuh see on Church Street most any day or night. You got any smokin' tobacco?'

She opened the glass case. 'What kind?'

'Camels.'

She handed over the cigarettes and took the money. He broke the pack and thrust one between his full, purple lips.

'You got a lil piece uh fire over dere, lady?'

They both laughed and she handed him two kitchen matches out of a box for that purpose. It was time for him to go but he didn't. He leaned on the counter with one elbow and cold-cocked her a look.

'Why ain't *you* at de ball game, too? Everybody else is dere.'

'Well, Ah see somebody else besides me ain't dere. Ah just sold some cigarettes.' They laughed again.

'Dat's 'cause Ah'm dumb. Ah got de thing all mixed up. Ah thought de game was gointuh be out at Hungerford. So Ah got uh ride tuh where dis road turns off from de Dixie Highway and walked over here and then Ah find out de game is in Winter Park.'

That was funny to both of them too.

'So what you gointuh do now? All de cars in Eatonville is gone.'

'How about playin' *you* some checkers? You looks hard tuh beat.'

'Ah is, 'cause Ah can't play uh lick.'

'You don't cherish de game, then?'

'Yes, Ah do, and then agin Ah don't know whether Ah do or not, 'cause nobody ain't never showed me how.'

'Dis is de last day for *dat* excuse. You got uh board round heah?'

'Yes indeed. De men folks treasures de game round heah. Ah just ain't never learnt how.'

He set it up and began to show her and she found herself glowing inside. Somebody wanted her to play. Somebody thought it natural for her to play. That was even nice. She looked him over and got little thrills from every one of his good points. Those full, lazy eyes with the lashes curling sharply away like drawn scimitars. The lean, over-padded shoulders and narrow waist. Even nice!

He was jumping her king! She screamed in protest against losing the king she had had such a hard time acquiring. Before she knew it she had grabbed his hand to stop him. He struggled gallantly to free himself. That is he struggled, but not hard enough to wrench a lady's fingers.

'Ah got uh right tuh take it. You left it right in mah way.'

'Yeah, but Ah wuz lookin' off when you went and stuck yo' men right up next tuh mine. No fair!'

'You ain't supposed tuh look off, Mis' Starks. It's de biggest part uh de game tuh watch out! Leave go mah hand.'

'No suh! Not mah king. You kin take another one, but not dat one.'

They scrambled and upset the board and laughed at that.

'Anyhow it's time for uh Coca-Cola,' he said. 'Ah'll come teach yuh some mo' another time.'

'It's all right tuh come teach me, but don't come tuh cheat me.'

'Yuh can't beat uh woman. Dey jes won't stand fuh it. But Ah'll come teach yuh agin. You gointuh be uh good player too, after while.'

'You reckon so? Jody useter tell me Ah never would learn. It wuz too heavy fuh mah brains.'

'Folks is playin' it wid sense and folks is playin' it without. But you got good meat on yo' head. You'll learn. Have uh cool drink on me.'

'Oh all right, thank yuh. Got plenty cold ones tuhday. Nobody ain't been heah tuh buy none. All gone off tuh de game.'

'You oughta be at de next game. 'Tain't no use in *you* stayin' heah if everybody else is gone. You don't buy from yo'self, do yuh?'

'You crazy thing! 'Course Ah don't. But Ah'm worried 'bout you uh little.'

'How come? 'Fraid Ah ain't gointuh pay fuh dese drinks?'

'Aw naw! How you gointuh git back home?'

'Wait round heah fuh a car. If none don't come, Ah got good shoe leather. 'Tain't but seben miles nohow. Ah could walk dat in no time. Easy.'

'If it wuz me, Ah'd wait on uh train. Seben miles is uh kinda long walk.'

'It would be for you, 'cause you ain't used to it. But Ah'm seen women walk further'n dat. You could too, if yuh had it tuh do.'

'Maybe so, but Ah'll ride de train long as Ah got railroad fare.'

'Ah don't need no pocket-full uh money to ride de train lak uh woman. When Ah takes uh notion Ah rides anyhow – money or no money.'

'Now ain't you somethin'! Mr er – er – You never did tell me whut yo' name wuz.'

'Ah sho didn't. Wuzn't expectin' fuh it to be needed. De name mah mama gimme is Vergible Woods. Dey calls me Tea Cake for short.'

'Tea Cake! So you sweet as all dat?' She laughed and he gave her a little cut-eye look to get her meaning.

'Ah may be guilty. You better try me and see.'

She did something half-way between a laugh and a frown and he set his hat on straight.

'B'lieve Ah done cut uh hawg, so Ah guess Ah better ketch air.' He made an elaborate act of tipping to the door stealthily. Then looked back at her with an irresistible grin on his face. Janie burst out laughing in spite of herself. 'You crazy thing!'

He turned and threw his hat at her feet. 'If she don't throw it at me, Ah'll take a chance on comin' back,' he announced, making gestures to indicate he was hidden behind a post. She picked up the hat and threw it after him with a laugh. 'Even if she had uh brick she couldn't hurt yuh wid it,' he said to an invisible companion. 'De lady can't throw.' He gestured to his companion, stepped out from behind the imaginary lamp post, set his coat and hat and strolled back to where Janie was as if he had just come in the store.

'Evenin' Mis' Starks. Could yuh lemme have uh pound uh knuckle puddin'* till Saturday? Ah'm sho tuh pay yuh then.'

'You needs ten pounds, Mr Tea Cake. Ah'll let yuh have all Ah got and you needn't bother 'bout payin' it back.'

They joked and went on till the people began to come in. Then he took a seat and made talk and laughter with the rest until closing time. When everyone else had left he said, 'Ah reckon Ah done over-layed mah leavin' time, but Ah figgured you needed somebody tuh help yuh shut up de place. Since nobody else ain't round heah, maybe Ah kin git de job.'

'Thankyuh, Mr Tea Cake. It is kinda strainin' fuh me.'

'Who ever heard of uh teacake bein' called Mister! If you wanta be real hightoned and call me Mr Woods, dat's de way you feel about it. If yuh wants tuh be uh lil friendly and call me Tea Cake, dat would be real nice.' He was closing and bolting windows all the time he talked.

'All right, then. Thank yuh, Tea Cake. How's dat?'

'Jes lak uh lil girl wid her Easter dress on. Even nice!' He locked the door and shook it to be sure and handed her the key. 'Come on now, Ah'll see yuh inside yo' door and git on down de Dixie.'

Janie was halfway down the palm-lined walk before she had a thought for her safety. Maybe this strange man was up to something! But it was no place to show her fear there in the darkness between the house and the store. He had hold of her arm too. Then in a moment it was gone. Tea Cake wasn't strange. Seemed as if she had known him all her life. Look

---

* A beating with the fist.

how she had been able to talk with him right off! He tipped his hat at the door and was off with the briefest good night.

So she sat on the porch and watched the moon rise. Soon its amber fluid was drenching the earth, and quenching the thirst of the day.

I I

Janie wanted to ask Hezekiah about Tea Cake, but she was afraid he might misunderstand her and think she was interested. In the first place he looked too young for her. Must be around twenty-five and here *she* was around forty. Then again he didn't look like he had too much. Maybe he was hanging around to get in with her and strip her of all that she had. Just as well if she never saw him again. He was probably the kind of man who lived with various women but never married. Fact is, she decided to treat him so cold if he ever did foot the place that he'd be sure not to come hanging around there again.

He waited a week exactly to come back for Janie's snub. It was early in the afternoon and she and Hezekiah were alone. She heard somebody humming like they were feeling for pitch and looked towards the door. Tea Cake stood there mimicking the tuning of a guitar. He frowned and struggled with the pegs of his imaginary instrument watching her out of the corner of his eye with that secret joke playing over his face. Finally she smiled and he sung middle C, put his guitar under his arm and walked on back to where she was.

'Evenin', folks. Thought y'all might lak uh lil music this evenin' so Ah brought long mah box.'

'Crazy thing!' Janie commented, beaming out with light.

He acknowledged the compliment with a smile and sat down on a box. 'Anybody have uh Coca-Cola wid me?'

'Ah just had one,' Janie temporized with her conscience.

'It'll hafter be done all over agin, Mis' Starks.'

'How come?'

''Cause it wasn't done right dat time. 'Kiah bring us two bottles from de bottom uh de box.'

'How you been makin' out since Ah seen yuh last, Tea Cake?'

'Can't kick. Could be worse. Made four days dis week and got de pay in mah pocket.'

'We got a rich man round here, then. Buyin' passenger trains uh battleships this week?'

'Which one do *you* want? It all depends on you.'

'Oh, if you'se treatin' me tuh it, Ah b'lieve Ah'll take de passenger train. If it blow up Ah'll still be on land.'

'Choose de battleship if dat's whut you really want. Ah know where one is right now. Seen one round Key West de other day.'

'How you gointuh git it?'

'Ah shucks, dem Admirals is always ole folks. Can't no ole man stop me from gittin' no ship for yuh if dat's whut you want. Ah'd git dat ship out from under him so slick till he'd be walkin' de water lak ole Peter befo' he knowed it.'

They played away the evening again. Everybody was surprised at Janie playing checkers but they liked it. Three or four stood behind her and coached her moves and generally made merry with her in a restrained way. Finally everybody went home but Tea Cake.

'You kin close up, 'Kiah,' Janie said. 'Think Ah'll g'wan home.'

Tea Cake fell in beside her and mounted the porch this time. So she offered him a seat and they made a lot of laughter out of nothing. Near eleven o'clock she remembered a piece of pound cake she had put away. Tea Cake went out to the lemon tree at the corner of the kitchen and picked some lemons and squeezed them for her. So they had lemonade too.

'Moon's too pretty fuh anybody tuh be sleepin' it away,' Tea Cake said after they had washed up the plates and glasses. 'Less us go fishin'.'

'Fishin'? Dis time uh night?'

'Unhhunh, fishin'. Ah know where de bream is beddin'. Seen 'em when Ah come round de lake dis evenin'. Where's yo' fishin' poles? Less go set on de lake.'

It was so crazy digging worms by lamp light and setting out for Lake Sabelia after midnight that she felt like a child breaking rules. That's what made Janie like it. They caught two or three and got home just before day. Then she had to smuggle Tea Cake out by the back gate and that made it seem like some great secret she was keeping from the town.

'Mis' Janie,' Hezekiah began sullenly next day, 'you oughtn't 'low dat Tea Cake tuh be walkin' tuh de house wid yuh. Ah'll go wid yuh mahself after dis, if you'se skeered.'

'What's de matter wid Tea Cake, 'Kiah? Is he uh thief uh somethin'?'

'Ah ain't never heard nobody say he stole nothin'.'

'Is he bad 'bout totin' pistols and knives tuh hurt people wid?'

'Dey don't say he ever cut nobody or shot nobody neither.'

'Well, is he – he – is he got uh wife or something lak dat? Not dat it's any uh mah business.' She held her breath for the answer.

'No'm. And nobody wouldn't marry Tea Cake tuh starve tuh death lessen it's somebody jes lak him – ain't used to nothin'. 'Course he always keep hisself in changin' clothes. Dat long-legged Tea Cake ain't got doodly squat. He ain't got no business makin' hissef familiar wid nobody lak you. Ah said Ah wuz goin' to tell yuh so yuh could know.'

'Oh dat's all right, Hezekiah. Thank yuh mighty much.'

The next night when she mounted her steps Tea Cake was there before her, sitting on the porch in the dark. He had a string of fresh-caught trout for a present.

'Ah'll clean 'em, you fry 'em and let's eat,' he said with the assurance of not being refused. They went out into the kitchen and fixed up the hot fish and corn muffins and ate. Then Tea Cake went to the piano without so much as asking and began playing blues and singing, and throwing grins over his shoulder. The sounds lulled Janie to soft slumber and she woke up with Tea Cake combing her hair and scratching the dandruff from her scalp. It made her more comfortable and drowsy.

'Tea Cake, where you git uh comb from tuh be combin' mah hair wid?'

'Ah brought it wid me. Come prepared tuh lay mah hands on it tuhnight.'

'Why, Tea Cake? Whut good do combin' mah hair do *you*? It's *mah* comfortable, not yourn.'

'It's mine too. Ah ain't been sleepin' so good for more'n uh week cause Ah been wishin' so bad tuh git mah hands in yo' hair. It's so pretty. It feels jus' lak underneath uh dove's wing next to mah face.'

'Umph! You'se mighty easy satisfied. Ah been had dis same hair next tuh mah face ever since Ah cried de fust time, and 'tain't never gimme me no thrill.'

'Ah tell you lak you told me – you'se mighty hard tuh satisfy. Ah betcha dem lips don't satisfy yuh neither.'

'Dat's right, Tea Cake. They's dere and Ah make use of 'em whenever it's necessary, but nothin' special tuh me.'

'Umph! umph! umph! Ah betcha you don't never go tuh de lookin' glass and enjoy yo' eyes yo'self. You lets other folks git all de enjoyment out of 'em 'thout takin' in any of it yo'self.'

'Naw, Ah never gazes at 'em in de lookin' glass. If anybody else gits any pleasure out of 'em Ah ain't been told about it.'

'See dat? You'se got de world in uh jug and make out you don't know it. But Ah'm glad tuh be de one tuh tell yuh.'

'Ah guess you done told plenty women all about it.'

'Ah'm de Apostle Paul tuh de Gentiles. Ah tells 'em and then agin Ah shows 'em.'

'Ah thought so.' She yawned and made to get up from the sofa. 'You done got me so sleepy wid yo' head-scratchin' Ah kin hardly make it tuh de bed.' She stood up at once, collecting her hair. He sat still.

'Naw, you ain't sleepy, Mis' Janie. You jus' want me tuh go. You figger Ah'm uh rounder and uh pimp and you done wasted too much time talkin' wid me.'

'Why, Tea Cake! Whut ever put dat notion in yo' head?'

'De way you looked at me when Ah said whut Ah did. Yo' face skeered me so bad till mah whiskers drawed up.'

'Ah ain't got no business bein' mad at nothin' you do and say. You got it all wrong. Ah ain't mad atall.'

'Ah know it and dat's what puts de shamery on me. You'se jus' disgusted wid me. Yo' face jus' left here and went off somewhere else. Naw, you ain't mad wid me. Ah be glad if you was, 'cause then Ah might do somethin' tuh please yuh. But lak it is—'

'Mah likes and dislikes ought not tuh make no difference wid you, Tea Cake. Dat's fuh yo' lady friend. Ah'm jus' uh sometime friend uh yourn.'

Janie walked towards the stairway slowly, and Tea Cake sat where he was, as if he had frozen to his seat, in fear that once he got up, he'd never get back in it again. He swallowed hard and looked at her walk away.

'Ah didn't aim tuh let on tuh yuh 'bout it, leastways not right away, but Ah ruther be shot wid tacks than fuh you tuh act wid me lak you is right now. You got me in de go-long.'

At the newel post Janie whirled around and for the space of a thought she was lit up like a transfiguration. Her next thought brought her crashing down. He's just saying anything for the time being, feeling he's got me so I'll b'lieve him. The next thought buried her under tons of cold futility. He's trading on being younger than me. Getting ready to laugh at me for an old fool. But oh, what wouldn't I give to be twelve years younger so I could b'lieve him!

'Aw, Tea Cake, you just say dat tuhnight because de fish and corn bread tasted sort of good. Tomorrow yo' mind would change.'

'Naw, it wouldn't neither. Ah know better.'

'Anyhow from what you told me when we wuz back dere in de kitchen Ah'm nearly twelve years older than you.'

'Ah done thought all about dat and tried tuh struggle aginst it, but it don't do me no good. De thought uh mah youngness don't satisfy me lak yo' presence do.'

'It makes uh whole heap uh difference wid most folks, Tea Cake.'

'Things lak dat got uh whole lot tuh do wid convenience, but it ain't got nothin' tuh do wid love.'

'Well, Ah love tuh find out whut you think after sun-up tomorrow. Dis is jus' yo' night thought.'

'You got yo' ideas and Ah got mine. Ah got uh dollar dat says you'se wrong. But Ah reckon you don't bet money, neither.'

'Ah never have done it so fur. But as de old folks always say, Ah'm born but Ah ain't dead. No tellin' whut Ah'm liable tuh do yet.'

He got up suddenly and took his hat. 'Good night Mis' Janie. Look lak we done run our conversation from grass roots tuh pine trees. G'bye.' He almost ran out of the door.

Janie hung over the newel post thinking so long that she all but went to sleep there. However, before she went to bed she took a good look at her mouth, eyes and hair.

All next day in the house and store she thought resisting thoughts about Tea Cake. She even ridiculed him in her mind and was a little ashamed of the association. But every hour or two the battle had to be fought all over again. She couldn't make him look just like any other man to her. He looked like the love thoughts of women. He could be a bee to a blossom – a pear tree blossom in the spring. He seemed to be crushing scent out of the world with his footsteps. Crushing aromatic herbs with every step he took. Spices hung about him. He was a glance from God.

So he didn't come that night and she laid in bed and pretended to think scornfully of him. 'Bet he's hangin' round some jook or 'nother. Glad Ah treated him cold. Whut do Ah want wid some trashy nigger out de streets? Bet he's livin' wid some woman or 'nother and takin' me for uh fool. Glad Ah caught mahself in time.' She tried to console herself that way.

The next morning she awoke hearing a knocking on the front door and found Tea Cake there.

'Hello, Mis' Janie, Ah hope Ah woke you up.'

'You sho did, Tea Cake. Come in and rest yo' hat. Whut you doin' out so soon dis mornin'?'

'Thought Ah'd try tuh git heah soon enough tuh tell yuh mah daytime thoughts. Ah see yuh needs tuh know mah daytime feelings. Ah can't sense yuh intuh it at night.'

'You crazy thing! Is dat whut you come here for at daybreak?'

'Sho is. You needs tellin' and showin', and dat's whut Ah'm doin'. Ah picked some strawberries too, Ah figgered you might like.'

'Tea Cake, Ah 'clare Ah don't know whut tuh make outa you. You'se so crazy. You better lemme fix you some breakfast.'

'Ain't got time. Ah got uh job uh work. Gottuh be back in Orlandah at eight o'clock. See yuh later, tell you straighter.'

He bolted down the walk and was gone. But that night when she left the store, he was stretched out in the hammock on the porch with his hat over his face pretending to sleep. She called him. He pretended not to hear. He snored louder. She went to the hammock to shake him and he seized and pulled her in with him. After a little, she let him adjust her in his arms and laid there for a while.

'Tea Cake, Ah don't know 'bout you, but Ah'm hongry, come on let's eat some supper.'

They went inside and their laughter rang out first from the kitchen and all over the house.

Janie awoke next morning by feeling Tea Cake almost kissing her breath away. Holding her and caressing her as if he feared she might escape his grasp and fly away. Then he must dress hurriedly and get to his job on time. He wouldn't let her get him any breakfast at all. He wanted her to get her rest. He made her stay where she was. In her heart she wanted to get his breakfast for him. But she stayed in bed long after he was gone.

So much had been breathed out by the pores that Tea Cake still was there. She could feel him and almost see him bucking around the room in the upper air. After a long time of passive happiness, she got up and opened the window and let Tea Cake leap forth and mount to the sky on a wind. That was the beginning of things.

In the cool of the afternoon the fiend from hell specially sent to lovers arrived at Janie's ear. Doubt. All the fears that circumstance could provide and the heart feel, attacked her on every side. This was a new sensation for her, but no less excruciating. If only Tea Cake would make her certain! He did not return that night nor the next and so she plunged into the abyss and descended to the ninth darkness where light has never been.

But the fourth day after he came in the afternoon driving a battered car. Jumped out like a deer and made the gesture of tying it to a post on the store porch. Ready with his grin! She adored him and hated him at the same time. How could he make her suffer so and then come grinning like that with that darling way he had? He pinched her arm as he walked inside the door.

'Brought me somethin' tuh haul you off in,' he told her with that secret chuckle. 'Git yo' hat if you gointuh wear one. We got tuh go buy groceries.'

'Ah sells groceries right here in dis store, Tea Cake, if you don't happen tuh know.' She tried to look cold but she was smiling in spite of herself.

'Not de kind we want fuh de occasion. You sells groceries for ordinary people. We'se gointuh buy for *you*. De big Sunday School picnic is tomorrow – bet you done forget it – and we got tuh be dere wid uh swell basket and ourselves.'

'Ah don't know 'bout dat, Tea Cake. Tell yuh whut you do. G'wan down tuh de house and wait for me. Be dere in uh minute.'

As soon as she thought it looked right she slipped out of the back and joined Tea Cake. No need of fooling herself. Maybe he was just being polite.

'Tea Cake, you sure you want me tuh go tuh dis picnic wid yuh?'

'Me scramble 'round tuh git de money tuh take yuh – been workin' lak uh dawg for two whole weeks – and she come astin' me if Ah want her tuh go! Puttin' mahself tuh uh whole heap uh trouble tuh git dis car so you kin go over tuh Winter Park or Orlandah tuh buy de things you might need and dis woman set dere and ast me if Ah want her tuh go!'

'Don't git mad, Tea Cake, Ah just didn't want you doin' nothin' outa politeness. If dere's somebody else you'd ruther take, it's all right wid me.'

'Naw, it ain't all right wid you. If it was you wouldn't be sayin' dat. Have de nerve tuh say whut you mean.'

'Well, all right, Tea Cake, Ah wants tuh go wid you real bad, but, – oh, Tea Cake, don't make no false pretense wid me!'

'Janie, Ah hope God may kill me, if Ah'm lyin'. Nobody else on earth kin hold uh candle tuh you, baby. You got de keys to de kingdom.'

12

It was after the picnic that the town began to notice things
and got mad. Tea Cake and Mrs Mayor Starks! All the men
that she could get, and fooling with somebody like Tea Cake!
Another thing, Joe Starks hadn't been dead but nine months
and here she goes sashaying off to a picnic in pink linen. Done
quit attending church, like she used to. Gone off to Sanford in
a car with Tea Cake and her all dressed in blue! It was a
shame. Done took to high heel slippers and a ten dollar hat!
Looking like some young girl, always in blue because Tea Cake
told her to wear it. Poor Joe Starks. Bet he turns over in his
grave every day. Tea Cake and Janie gone hunting. Tea Cake
and Janie gone fishing. Tea Cake and Janie gone to Orlando
to the movies. Tea Cake and Janie gone to a dance. Tea Cake
making flower beds in Janie's yard and seeding the garden for
her. Chopping down that tree she never did like by the dining
room window. All those signs of possession. Tea Cake in a borrowed car teaching Janie to drive. Tea Cake and Janie playing
checkers; playing coon-can; playing Florida flip on the store

porch all afternoon as if nobody else was there. Day after day and week after week.

'Pheoby,' Sam Watson said one night as he got in the bed, 'Ah b'lieve yo' buddy is all tied up with dat Tea Cake sho-nough. Didn't b'lieve it at first.'

'Aw she don't mean nothin' by it. Ah think she's sort of stuck on dat undertaker up at Sanford.'

'It's somebody 'cause she looks mighty good dese days. New dresses and her hair combed a different way nearly every day. You got to have something to comb hair over. When you see uh woman doin' so much rakin' in her head, she's combin' at some man or 'nother.'

''Course she kin do as she please, but dat's uh good chance she got up at Sanford. De man's wife died and he got uh lovely place tuh take her to – already furnished. Better'n her house Joe left her.'

'You better sense her intuh things then 'cause Tea Cake can't do nothin' but help her spend whut she got. Ah reckon dat's whut he's after. Throwin' away whut Joe Starks worked hard tuh git tuhgether.'

'Dat's de way it looks. Still and all, she's her own woman. She oughta know by now whut she wants tuh do.'

'De men wuz talkin' 'bout it in de grove tuhday and givin' her and Tea Cake both de devil. Dey figger he's spendin' on her now in order tuh make her spend on him later.'

'Umph! Umph! Umph!'

'Oh dey got it all figgered out. Maybe it ain't as bad as they say, but they talk it and make it sound real bad on her part.'

'Dat's jealousy and malice. Some uh dem very mens wants tuh do whut dey claim deys skeered Tea Cake is doin'.'

'De Pastor claim Tea Cake don't 'low her tuh come tuh church only once in awhile 'cause he want dat change tuh buy gas wid. Just draggin' de woman away from church. But anyhow, she's yo' bosom friend, so you better go see 'bout her. Drop uh lil hint here and dere and if Tea Cake is tryin' tuh rob her she kin see and know. Ah laks de woman and Ah sho would hate tuh see her come up lak Mis' Tyler.'

'Aw mah God, naw! Reckon Ah better step over dere tomorrow and have some chat wid Janie. She jus' ain't thinkin' whut she doin', dat's all.'

The next morning Pheoby picked her way over to Janie's house like a hen to a neighbor's garden. Stopped and talked a little with everyone she met, turned aside momentarily to pause at a porch or two – going straight by walking crooked. So her firm intention looked like an accident and she didn't have to give her opinion to folks along the way.

Janie acted glad to see her and after a while Pheoby broached her with, 'Janie, everybody's talkin' 'bout how dat Tea Cake is draggin' you round tuh places you ain't used tuh. Baseball games and huntin' and fishin'. He don't know you'se useter uh more high time crowd than dat. You always did class off.'

'Jody classed me off. Ah didn't. Naw, Pheoby, Tea Cake ain't draggin' me off nowhere Ah don't want tuh go. Ah always did want tuh git round uh whole heap, but Jody wouldn't 'low me tuh. When Ah wasn't in de store he wanted me tuh jes sit wid folded hands and sit dere. And Ah'd sit dere wid de walls creepin' up on me and squeezin' all de life outa me. Pheoby, dese educated women got uh heap of things to sit down and consider. Somebody done tole 'em what to set down for. Nobody ain't told poor me, so sittin' still worries me. Ah wants tuh utilize mahself all over.'

'But, Janie, Tea Cake, whilst he ain't no jail-bird, he ain't got uh dime tuh cry. Ain't you skeered he's jes after yo' money – him bein' younger than you?'

'He ain't never ast de first penny from me yet, and if he love property he ain't no different from all de rest of us. All dese ole men dat's settin' round me is after de same thing. They's three mo' widder women in town, how come dey don't break dey neck after dem? 'Cause dey ain't got nothin', dat's why.'

'Folks seen you out in colors and dey thinks you ain't payin' de right amount uh respect tuh yo' dead husband.'

'Ah ain't grievin' so why do Ah hafta mourn? Tea Cake love me in blue, so Ah wears it. Jody ain't never in his life picked out no color for me. De world picked out black and white for mournin', Joe didn't. So Ah wasn't wearin' it for him. Ah was wearin' it for de rest of y'all.'

'But anyhow, watch yo'self, Janie, and don't be took advantage of. You know how dese young men is wid older women. Most of de time dey's after whut dey kin git, then dey's gone lak uh turkey through de corn.'

'Tea Cake don't talk dat way. He's aimin' tuh make hisself permanent wid me. We done made up our mind tuh marry.'

'Janie, you'se yo' own woman, and Ah hope you know whut you doin'. Ah sho hope you ain't lak uh possum – de older you gits, de less sense yuh got. Ah'd feel uh whole heap better 'bout yuh if you wuz marryin' dat man up dere in Sanford. He got somethin' tuh put long side uh whut you got and dat make it more better. He's endurable.'

'Still and all Ah'd ruther be wid Tea Cake.'

'Well, if yo' mind is already made up, 'tain't nothin' nobody kin do. But you'se takin' uh awful chance.'

'No mo' than Ah took befo' and no mo' than anybody else takes when dey gits married. It always changes folks, and sometimes it brings out dirt and meanness dat even de person didn't know they had in 'em theyselves. You know dat. Maybe Tea Cake might turn out lak dat. Maybe not. Anyhow Ah'm ready and willin' tuh try 'im.'

'Well, when you aim tuh step off?'

'Dat we don't know. De store is got tuh be sold and then we'se goin' off somewhere tuh git married.'

'How come you sellin' out de store?'

''Cause Tea Cake ain't no Jody Starks, and if he tried tuh be, it would be uh complete flommuck. But de minute Ah marries 'im everybody is gointuh be makin' comparisons. So us is goin' off somewhere and start all over in Tea Cake's way. Dis ain't no business proposition, and no race after property and titles. Dis is uh love game. Ah done lived Grandma's way, now Ah means tuh live mine.'

'What you mean by dat, Janie?'

'She was borned in slavery time when folks, dat is black folks, didn't sit down anytime dey felt lak it. So sittin' on porches lak de white madam looked lak uh mighty fine thing tuh her. Dat's whut she wanted for me – don't keer whut it cost. Git up on uh high chair and sit dere. She didn't have time tuh think whut tuh do after you got up on de stool uh do nothin'. De object wuz tuh git dere. So Ah got up on de high stool lak she told me, but Pheoby, Ah done nearly languished tuh death up dere. Ah felt like de world wuz cryin' extry and Ah ain't read de common news yet.'

'Maybe so, Janie. Still and all Ah'd love tuh experience it for just one year. It look lak heben tuh me from where Ah'm at.'

'Ah reckon so.'

'But anyhow, Janie, you be keerful 'bout dis sellin' out and goin' off wid strange men. Look whut happened tuh Annie Tyler. Took whut little she had and went off tuh Tampa wid dat boy dey call Who Flung. It's somethin' tuh think about.'

'It sho is. Still Ah ain't Mis' Tyler and Tea Cake ain't no Who Flung, and he ain't no stranger tuh me. We'se just as good as married already. But Ah ain't puttin' it in de street. Ah'm tellin' *you*.'

'Ah jus lak uh chicken. Chicken drink water, but he don't pee-pee.'

'Oh, Ah know you don't talk. We ain't shame faced. We jus' ain't ready tuh make no big kerflommuck as yet.'

'You doin' right not tuh talk it, but Janie, you'se takin' uh mighty big chance.'

'''Tain't so big uh chance as it seem lak, Pheoby. Ah'm older than Tea Cake, yes. But he done showed me where it's de thought dat makes de difference in ages. If people thinks de same they can make it all right. So in the beginnin' new thoughts had tuh be thought and new words said. After Ah got used tuh dat, we gits 'long jus' fine. He done taught me de maiden language all over. Wait till you see de new blue satin Tea Cake done picked out for me tuh stand up wid him in. High heel slippers, necklace, earrings, *everything* he wants tuh see me in. Some of dese mornin's and it won't be long, you gointuh wake up callin' me and Ah'll be gone.'

13

Jacksonville. Tea Cake's letter had said Jacksonville. He had worked in the railroad shops up there before and his old boss had promised him a job come next pay day. No need for Janie to wait any longer. Wear the new blue dress because he meant to marry her right from the train. Hurry up and come because he was about to turn into pure sugar thinking about her. Come on, baby, papa Tea Cake never could be mad with you!

Janie's train left too early in the day for the town to witness much, but the few who saw her leave bore plenty witness. They had to give it to her, she sho looked good, but she had no business to do it. It was hard to love a woman that always made you feel so wishful.

The train beat on itself and danced on the shiny steel rails mile after mile. Every now and then the engineer would play on his whistle for the people in the towns he passed by. And the train shuffled on to Jacksonville, and to a whole lot of things she wanted to see and to know.

And there was Tea Cake in the big old station in a new blue suit and straw hat, hauling her off to a preacher's house first thing. Then right on to the room he had been sleeping in for two weeks all by himself waiting for her to come. And such another hugging and kissing and carrying on you never saw. It made her so glad she was scared of herself. They stayed at home and rested that night, but the next night they went to a show and after that they rode around on the trolley cars and sort of looked things over for themselves. Tea Cake was spending and doing out of his own pocket, so Janie never told him about the two hundred dollars she had pinned inside her shirt next to her skin. Pheoby had insisted that she bring it along and keep it secret just to be on the safe side. She had ten dollars over her fare in her pocket book. Let Tea Cake think that was all she had. Things might not turn out like she thought. Every minute since she had stepped off the train she had been laughing at Pheoby's advice. She meant to tell Tea Cake the joke some time when she was sure she wouldn't hurt his feelings. So it came around that she had been married a week and sent Pheoby a card with a picture on it.

That morning Tea Cake got up earlier than Janie did. She felt sleepy and told him to go get some fish to fry for breakfast. By the time he had gone and come back she would have finished her nap out. He told her he would and she turned over and went back to sleep. She woke up and Tea Cake still wasn't there and the clock said it was getting late, so she got up and washed her face and hands. Perhaps he was down in the kitchen fixing around to let her sleep. Janie went down and the landlady made her drink some coffee with her because she said her husband was dead and it was bad to be having your morning coffee by yourself.

'Yo' husband gone tuh work dis mornin', Mis' Woods? Ah seen him go out uh good while uh go. Me and you kin be comp'ny for one 'nother, can't us?'

'Oh yes, indeed, Mis' Samuels. You puts me in de mind uh mah friend back in Eatonville. Yeah, you'se nice and friendly jus' lak her.'

Therefore Janie drank her coffee and sankled on back to her room without asking her landlady anything. Tea Cake must be hunting all over the city for that fish. She kept that thought in front of her in order not to think too much. When she heard the twelve o'clock whistle she decided to get up and dress. That was when she found out her two hundred dollars was gone. There was the little cloth purse with the safety pin on the chair beneath her clothes and the money just wasn't nowhere in the room. She knew from the beginning that the money wasn't any place she knew of if it wasn't in that little pocket book pinned to her pink silk vest. But the exercise of searching the room kept her busy and that was good for her to keep moving, even though she wasn't doing anything but turning around in her tracks.

But, don't care how firm your determination is, you can't keep turning round in one place like a horse grinding sugar cane. So Janie took to sitting over the room. Sit and look. The room inside looked like the mouth of an alligator – gaped wide open to swallow something down. Outside the window Jacksonville looked like it needed a fence around it to keep it from running out on ether's bosom. It was too big to be warm, let alone to need somebody like her. All day and night she worried time like a bone.

Way late in the morning the thought of Annie Tyler and Who Flung came to pay her a visit. Annie Tyler who at fifty-two had been left a widow with a good home and insurance money.

Mrs Tyler with her dyed hair, newly straightened and her uncomfortable new false teeth, her leathery skin, blotchy with powder and her giggle. Her love affairs, affairs with boys in their late teens or early twenties for all of whom she spent her money on suits of clothes, shoes, watches and things like that and how they all left her as soon as their wants were satisfied. Then when her ready cash was gone, had come Who Flung to denounce his predecessor as a scoundrel and took up around the house himself. It was he who persuaded her to sell her house and come to Tampa with him. The town had seen her limp off. The undersized high-heel slippers were punishing her tired feet that looked like bunions all over. Her body squeezed and crowded into a tight corset that shoved her middle up under her chin. But she had gone off laughing and sure. As sure as Janie had been.

Then two weeks later the porter and conductor of the north bound local had helped her off the train at Maitland. Hair all gray and black and bluish and reddish in streaks. All the capers that cheap dye could cut was showing in her hair. Those slippers bent and griped just like her work-worn feet. The corset gone and the shaking old woman hanging all over herself. Everything that you could see was hanging. Her chin hung from her ears and rippled down her neck like drapes. Her hanging bosom and stomach and buttocks and legs that draped down over her ankles. She groaned but never giggled.

She was broken and her pride was gone, so she told those who asked what had happened. Who Flung had taken her to a shabby room in a shabby house in a shabby street and promised to marry her next day. They stayed in the room two whole days then she woke up to find Who Flung and her money gone. She got up to stir around and see if she could find him, and found herself too worn out to do much. All she found out was that she was too old a vessel for new wine. The next day hunger had driven her out to shift. She had stood on the streets and smiled and smiled, and then smiled and begged and then just begged. After a week of world-bruising a young man from home had come along and seen her. She couldn't tell him how it was. She just told him she got off the train and somebody had stolen her purse. Naturally, he had believed her and taken her home with him to give her time to rest up a day or two, then he had bought her a ticket for home.

They put her to bed and sent for her married daughter from up around Ocala to come see about her. The daughter came as soon as she could and took Annie Tyler away to die in peace. She had waited all her life for something, and it had killed her when it found her.

The thing made itself into pictures and hung around Janie's bedside all night long. Anyhow, she wasn't going back to Eatonville to be laughed at and pitied. She had ten dollars in her pocket and twelve hundred in the bank. But oh God, don't let Tea Cake be off somewhere hurt and Ah not know nothing about it. And God, please suh, don't let him love nobody else but me. Maybe Ah'm is uh fool, Lawd, lak dey say, but Lawd, Ah been so lonesome, and Ah been waitin', Jesus. Ah done waited uh long time.

Janie dozed off to sleep but she woke up in time to see the sun sending up spies ahead of him to mark out the road through the dark. He peeped up over the door sill of the world and made a little foolishness with red. But pretty soon, he laid all that aside and went about his business dressed all in white. But it was always going to be dark to Janie if Tea Cake didn't soon come back. She got out of the bed but a chair couldn't hold her. She dwindled down on the floor with her head in a rocking chair.

After a while there was somebody playing a guitar outside her door. Played right smart while. It sounded lovely too. But it was sad to hear it feeling blue like Janie was. Then whoever it was started to singing 'Ring de bells of mercy. Call de sinner man home.' Her heart all but smothered her.

'Tea Cake is dat you?'

'You know so well it's me, Janie. How come you don't open de door?'

But he never waited. He walked on in with a guitar and a grin. Guitar hanging round his neck with a red silk cord and a grin hanging from his ears.

'Don't need tuh ast me where Ah been all dis time, 'cause it's mah all day job tuh tell yuh.'

'Tea Cake, Ah—'

'Good Lawd, Janie, whut you doin' settin' on de floor?'

He took her head in his hands and eased himself into the

chair. She still didn't say anything. He sat stroking her head and looking down into her face.

'Ah see whut it is. You doubted me 'bout de money. Thought Ah had done took it and gone. Ah don't blame yuh but it wasn't lak you think. De girl baby ain't born and her mama is dead, dat can git me tuh spend our money on her. Ah told yo' before dat you got de keys tuh de kingdom. You can depend on dat.'

'Still and all you went off and left me all day and all night.'

''Twasn't 'cause Ah wanted tuh stay off lak dat, and it sho Lawd, wuzn't no woman. If you didn't have de power tuh hold me and hold me tight, Ah wouldn't be callin' yuh Mis' Woods. Ah met plenty women before Ah knowed you tuh talk tuh. You'se de onliest woman in de world Ah ever even mentioned gitting married tuh. You bein' older don't make no difference. Don't never consider dat no mo'. If Ah ever gits tuh messin' round another woman it won't be on account of her age. It'll be because she got me in de same way you got me – so Ah can't help mahself.'

He sat down on the floor beside her and kissed and playfully turned up the corner of her mouth until she smiled.

'Looka here, folks,' he announced to an imaginary audience, 'Sister Woods is 'bout tuh quit her husband!'

Janie laughed at that and let herself lean on him. Then she announced to the same audience, 'Mis' Woods got herself uh new lil boy rooster, but he been off somewhere and won't tell her.'

'First thing, though, us got tuh eat together, Janie. Then we can talk.'

'One thing, Ah won't send you out after no fish.'

He pinched her in the side and ignored what she said.

"Tain't no need of neither one of us workin' dis mornin'. Call Mis' Samuels and let her fix whatever you want.'

'Tea Cake, if you don't hurry up and tell me, Ah'll take and beat yo' head flat as uh dime.'

Tea Cake stuck out till he had some breakfast, then he talked and acted out the story.

He spied the money while he was tying his tie. He took it up and looked at it out of curiosity and put it in his pocket to count it while he was out to find some fish to fry. When he found out how much it was, he was excited and felt like letting folks know who he was. Before he found the fish market he met a fellow he used to work with at the round house. One word brought on another one and pretty soon he made up his mind to spend some of it. He never had had his hand on so much money before in his life, so he made up his mind to see how it felt to be a millionaire. They went on out to Callahan round the railroad shops and he decided to give a big chicken and macaroni supper that night, free to all.

He bought up the stuff and they found somebody to pick the guitar so they could all dance some. So they sent the message all around for people to come. And come they did. A big table loaded down with fried chicken and biscuits and a wash-tub full of macaroni with plenty cheese in it. When the fellow began to pick the box the people begin to come from east, west, north and Australia. And he stood in the door and paid all the ugly women two dollars *not* to come in. One big meriny colored woman was so ugly till it was worth five dollars for her not to come in, so he gave it to her.

They had a big time till one man come in who thought he was bad. He tried to pull and haul over all the chickens and pick out the livers and gizzards to eat. Nobody else couldn't pacify him so they called Tea Cake to come see if he could stop him. So Tea Cake walked up and asked him, 'Say, whut's de matter wid you, nohow?'

'Ah don't want nobody handin' me nothin'. Specially don't issue me out no rations. Ah always chooses mah rations.' He kept right on plowing through the pile uh chicken. So Tea Cake got mad.

'You got mo' nerve than uh brass monkey. Tell me, what post office did *you* ever pee in? Ah craves tuh know.'

'Whut you mean by dat now?' the fellow asked.

'Ah means dis – it takes jus' as much nerve tuh cut caper lak dat in uh United States Government Post Office as it do tuh comes pullin' and haulin' over any chicken Ah pay for. Hit de ground. Damned if Ah ain't gointuh try you dis night.'

So they all went outside to see if Tea Cake could handle the boogerboo. Tea Cake knocked out two of his teeth, so that man went on off from there. Then two men tried to pick a fight with one another, so Tea Cake said they had to kiss and make up. They didn't want to do it. They'd rather go to jail, but everybody else liked the idea, so they made 'em do it. Afterwards, both of them spit and gagged and wiped their mouths with the back of their hands. One went outside and chewed a little grass like a sick dog, he said to keep it from killing him.

Then everybody began to holler at the music because the man couldn't play but three pieces. So Tea Cake took the guitar and played himself. He was glad of the chance because he hadn't had his hand on a box since he put his in the pawn shop to get some money to hire a car for Janie soon after he met her. He missed his music. So that put him in the notion he ought to have one. He bought the guitar on the spot and paid fifteen dollars cash. It was really worth sixty-five any day.

Just before day the party wore out. So Tea Cake hurried on back to his new wife. He had done found out how rich people feel and he had a fine guitar and twelve dollars left in his pocket and all he needed now was a great big old hug and kiss from Janie.

'You musta thought yo' wife was powerful ugly. Dem ugly women dat you paid two dollars not to come in, could git tuh de door. You never even 'lowed me tuh git dat close.' She pouted.

'Janie, Ah would have give Jacksonville wid Tampa for a jump-back for you to be dere wid me. Ah started to come git yuh two three times.'

'Well, how come yuh didn't come git me?'

'Janie, would you have come if Ah did?'

'Sho Ah would. Ah laks fun just as good as you do.'

'Janie, Ah wanted tuh, mighty much, but Ah was skeered. Too skeered Ah might lose yuh.'

'Why?'

'Dem wuzn't no high muckty mucks. Dem wuz railroad hands and dey womenfolks. You ain't usetuh folks lak dat and Ah wuz skeered you might git all mad and quit me for takin' you 'mongst 'em. But Ah wanted yuh wid me jus' de same. Befo' us got married Ah made up mah mind not tuh let you see no commonness in me. When Ah git mad habits on, Ah'd go off and keep it out yo' sight. 'Tain't mah notion tuh drag *you* down wid me.'

'Looka heah, Tea Cake, if you ever go off from me and have a good time lak dat and then come back heah tellin' me how nice Ah is, Ah specks tuh kill yuh dead. You heah me?'

'So you aims tuh partake wid everything, hunh?'

'Yeah, Tea Cake, don't keer what it is.'

'Dat's all Ah wants tuh know. From now on you'se mah wife and mah woman and everything else in de world Ah needs.'

'Ah hope so.'

'And honey, don't you worry 'bout yo' lil ole two hundred dollars. It's big pay day dis comin' Saturday at de railroad yards. Ah'm gointuh take dis twelve dollars in mah pocket and win it all back and mo'.'

'How?'

'Honey, since you loose me and gimme privilege tuh tell yuh all about mahself, Ah'll tell yuh. You done married one uh de best gamblers God ever made. Cards or dice either one. Ah can take uh shoe string and win uh tan-yard. Wish yuh could see me rollin'. But dis time it's gointuh be nothin' but tough men's talkin' all kinds uh talk so it ain't no place for you tuh be, but 'twon't be long befo' you see me.'

All the rest of the week Tea Cake was busy practising up on his dice. He would flip them on the bare floor, on the rug and on the bed. He'd squat and throw, sit in a chair and throw and stand and throw. It was very exciting to Janie who had never touched dice in her life. Then he'd take his deck of cards and shuffle and cut, shuffle and cut and deal out then examine each hand carefully, and do it again. So Saturday came. He went out and bought a new switch-blade knife and two decks of star-back playing cards that morning and left Janie around noon.

'They'll start to paying off, pretty soon now. Ah wants tuh git in de game whilst de big money is in it. Ah ain't fuh no spuddin' tuhday. Ah'll come home wid de money or Ah'll come back on uh stretcher.' He cut nine hairs out of the mole of her head for luck and went off happy.

Janie waited till midnight without worrying, but after that she began to be afraid. So she got up and sat around scared and miserable. Thinking and fearing all sorts of dangers. Wondering at herself as she had many times this week that she was not shocked at Tea Cake's gambling. It was part of him, so it was all right. She rather found herself angry at imaginary people who might try to criticize. Let the old hypocrites learn to mind their own business, and leave other folks alone. Tea Cake wasn't doing a bit more harm trying to win hisself a little money than they was always doing with their lying tongues. Tea Cake had more good nature under his toe-nails than they had in their so-called Christian hearts. She better not hear none of them old backbiters talking about *her* husband! Please, Jesus, don't let them nasty niggers hurt her boy. If they do, Master Jesus, grant her a good gun and a chance to shoot 'em. Tea Cake had a knife it was true, but that was only to protect hisself. God knows, Tea Cake wouldn't harm a fly.

Daylight was creeping around the cracks of the world when

Janie heard a feeble rap on the door. She sprung to the door and flung it wide. Tea Cake was out there looking like he was asleep standing up. In some strange way it was frightening. Janie caught his arm to arouse him and he stumbled into the room and fell.

'Tea Cake! You chile! What's de matter, honey?'

'Dey cut me, dat's all. Don't cry. Git me out dis coat quick as yuh can.'

He told her he wasn't cut but twice but she had to have him naked so she could look him all over and fix him up to a certain extent. He told her not to call a doctor unless he got much worse. It was mostly loss of blood anyhow.

'Ah won the money jus' lak ah told yuh. Round midnight Ah had yo' two hundred dollars and wuz ready tuh quit even though it wuz uh heap mo' money in de game. But dey wanted uh chance tuh win it back so Ah set back down tuh play some mo'. Ah knowed ole Double-Ugly wuz 'bout broke and wanted tuh fight 'bout it, so Ah set down tuh give 'im his chance tuh git back his money and then to give 'im uh quick trip tuh hell if he tried tuh pull dat razor Ah glimpsed in his pocket. Honey, no up-to-date man don't fool wid no razor. De man wid his switch-blade will be done cut yuh tuh death while you foolin' wid uh razor. But Double-Ugly brags he's too fast wid it tuh git hurt, but Ah knowed better.

'So round four o'clock Ah had done cleaned 'em out complete – all except two men dat got up and left while dey had money for groceries, and one man dat wuz lucky. Then Ah rose tuh bid 'em good bye agin. None of 'em didn't lak it, but dey all realized it wuz fair. Ah had done give 'em a fair chance.

All but Double-Ugly. He claimed Ah switched de dice. Ah shoved de money down deep in mah pocket and picked up mah hat and coat wid mah left hand and kept mah right hand on mah knife. Ah didn't keer what he *said* long as he didn't try tuh *do* nothin'. Ah got mah hat on and one arm in mah coat as Ah got to de door. Right dere he jumped at me as Ah turned to see de doorstep outside and cut me twice in de back.

'Baby, Ah run mah other arm in mah coat-sleeve and grabbed dat nigger by his necktie befo' he could bat his eye and then Ah wuz all over 'im jus' lak gravy over rice. He lost his razor tryin' tuh git loose from me. He wuz hollerin' for me tuh turn him loose, but baby, Ah turnt him every way *but* loose. Ah left him on the doorstep and got here to yuh de quickest way Ah could. Ah know Ah ain't cut too deep 'cause he was too skeered tuh run up on me close enough. Sorta pull de flesh together with stickin' plaster. Ah'll be all right in uh day or so.'

Janie was painting on iodine and crying.

'You ain't de one to be cryin', Janie. It's his ole lady oughta do dat. You done gimme luck. Look in mah left hand pants pocket and see whut yo' daddy brought yuh. When Ah tell yuh Ah'm gointuh bring it, Ah don't lie.'

They counted it together – three hundred and twenty-two dollars. It was almost like Tea Cake had held up the Paymaster. He made her take the two hundred and put it back in the secret place. Then Janie told him about the other money she had in the bank.

'Put dat two hundred back wid de rest, Janie. Mah dice. Ah no need no assistance tuh help me feed mah woman. From now on, you gointuh eat whutever mah money can buy yuh and wear de same. When Ah ain't got nothin' you don't git nothin'.'

'Dat's all right wid me.'

He was getting drowsy, but he pinched her leg playfully because he was glad she took things the way he wanted her to. 'Listen, mama, soon as Ah git over dis lil cuttin' scrape, we gointuh do somethin' crazy.'

'Whut's dat?'

'We goin' on de muck.'

'Whut's de muck, and where is it at?'

'Oh down in de Everglades round Clewiston and Belle Glade where dey raise all dat cane and string-beans and tomatuhs. Folks don't do nothin' down dere but make money and fun and foolishness. We must go dere.'

He drifted off into sleep and Janie looked down on him and felt a self-crushing love. So her soul crawled out from its hiding place.

14

To Janie's strange eyes, everything in the Everglades was big and new. Big Lake Okechobee, big beans, big cane, big weeds, big everything. Weeds that did well to grow waist high up the state were eight and often ten feet tall down there. Ground so rich that everything went wild. Volunteer cane just taking the place. Dirt roads so rich and black that a half mile of it would have fertilized a Kansas wheat field. Wild cane on either side of the road hiding the rest of the world. People wild too.

'Season don't open up till last of September, but we had tuh git heah ahead uh time tuh git us uh room,' Tea Cake explained. 'Two weeks from now, it'll be so many folks heah dey won't be lookin' fuh rooms, dey'll be jus' looking fuh somewhere tuh sleep. Now we got uh chance tuh git uh room at de hotel, where dey got uh bath tub. Yuh can't live on de muck 'thout yuh take uh bath every day. Do dat muck'll itch yuh lak ants. 'Tain't but one place round heah wid uh bath tub. 'Tain't nowhere near enough rooms.'

'Whut we gointuh do round heah?'

'All day Ah'm pickin' beans. All night Ah'm pickin' mah box and rollin' dice. Between de beans and de dice Ah can't lose. Ah'm gone right now tuh pick me uh job uh work wid de best man on de muck. Before de rest of 'em gits heah. You can always git jobs round heah in de season, but not wid de right folks.'

'When do de job open up, Tea Cake? Everybody round here look lak dey waitin' too.'

'Dat's right. De big men haves uh certain time tuh open de season jus' lak in everything else. Mah bossman didn't get sufficient seed. He's out huntin' up uh few mo' bushels. Den we'se gointuh plantin'.'

'Bushels?'

'Yeah, bushels. Dis ain't no game fuh pennies. Po' man ain't got no business at de show.'

The very next day he burst into the room in high excitement. 'Boss done bought out another man and want me down on de lake. He got houses fuh de first ones dat git dere. Less go!'

They rattled nine miles in a borrowed car to the quarters that squatted so close that only the dyke separated them from great, sprawling Okechobee. Janie fussed around the shack making a home while Tea Cake planted beans. After hours they fished. Every now and then they'd run across a party of Indians in their long, narrow dug-outs calmly winning their living in the trackless ways of the 'Glades. Finally the beans were in. Nothing much to do but wait to pick them. Tea Cake picked his box a great deal for Janie, but he still didn't have enough to do. No need of gambling yet. The people who were pouring in were broke. They didn't come bringing money, they were coming to make some.

'Tell yuh whut, Janie, less buy us some shootin' tools and go huntin' round heah.'

'Dat would be fine, Tea Cake, exceptin' you know Ah can't shoot. But Ah'd love tuh go wid *you*.'

'Oh, you needs tuh learn how. 'Tain't no need uh you not knowin' how tuh handle shootin' tools. Even if you didn't never find no game, it's always some trashy rascal dat needs uh good killin',' he laughed. 'Less go intuh Palm Beach and spend some of our money.'

Every day they were practising. Tea Cake made her shoot at little things just to give her good aim. Pistol and shot gun and rifle. It got so the others stood around and watched them. Some of the men would beg for a shot at the target themselves. It was the most exciting thing on the muck. Better than the jook and the pool-room unless some special band was playing for a dance. And the thing that got everybody was the way Janie caught on. She got to the place she could shoot a hawk out of a pine tree and not tear him up. Shoot his head off. She got to be a better shot than Tea Cake. They'd go out any late afternoon and come back loaded down with game. One night they got a boat and went out hunting alligators. Shining their phosphorescent eyes and shooting them in the dark. They could sell the hides and teeth in Palm Beach besides having fun together till work got pressing.

Day by day now, the hordes of workers poured in. Some came limping in with their shoes and sore feet from walking.

It's hard trying to follow your shoe instead of your shoe following you. They came in wagons from way up in Georgia and they came in truck loads from east, west, north and south. Permanent transients with no attachments and tired looking men with their families and dogs in flivvers. All night, all day, hurrying in to pick beans. Skillets, beds, patched up spare inner tubes all hanging and dangling from the ancient cars on the outside and hopeful humanity, herded and hovered on the inside, chugging on to the muck. People ugly from ignorance and broken from being poor.

All night now the jooks clanged and clamored. Pianos living three lifetimes in one. Blues made and used right on the spot. Dancing, fighting, singing, crying, laughing, winning and losing love every hour. Work all day for money, fight all night for love. The rich black earth clinging to bodies and biting the skin like ants.

Finally no more sleeping places. Men made big fires and fifty or sixty men slept around each fire. But they had to pay the man whose land they slept on. He ran the fire just like his boarding place – for pay. But nobody cared. They made good money, even to the children. So they spent good money. Next month and next year were other times. No need to mix them up with the present.

Tea Cake's house was a magnet, the unauthorized center of the 'job.' The way he would sit in the doorway and play his guitar made people stop and listen and maybe disappoint the jook for that night. He was always laughing and full of fun too. He kept everybody laughing in the bean field.

Janie stayed home and boiled big pots of black-eyed peas

and rice. Sometimes baked big pans of navy beans with plenty of sugar and hunks of bacon laying on top. That was something Tea Cake loved so no matter if Janie had fixed beans two or three times during the week, they had baked beans again on Sunday. She always had some kind of dessert too, as Tea Cake said it give a man something to taper off on. Sometimes she'd straighten out the two-room house and take the rifle and have fried rabbit for supper when Tea Cake got home. She didn't leave him itching and scratching in his work clothes, either. The kettle of hot water was already waiting when he got in.

Then Tea Cake took to popping in at the kitchen door at odd hours. Between breakfast and dinner, sometimes. Then often around two o'clock he'd come home and tease and wrestle with her for a half hour and slip on back to work. So one day she asked him about it.

'Tea Cake, whut you doin' back in de quarters when everybody else is still workin'?'

'Come tuh see 'bout you. De boogerman liable tuh tote yuh off whilst Ah'm gone.'

''Tain't no boogerman got me tuh study 'bout. Maybe you think Ah ain't treatin' yuh right and you watchin' me.'

'Naw, naw, Janie. Ah *know* better'n dat. But since you got dat in yo' head, Ah'll have tuh tell yuh de real truth, so yuh can know. Janie, Ah gits lonesome out dere all day 'thout yuh. After dis, you betta come git uh job uh work out dere lak de rest uh de women – so Ah won't be losin' time comin' home.'

'Tea Cake, you'se uh mess! Can't do 'thout me dat lil time.'

''Tain't no lil time. It's near 'bout all day.'

So the very next morning Janie got ready to pick beans along with Tea Cake. There was a suppressed murmur when she picked up a basket and went to work. She was already getting to be a special case on the muck. It was generally assumed that she thought herself too good to work like the rest of the women and that Tea Cake 'pomped her up tuh dat.' But all day long the romping and playing they carried on behind the boss's back made her popular right away. It got the whole field to playing off and on. Then Tea Cake would help get supper afterwards.

'You don't think Ah'm tryin' tuh git outa takin' keer uh yuh, do yuh, Janie, 'cause Ah ast yuh tuh work long side uh me?' Tea Cake asked her at the end of her first week in the field.

'Ah naw, honey. Ah laks it. It's mo' nicer than settin' round dese quarters all day. Clerkin' in dat store wuz hard, but heah, we ain't got nothin' tuh do but do our work and come home and love.'

The house was full of people every night. That is, all around the doorstep was full. Some were there to hear Tea Cake pick the box; some came to talk and tell stories, but most of them came to get into whatever game was going on or might go on. Sometimes Tea Cake lost heavily, for there were several good gamblers on the lake. Sometimes he won and made Janie proud of his skill. But outside of the two jooks, everything on that job went on around those two.

Sometimes Janie would think of the old days in the big white house and the store and laugh to herself. What if Eatonville could see her now in her blue denim overalls and heavy shoes? The crowd of people around her and a dice game on her floor! She was sorry for her friends back there and scornful of the others. The men held big arguments here like they used to do on the store porch. Only here, she could listen and laugh and even talk some herself if she wanted to. She got so she could tell big stories herself from listening to the rest. Because she loved to hear it, and the men loved to hear themselves, they would 'woof' and 'boogerboo' around the games to the limit. No matter how rough it was, people seldom got mad, because everything was done for a laugh. Everybody loved to hear Ed Dockery, Bootyny, and Sop-de-Bottom in a skin game. Ed Dockery was dealing one night and he looked over at Sop-de-Bottom's card and he could tell Sop thought he was going to win. He hollered, 'Ah'll break up *dat* settin' uh eggs.' Sop looked and said, 'Root de peg.' Bootyny asked, 'What are you goin' tuh do? Do do!' Everybody was watching that next card fall. Ed got ready to turn. 'Ah'm gointuh sweep out hell and burn up de broom.' He slammed down another dollar. 'Don't oversport yourself, Ed,' Bootyny challenged. 'You gittin' too yaller.' Ed caught hold of the corner of the card. Sop dropped a dollar. 'Ah'm gointuh shoot in de hearse, don't keer how sad de funeral be.' Ed said, 'You see how this man is teasin' hell?' Tea Cake nudged Sop not to bet. 'You gointuh git caught in uh bullet storm if you don't watch out.' Sop said, 'Aw 'tain't nothin' tuh dat bear but his curly hair. Ah can look through muddy water and see dry land.' Ed turned off the card and hollered, 'Zachariah, Ah says come down out dat sycamore tree. You can't do no business.' Nobody fell on that card. Everybody was scared of the next one. Ed looked around and saw Gabe standing behind his chair and hollered, 'Move, from over me, Gabe! You too black. You draw heat! Sop, you wanta pick up dat bet whilst you got uh chance?' 'Naw, man, Ah wish Ah had uh thousand-leg tuh put on it.' 'So yuh won't lissen, huh? Dumb niggers and free schools. Ah'm gointuh take and teach yuh. Ah'll main-line but Ah won't side-track.' Ed flipped the next card and Sop fell and lost. Everybody hollered and laughed. Ed laughed and said, 'Git off de muck! You ain't nothin'. Dat's all! Hot boilin' water won't help yuh none.' Ed kept on laughing because he had been so scared before. 'Sop, Bootyny, all y'all dat lemme win yo' money: Ah'm sending it straight off to Sears and Roebuck and buy me some clothes, and when Ah turn out Christmas day, it would take a doctor to tell me how near Ah is dressed tuh death.'

15

Janie learned what it felt like to be jealous. A little chunky girl took to picking a play out of Tea Cake in the fields and in the quarters. If he said anything at all, she'd take the opposite side and hit him or shove him and run away to make him chase her. Janie knew what she was up to – luring him away from the crowd. It kept up for two or three weeks with Nunkie getting bolder all the time. She'd hit Tea Cake playfully and the minute he so much as tapped her with his finger she'd fall against him or fall on the ground and have to be picked up. She'd be almost helpless. It took a good deal of handling to set her on her feet again. And another thing. Tea Cake didn't seem to be able to fend her off as promptly as Janie thought he ought to. She began to be snappish a little. A little seed of fear was growing into a tree. Maybe some day Tea Cake would weaken. Maybe he had already given secret encouragement and this was Nunkie's way of bragging about it. Other people began to notice too, and that put Janie more on a wonder.

One day they were working near where the beans ended and the sugar cane began. Janie had marched off a little from Tea Cake's side with another woman for a chat. When she glanced around Tea Cake was gone. Nunkie too. She knew because she looked.

'Where's Tea Cake?' she asked Sop-de-Bottom.

He waved his hand towards the cane field and hurried away. Janie never thought at all. She just acted on feelings. She rushed into the cane and about the fifth row down she found Tea Cake and Nunkie struggling. She was on them before either knew.

'Whut's de matter heah?' Janie asked in a cold rage. They sprang apart.

'Nothin',' Tea Cake told her, standing shamefaced.

'Well, whut you doin' in heah? How come you ain't out dere wid de rest?'

'She grabbed mah workin' tickets outa mah shirt pocket and Ah run tuh git 'em back,' Tea Cake explained, showing the tickets, considerably mauled about in the struggle.

Janie made a move to seize Nunkie but the girl fled. So she took out behind her over the humped-up cane rows. But Nunkie did not mean to be caught. So Janie went on home. The sight of the fields and the other happy people was too much for her that day. She walked slowly and thoughtfully to the quarters. It wasn't long before Tea Cake found her there and tried to talk. She cut him short with a blow and they fought from one room to the other, Janie trying to beat him, and Tea Cake kept holding her wrists and wherever he could to keep her from going too far.

'Ah b'lieve you been messin' round her!' she panted furiously.

'No sich uh thing!' Tea Cake retorted.

'Ah b'lieve yuh did.'

'Don't keer how big uh lie get told, somebody kin b'lieve it!'

They fought on. 'You done hurt mah heart, now you come wid uh lie tuh bruise mah ears! Turn go mah hands!' Janie seethed. But Tea Cake never let go. They wrestled on until they were doped with their own fumes and emanations; till their clothes had been torn away; till he hurled her to the floor and held her there melting her resistance with the heat of his body, doing things with their bodies to express the inexpressible; kissed her until she arched her body to meet him and they fell asleep in sweet exhaustion.

The next morning Janie asked like a woman, 'You still love ole Nunkie?'

'Naw, never did, and you know it too. Ah didn't want her.'

'Yeah, you did.' She didn't say this because she believed it. She wanted to hear his denial. She had to crow over the fallen Nunkie.

'Whut would Ah do wid dat lil chunk of a woman wid you around? She ain't good for nothin' exceptin' tuh set up in uh corner by de kitchen stove and break wood over her head. You'se something tuh make uh man forgit tuh git old and forgit tuh die.'

16

The season closed and people went away like they had come – in droves. Tea Cake and Janie decided to stay since they wanted to make another season on the muck. There was nothing to do, after they had gathered several bushels of dried beans to save over and sell to the planters in the fall. So Janie began to look around and see people and things she hadn't noticed during the season.

For instance during the summer when she heard the subtle but compelling rhythms of the Bahaman drummers, she'd walk over and watch the dances. She did not laugh the 'Saws' to scorn as she had heard the people doing in the season. She got to like it a lot and she and Tea Cake were on hand every night till the others teased them about it.

Janie came to know Mrs Turner now. She had seen her several times during the season, but neither ever spoke. Now they got to be visiting friends.

Mrs Turner was a milky sort of a woman that belonged to child-bed. Her shoulders rounded a little, and she must have been conscious of her pelvis because she kept it stuck out in front of her so she could always see it. Tea Cake made a lot of fun about Mrs Turner's shape behind her back. He claimed that she had been shaped up by a cow kicking her from behind. She was an ironing board with things throwed at it. Then that same cow took and stepped in her mouth when she was a baby and left it wide and flat with her chin and nose almost meeting.

But Mrs Turner's shape and features were entirely approved by Mrs Turner. Her nose was slightly pointed and she was proud. Her thin lips were an ever delight to her eyes. Even her buttocks in bas-relief were a source of pride. To her way of thinking all these things set her aside from Negroes. That was why she sought out Janie to friend with. Janie's coffee-and-cream complexion and her luxurious hair made Mrs Turner forgive her for wearing overalls like the other women who worked in the fields. She didn't forgive her for marrying a man as dark as Tea Cake, but she felt that she could remedy that. That was what her brother was born for. She seldom stayed long when she found Tea Cake at home, but when she happened to drop in and catch Janie alone, she'd spend hours chatting away. Her disfavorite subject was Negroes.

'Mis' Woods, Ah have often said to mah husband, Ah don't see how uh lady like Mis' Woods can stand all them common niggers round her place all de time.'

'They don't worry me atall, Mis' Turner. Fact about de thing is, they tickles me wid they talk.'

'You got mo' nerve than me. When somebody talked mah

husband intuh comin' down heah tuh open up uh eatin' place Ah never dreamt so many different kins uh black folks could colleck in one place. Did Ah never woulda come. Ah ain't useter 'ssociatin' wid black folks. Mah son claims dey draws lightnin'.' They laughed a little and after many of these talks Mrs Turner said, 'Yo' husband musta had plenty money when y'all got married.'

'Whut make you think dat, Mis' Turner?'

'Tuh git hold of uh woman lak you. You got mo' nerve than me. Ah jus' couldn't see mahself married to no black man. It's too many black folks already. We oughta lighten up de race.'

'Naw, mah husband didn't had nothin' but hisself. He's easy tuh love if you mess round 'im. Ah loves 'im.'

'Why you, Mis' Woods! Ah don't b'lieve it. You'se jus' sorter hypnotized dat's all.'

'Naw, it's real. Ah couldn't stand it if he wuz tuh quit me. Don't know whut Ah'd do. He kin take most any lil thing and make summertime out of it when times is dull. Then we lives offa dat happiness he made till some mo' happiness come along.'

'You'se different from me. Ah can't stand black niggers. Ah don't blame de white folks from hatin' 'em 'cause Ah can't stand 'em mahself. 'Nother thing, Ah hates tuh see folks lak me and you mixed up wid 'em. Us oughta class off.'

'Us can't *do* it. We'se uh mingled people and all of us got black kinfolks as well as yaller kinfolks. How come you so against black?'

'And dey makes me tired. Always laughin'! Dey laughs too much and dey laughs too loud. Always singin' ol' nigger songs!

Always cuttin' de monkey for white folks. If it wuzn't for so many black folks it wouldn't be no race problem. De white folks would take us in wid dem. De black ones is holdin' us back.'

'You reckon? 'course Ah ain't never thought about it too much. But Ah don't figger dey even gointuh want us for comp'ny. We'se too poor.'

''Tain't de poorness, it's de color and de features. Who want any lil ole black baby layin' up in de baby buggy lookin' lak uh fly in buttermilk? Who wants to be mixed up wid uh rusty black man, and uh black woman goin' down de street in all dem loud colors, and whoopin' and hollerin' and laughin' over nothin'? Ah don't know. Don't bring me no nigger doctor tuh hang over mah sick-bed. Ah done had six chillun – wuzn't lucky enough tuh raise but dat one – and ain't never had uh nigger tuh even feel mah pulse. White doctors always gits mah money. Ah don't go in no nigger store tuh buy nothin' neither. Colored folks don't know nothin' 'bout no business. Deliver me!'

Mrs Turner was almost screaming in fanatical earnestness by now. Janie was dumb and bewildered before and she clucked sympathetically and wished she knew what to say. It was so evident that Mrs Turner took black folk as a personal affront to herself.

'Look at me! Ah ain't got no flat nose and liver lips. Ah'm uh featured woman. Ah got white folks' features in mah face. Still and all Ah got tuh be lumped in wid all de rest. It ain't fair. Even if dey don't take us in wid de whites, dey oughta make us uh class tuh ourselves.'

'It don't worry me atall, but Ah reckon Ah ain't got no real head fur thinkin'.'

'You oughta meet mah brother. He's real smart. Got dead straight hair. Dey made him uh delegate tuh de Sunday School Convention and he read uh paper on Booker T. Washington and tore him tuh pieces!'

'Booker T.? He wuz a great big man, wusn't he?'

'"Sposed tuh be. All he ever done was cut de monkey for white folks. So dey pomped him up. But you know whut de ole folks say "de higher de monkey climbs de mo' he show his behind" so dat's de way it wuz wid Booker T. Mah brother hit 'im every time dey give 'im chance tuh speak.'

'Ah was raised on de notion dat he wuz uh great big man,' was all that Janie knew to say.

'He didn't do nothin' but hold us back – talkin' 'bout work when de race ain't never done nothin' else. He wuz uh enemy tuh us, dat's whut. He wuz uh white folks' nigger.'

According to all Janie had been taught this was sacrilege so she sat without speaking at all. But Mrs Turner went on.

'Ah done sent fuh mah brother tuh come down and spend uh while wid us. He's sorter outa work now. Ah wants yuh tuh meet him mo' special. You and him would make up uh swell couple if you wuzn't already married. He's uh fine carpenter, when he kin git anything tuh do.'

'Yeah, maybe so. But Ah *is* married now, so 'tain't no use in considerin'.'

Mrs Turner finally rose to go after being very firm about several other view-points of either herself, her son or her brother. She begged Janie to drop in on her anytime, but never once mentioning Tea Cake. Finally she was gone and Janie hurried to her kitchen to put on supper and found Tea Cake sitting in there with his head between his hands.

'Tea Cake! Ah didn't know you wuz home.'

'Ah know yuh didn't. Ah been heah uh long time listenin' to dat heifer run me down tuh de dawgs uh try tuh tole you off from me.'

'So dat whut she wuz up to? Ah didn't know.'

''Course she is. She got some no-count brother she wants yuh tuh hook up wid and take keer of Ah reckon.'

'Shucks! If dat's her notion she's barkin' up de wrong tree. Mah hands is full already.'

'Thanky Ma'am. Ah hates dat woman lak poison. Keep her from round dis house. Her look lak uh white woman! Wid dat meriny skin and hair jus' as close tuh her head as ninety-nine is tuh uh hundred! Since she hate black folks so, she don't need our money in her ol' eatin' place. Ah'll pass de word along. We kin go tuh dat white man's place and git good treatment. Her and dat whittled-down husband uh hers! And dat son! He's jus' uh dirty trick her womb played on her. Ah'm telling her husband tuh keep her home. Ah don't want her round dis house.'

One day Tea Cake met Turner and his son on the street. He was a vanishing-looking kind of a man as if there used to be parts about him that stuck out individually but now he hadn't a thing about him that wasn't dwindled and blurred. Just like he had been sand-papered down to a long oval mass. Tea Cake felt sorry for him without knowing why. So he didn't blurt out the insults he had intended. But he couldn't hold in everything. They talked about the prospects for the coming season for a moment, then Tea Cake said, 'Yo' wife don't seem tuh have nothin' much tuh do, so she kin visit uh lot. Mine got too much tuh do tuh go visitin' and too much tuh spend time talkin' tuh folks dat visit her.'

'Mah wife takes time fuh whatever she wants tuh do. Real strong headed dat way. Yes indeed.' He laughed a high lungless laugh. 'De chillun don't keep her in no mo' so she visits when she chooses.'

'De chillun?' Tea Cake asked him in surprise. 'You got any smaller than him?' He indicated the son who seemed around twenty or so. 'Ah ain't seen yo' others.'

'Ah reckon you ain't 'cause dey all passed on befo' dis one wuz born. We ain't had no luck atall wid our chillun. We lucky to raise him. He's de last stroke of exhausted nature.'

He gave his powerless laugh again and Tea Cake and the boy joined in with him. Then Tea Cake walked on off and went home to Janie.

'Her husband can't do nothin' wid dat butt-headed woman. All you can do is treat her cold whenever she come round here.'

Janie tried that, but short of telling Mrs Turner bluntly, there was nothing she could do to discourage her completely. She felt honored by Janie's acquaintance and she quickly forgave and forgot snubs in order to keep it. Anyone who looked more white folkish than herself was better than she was in her criteria, therefore it was right that they should be cruel to her at times, just as she was cruel to those more negroid than herself in direct ratio to their negroness. Like the pecking-order in a chicken yard. Insensate cruelty to those you can whip, and grovelling submission to those you can't. Once having set up her idols and built altars to them it was inevitable that she would worship there. It was inevitable that she should accept any inconsistency and cruelty from her deity as all good worshippers do from theirs. All gods who receive homage are cruel. All gods dispense suffering without reason. Otherwise they would not be worshipped. Through indiscriminate suffering men know fear and fear is the most divine emotion. It is the stones for altars and the beginning of wisdom. Half gods are worshipped in wine and flowers. Real gods require blood.

Mrs Turner, like all other believers, had built an altar to the unattainable – Caucasian characteristics for all. Her god would smite her, would hurl her from pinnacles and lose her in deserts. But she would not forsake his altars. Behind her crude words was a belief that somehow she and others through worship could attain her paradise – a heaven of straight-haired, thin-lipped, high-nose boned white seraphs. The physical impossibilities in no way injured faith. That was the mystery and mysteries are the chores of gods. Beyond her faith was a fanaticism to defend the altars of her god. It was distressing to emerge from her inner temple and find these black desecrators howling with laughter before the door. Oh, for an army, terrible with banners *and swords!*

So she didn't cling to Janie Woods the woman. She paid homage to Janie's Caucasian characteristics as such. And when she was with Janie she had a feeling of transmutation, as if she herself had become whiter and with straighter hair and she hated Tea Cake first for his defilement of divinity and next for his telling mockery of her. If she only knew something she could do about it! But she didn't. Once she was complaining about the carryings-on at the jook and Tea Cake snapped, 'Aw, don't make God look so foolish – findin' fault wid everything He made.'

So Mrs Turner frowned most of the time. She had so much to disapprove of. It didn't affect Tea Cake and Janie too much. It just gave them something to talk about in the summertime when everything was dull on the muck. Otherwise they made little trips to Palm Beach, Fort Myers and Fort Lauderdale for their fun. Before they realized it the sun was cooler and the crowds came pouring onto the muck again.

17

A great deal of the old crowd were back. But there were lots of new ones too. Some of these men made passes at Janie, and women who didn't know took out after Tea Cake. Didn't take them long to be put right, however. Still and all, jealousies arose now and then on both sides. When Mrs Turner's brother came and she brought him over to be introduced, Tea Cake had a brainstorm. Before the week was over he had whipped Janie. Not because her behavior justified his jealousy, but it relieved that awful fear inside him. Being able to whip her reassured him in possession. No brutal beating at all. He just slapped her around a bit to show he was boss. Everybody talked about it next day in the fields. It aroused a sort of envy in both men and women. The way he petted and pampered her as if those two or three face slaps had nearly killed her made the women see visions and the helpless way she hung on him made men dream dreams.

'Tea Cake, you sho is a lucky man,' Sop-de-Bottom told him. 'Uh person can see every place you hit her. Ah bet she never raised her hand tuh hit yuh back, neither. Take some uh dese ol' rusty black women and dey would fight yuh all night long and next day nobody couldn't tell you ever hit 'em. Dat's de reason Ah done quit beatin' mah woman. You can't make no mark on 'em at all. Lawd! wouldn't Ah love tuh whip uh tender woman lak Janie! Ah bet she don't even holler. She jus' cries, eh Tea Cake?'

'Dat's right.'

'See dat! Mah woman would spread her lungs all over Palm Beach County, let alone knock out mah jaw teeth. You don't know dat woman uh mine. She got ninety-nine rows uh jaw teeth and git her good and mad, she'll wade through solid rock up to her hip pockets.'

'Mah Janie is uh high time woman and useter things. Ah didn't git her outa de middle uh de road. Ah got her outa uh big fine house. Right now she got money enough in de bank tuh buy up dese ziggaboos and give 'em away.'

'Hush yo' mouf! And she down heah on de muck lak anybody else!'

'Janie is wherever *Ah* wants tuh be. Dat's de kind uh wife she is and Ah love her for it. Ah wouldn't be knockin' her around. Ah didn't wants whup her last night, but ol' Mis' Turner done sent for her brother tuh come tuh bait Janie in and take her way from me. Ah didn't whup Janie 'cause *she* done nothin'. Ah beat her tuh show dem Turners who is boss. Ah set in de kitchen one day and heard dat woman tell mah wife Ah'm too black fuh her. She don't see how Janie can stand me.'

'Tell her husband on her.'

'Shucks! Ah b'lieve he's skeered of her.'

'Knock her teeth down her throat.'

'Dat would look like she had some influence when she ain't. Ah jus' let her see dat Ah got control.'

'So she live offa our money and don't lak black folks, huh? O.K. we'll have her gone from here befo' two weeks is up. Ah'm goin' right off tuh all de men and drop rocks aginst her.'

'Ah ain't mad wid her for whut she done, 'cause she ain't done me nothin' yet. Ah'm mad at her for thinkin'. Her and her gang got tuh go.'

'Us is wid yuh, Tea Cake. You know dat already. Dat Turner woman is real smart, accordin' tuh her notions. Reckon she done heard 'bout dat money yo' wife got in de bank and she's bound tuh rope her in tuh her family one way or another.'

'Sop, Ah don't think it's half de money as it is de looks. She's color-struck. She ain't got de kind of uh mind you meet every day. She ain't a fact and neither do she make a good story when you tell about her.'

'Ah yeah, she's too smart tuh stay round heah. She figgers we'se jus' uh bunch uh dumb niggers so she think she'll grow horns. But dat's uh lie. She'll die butt-headed.'

Saturday afternoon when the work tickets were turned into cash everybody began to buy coon-dick and get drunk. By dusk dark Belle Glade was full of loud-talking, staggering men. Plenty women had gotten their knots charged too. The police chief in his speedy Ford was rushing from jook to jook and eating house trying to keep order, but making few arrests. Not enough jail-space for all the drunks so why bother with a few?

All he could do to keep down fights and get the white men out of colored town by nine o'clock. Dick Sterrett and Coodemay seemed to be the worst off. Their likker told them to go from place to place pushing and shoving and loud-talking and they were doing it.

Way after awhile they arrived at Mrs Turner's eating house and found the place full to the limit. Tea Cake, Stew Beef, Sop-de-Bottom, Bootyny, Motor Boat and all the familiar crowd was there. Coodemay straightened up as if in surprise and asked, 'Say, whut y'all doin' in heah?'

'Eatin'',' Stew Beef told him. 'Dey got beef stew, so you *know* Ah'd be heah.'

'We all laks tuh take uh rest from our women folks' cookin' once in uh while, so us all eatin' way from home tuhnight. Anyhow Mis' Turner got de best ole grub in town.'

Mrs Turner back and forth in the dining room heard Sop when he said this and beamed.

'Ah speck you two last ones tuh come in is gointuh have tuh wait for uh seat. Ah'm all full up now.'

'Dat's all right,' Sterrett objected. 'You fry me some fish. Ah kin eat dat standin' up. Cuppa coffee on de side.'

'Sling me up uh plate uh dat stew beef wid some coffee too, please ma'am. Sterrett is jus' ez drunk ez Ah is; and if he kin eat standin' up, Ah kin do de same.' Coodemay leaned drunkenly against the wall and everybody laughed.

Pretty soon the girl that was waiting table for Mrs Turner brought in the order and Sterrett took his fish and coffee in his hands and stood there. Coodemay wouldn't take his off the tray like he should have.

'Naw, you hold it fuh me, baby, and lemme eat,' he told the waitress. He took the fork and started to eat off the tray.

'Nobody ain't got no time tuh hold yo' grub up in front uh yo' face,' she told Coodemay. 'Heah, take it yo'self.'

'You'se right,' Coodemay told her. 'Gimme it heah. Sop kin gimme his chear.'

'You'se uh lie,' Sop retorted. 'Ah ain't through and Ah ain't ready tuh git up.'

Coodemay tried to shove Sop out of the chair and Sop resisted. That brought on a whole lot of shoving and scrambling and coffee got spilt on Sop. So he aimed at Coodemay with a saucer and hit Bootyny. Bootyny threw his thick coffee cup at Coodemay and just missed Stew Beef. So it got to be a big fight. Mrs Turner came running in out of the kitchen. Then Tea Cake got up and caught hold of Coodemay by the collar.

'Looka heah, y'all, don't come in heah and raise no disturbance in de place. Mis' Turner is too nice uh woman fuh dat. In fact, she's more nicer than anybody else on de muck.' Mrs Turner beamed on Tea Cake.

'Ah knows dat. All of us knows it. But Ah don't give uh damn how nice she is, Ah got tuh have some place tuh set down and eat. Sop ain't gointuh bluff me, neither. Let 'im fight lak a man. Take yo' hands off me, Tea Cake.'

'Naw, Ah won't neither. You comin' on outa de place.'

'Who gointuh make me come out?'

'Me, dat's who. Ah'm in heah, ain't Ah? If you don't want tuh respect nice people lak Mrs Turner, God knows you gointuh respect me! Come on outa heah, Coodemay.'

'Turn him loose, Tea Cake!' Sterrett shouted. 'Dat's *mah*

buddy. Us come in heah together and he ain't goin' nowhere until Ah go mahself.'

'Well, both of yuh is goin'!' Tea Cake shouted and fastened down on Coodemay. Dockery grabbed Sterrett and they wrassled all over the place. Some more joined in and dishes and tables began to crash.

Mrs Turner saw with dismay that Tea Cake's taking them out was worse than letting them stay in. She ran out in the back somewhere and got her husband to put a stop to things. He came in, took a look and squinched down into a chair in an off corner and didn't open his mouth. So Mrs Turner struggled into the mass and caught Tea Cake by the arm.

'Dat's all right, Tea Cake, Ah 'preciate yo' help, but leave 'em alone.'

'Naw suh, Mis' Turner, Ah'm gointuh show 'em dey can't come runnin' over nice people and loud-talk no place whilst Ah'm around. Dey goin' outa heah!'

By that time everybody in and around the place was taking sides. Somehow or other Mrs Turner fell down and nobody knew she was down there under all the fighting, and broken dishes and crippled up tables and broken-off chair legs and window panes and such things. It got so that the floor was knee-deep with something no matter where you put your foot down. But Tea Cake kept right on until Coodemay told him, 'Ah'm wrong. Ah'm wrong! Y'all tried tuh tell me right and Ah wouldn't lissen. Ah ain't mad wid nobody. Just tuh show y'all Ah ain't mad, me and Sterrett gointuh buy everybody somethin' tuh drink. Ole man Vickers got some good coon-dick over round Pahokee. Come on everybody.

Let's go git our knots charged.' Everybody got in a good humor and left.

Mrs Turner got up off the floor hollering for the police. Look at her place! How come nobody didn't call the police? Then she found out that one of her hands was all stepped on and her fingers were bleeding pretty peart. Two or three people who were not there during the fracas poked their heads in at the door to sympathize but that made Mrs Turner madder. She told them where to go in a hurry. Then she saw her husband sitting over there in the corner with his long bony legs all crossed up smoking his pipe.

'What kinda man is *you*, Turner? You see dese no count niggers come in heah and break up mah place! How kin you set and see yo' wife all trompled on? You ain't no kinda man at all. You seen dat Tea Cake shove me down! Yes you did! You ain't raised yo' hand tuh do nothin' about it.'

Turner removed his pipe and answered: 'Yeah, and you see how Ah did swell up too, didn't yuh? You tell Tea Cake he better be keerful Ah don't swell up again.' At that Turner crossed his legs the other way and kept right on smoking his pipe.

Mrs Turner hit at him the best she could with her hurt hand and then spoke her mind for half an hour.

'It's a good thing mah brother wuzn't round heah when it happened do he would uh kilt somebody. Mah son too. Dey got some manhood about 'em. We'se goin' back tuh Miami where folks is civilized.'

Nobody told her right away that her son and brother were already on their way after pointed warnings outside the café.

No time for fooling around. They were hurrying into Palm Beach. She'd find out about that later on.

Monday morning Coodemay and Sterrett stopped by and begged her pardon profusely and gave her five dollars apiece. Then Coodemay said, 'Dey tell me Ah wuz drunk Sat'day night and clownin' down. Ah don't 'member uh thing 'bout it. But when Ah git tuh peepin' through mah likker, dey tell me Ah'm uh mess.'

18

Since Tea Cake and Janie had friended with the Bahaman workers in the 'Glades, they, the 'Saws,' had been gradually drawn into the American crowd. They quit hiding out to hold their dances when they found that their American friends didn't laugh at them as they feared. Many of the Americans learned to jump and liked it as much as the 'Saws.' So they began to hold dances night after night in the quarters, usually behind Tea Cake's house. Often now, Tea Cake and Janie stayed up so late at the fire dances that Tea Cake would not let her go with him to the field. He wanted her to get her rest.

So she was home by herself one afternoon when she saw a band of Seminoles passing by. The men walking in front and the laden, stolid women following them like burros. She had seen Indians several times in the 'Glades, in twos and threes, but this was a large party. They were headed towards the Palm Beach road and kept moving steadily. About an hour later another party appeared and went the same way. Then another just before sundown. This time she asked where they were all going and at last one of the men answered her.

'Going to high ground. Saw-grass bloom. Hurricane coming.'

Everybody was talking about it that night. But nobody was worried. The fire dance kept up till nearly dawn. The next day, more Indians moved east, unhurried but steady. Still a blue sky and fair weather. Beans running fine and prices good, so the Indians could be, *must* be, wrong. You couldn't have a hurricane when you're making seven and eight dollars a day picking beans. Indians are dumb anyhow, always were. Another night of Stew Beef making dynamic subtleties with his drum and living, sculptural, grotesques in the dance. Next day, no Indians passed at all. It was hot and sultry and Janie left the field and went home.

Morning came without motion. The winds, to the tiniest, lisping baby breath had left the earth. Even before the sun gave light, dead day was creeping from bush to bush watching man.

Some rabbits scurried through the quarters going east. Some possums slunk by and their route was definite. One or two at a time, then more. By the time the people left the fields the procession was constant. Snakes, rattlesnakes began to cross the quarters. The men killed a few, but they could not be missed from the crawling horde. People stayed indoors until daylight. Several times during the night Janie heard the snort of big animals like deer. Once the muted voice of a panther. Going east and east. That night the palm and banana trees began that long distance talk with rain. Several people took fright and picked up and went in to Palm Beach anyway. A thousand buzzards held a flying meet and then went above the clouds and stayed.

One of the Bahaman boys stopped by Tea Cake's house in a car and hollered. Tea Cake came out throwin' laughter over his shoulder into the house.

'Hello Tea Cake.'

'Hello 'Lias. You leavin', Ah see.'

'Yeah man. You and Janie wanta go? Ah wouldn't give nobody else uh chawnce at uh seat till Ah found out if you all had anyway tuh go.'

'Thank yuh ever so much, Lias. But we 'bout decided tuh stay.'

'De crow gahn up, man.'

'Dat ain't nothin'. You ain't seen de bossman go up, is yuh? Well all right now. Man, de money's too good on the muck. It's liable tuh fair off by tuhmorrer. Ah wouldn't leave if Ah wuz you.'

'Mah uncle come for me. He say hurricane warning out in Palm Beach. Not so bad dere, but man, dis muck is too low and dat big lake is liable tuh bust.'

'Ah naw, man. Some boys in dere now talkin' 'bout it. Some of 'em been in de 'Glades fuh years. 'Tain't nothin' but uh lil blow. You'll lose de whole day tuhmorrer tryin' tuh git back out heah.'

'De Indians gahn east, man. It's dangerous.'

'Dey don't always know. Indians don't know much uh nothin', tuh tell de truth. Else dey'd own dis country still. De white folks ain't gone nowhere. Dey oughta know if it's dangerous. You better stay heah, man. Big jumpin' dance tuhnight right heah, when it fair off.'

Lias hesitated and started to climb out, but his uncle wouldn't let him. 'Dis time tuhmorrer you gointuh wish you follow crow,' he snorted and drove off. Lias waved back to them gaily.

'If Ah never see you no mo' on earth, Ah'll meet you in Africa.'

Others hurried east like the Indians and rabbits and snakes and coons. But the majority sat around laughing and waiting for the sun to get friendly again.

Several men collected at Tea Cake's house and sat around stuffing courage into each other's ears. Janie baked a big pan of beans and something she called sweet biscuits and they all managed to be happy enough.

Most of the great flame-throwers were there and naturally, handling Big John de Conquer and his works. How he had done everything big on earth, then went up tuh heben without dying atall. Went up there picking a guitar and got all de angels doing the ring-shout round and round de throne. Then everybody but God and Old Peter flew off on a flying race to Jericho and back and John de Conquer won the race; went on down to hell, beat the old devil and passed out ice water to everybody down there. Somebody tried to say that it was a mouth organ harp that John was playing, but the rest of them would not hear that. Don't care how good anybody could play a harp, God would rather to hear a guitar. That brought them back to Tea Cake. How come he couldn't hit that box a lick or two? Well, all right now, make us know it.

When it got good to everybody, Muck-Boy woke up and

began to chant with the rhythm and everybody bore down on the last word of the line:

> Yo' mama don't wear no *Draws*
> Ah seen her when she took 'em *Off*
> She soaked 'em in alco*Hol*
> She sold 'em tuh de Santy *Claus*
> He told her 'twas aginst de *Law*
> To wear dem dirty *Draws*

Then Muck-Boy went crazy through the feet and danced himself and everybody else crazy. When he finished he sat back down on the floor and went to sleep again. Then they got to playing Florida flip and coon-can. Then it was dice. Not for money. This was a show-off game. Everybody posing his fancy shots. As always it broiled down to Tea Cake and Motor Boat. Tea Cake with his shy grin and Motor Boat with his face like a little black cherubim just from a church tower doing amazing things with anybody's dice. The others forgot the work and the weather watching them throw. It was art. A thousand dollars a throw in Madison Square Garden wouldn't have gotten any more breathless suspense. It would have just been more people holding in.

After a while somebody looked out and said, 'It ain't gitting no fairer out dere. B'lieve Ah'll git on over tuh mah shack.' Motor Boat and Tea Cake were still playing so everybody left them at it.

Sometime that night the winds came back. Everything in the world had a strong rattle, sharp and short like Stew Beef vibrating the drum head near the edge with his fingers. By morning Gabriel was playing the deep tones in the center of the drum. So when Janie looked out of her door she saw the drifting mists gathered in the west – that cloud field of the sky – to arm themselves with thunders and march forth against the world. Louder and higher and lower and wider the sound and motion spread, mounting, sinking, darking.

It woke up old Okechobee and the monster began to roll in his bed. Began to roll and complain like a peevish world on a grumble. The folks in the quarters and the people in the big houses further around the shore heard the big lake and wondered. The people felt uncomfortable but safe because there were the seawalls to chain the senseless monster in his bed. The folks let the people do the thinking. If the castles thought themselves secure, the cabins needn't worry. Their decision was already made as always. Chink up your cracks, shiver in your wet beds and wait on the mercy of the Lord. The bossman might have the thing stopped before morning anyway. It is so easy to be hopeful in the day time when you can see the things you wish on. But it was night, it stayed night. Night was striding across nothingness with the whole round world in his hands.

A big burst of thunder and lightning that trampled over the roof of the house. So Tea Cake and Motor stopped playing. Motor looked up in his angel-looking way and said, 'Big Massa draw him chair upstairs.'

'Ah'm glad y'all stop dat crap-shootin' even if it wasn't for money,' Janie said. 'Ole Massa is doin' *His* work now. Us oughta keep quiet.'

They huddled closer and stared at the door. They just didn't use another part of their bodies, and they didn't look at anything but the door. The time was past for asking the white folks what to look for through that door. Six eyes were questioning *God*.

Through the screaming wind they heard things crashing and things hurtling and dashing with unbelievable velocity. A baby rabbit, terror ridden, squirmed through a hole in the floor and squatted off there in the shadows against the wall, seeming to know that nobody wanted its flesh at such a time. And the lake got madder and madder with only its dikes between them and him.

In a little wind-lull, Tea Cake touched Janie and said, 'Ah reckon you wish now you had of stayed in yo' big house 'way from such as dis, don't yuh?'

'Naw.'

'Naw?'

'Yeah, naw. People don't die till dey time come nohow, don't keer where you at. Ah'm wid mah husband in uh storm, dat's all.'

'Thanky, Ma'am. But 'sposing you wuz tuh die, now. You wouldn't git mad at me for draggin' yuh heah?'

'Naw. We been tuhgether round two years. If you kin see de light at daybreak, you don't keer if you die at dusk. It's so many people never seen de light at all. Ah wuz fumblin' round and God opened de door.'

He dropped to the floor and put his head in her lap. 'Well then, Janie, you meant whut you didn't say, 'cause Ah never *knowed* you wuz so satisfied wid me lak dat. Ah kinda thought—'

The wind came back with triple fury, and put out the light for the last time. They sat in company with the others in other shanties, their eyes straining against crude walls and their souls asking if He meant to measure their puny might against His. They seemed to be staring at the dark, but their eyes were watching God.

As soon as Tea Cake went out pushing wind in front of him, he saw that the wind and water had given life to lots of things that folks think of as dead and given death to so much that had been living things. Water everywhere. Stray fish swimming in the yard. Three inches more and the water would be in the house. Already in some. He decided to try to find a car to take them out of the 'Glades before worse things happened. He turned back to tell Janie about it so she could be ready to go.

'Git our insurance papers tuhgether, Janie. Ah'll tote mah box mahself and things lak dat.'

'You got all de money out de dresser drawer, already?'

'Naw, git it quick and cut up piece off de tablecloth tuh wrap it up in. Us liable tuh git wet tuh our necks. Cut uh piece uh dat oilcloth quick fuh our papers. We got tuh go, if it ain't too late. De dish can't bear it out no longer.'

He snatched the oilcloth off the table and took out his knife. Janie held it straight while he slashed off a strip.

'But Tea Cake, it's too awful out dere. Maybe it's better tuh stay heah in de wet than it is tuh try tuh—'

He stunned the argument with half a word. 'Fix,' he said and fought his way outside. He had seen more than Janie had.

Janie took a big needle and ran up a longish sack. Found

some newspaper and wrapped up the paper money and papers and thrust them in and whipped over the open end with her needle. Before she could get it thoroughly hidden in the pocket of her overalls, Tea Cake burst in again.

'Tain't no cars, Janie.'

'Ah thought not! Whut we gointuh do now?'

'We got tuh walk.'

'In all dis weather, Tea Cake? Ah don't b'lieve Ah could make it out de quarters.'

'Oh yeah you kin. Me and you and Motor Boat kin all lock arms and hold one 'nother down. Eh, Motor?'

'He's sleep on de bed in yonder,' Janie said. Tea Cake called without moving.

'Motor Boat! You better git up from dere! Hell done broke loose in Georgy. Dis minute! How kin you sleep at uh time lak dis? Water knee deep in de yard.'

They stepped out in water almost to their buttocks and managed to turn east. Tea Cake had to throw his box away, and Janie saw how it hurt him. Dodging flying missiles, floating dangers, avoiding stepping in holes and warmed on the wind now at their backs until they gained comparatively dry land. They had to fight to keep from being pushed the wrong way and to hold together. They saw other people like themselves struggling along. A house down, here and there, frightened cattle. But above all the drive of the wind and the water. And the lake. Under its multiplied roar could be heard a mighty sound of grinding rock and timber and a wail. They looked back. Saw people trying to run in raging waters and screaming when they found they couldn't. A huge barrier of the makings of the dike to which the cabins had been added was rolling and tumbling forward. Ten feet higher and as far as they could see the muttering wall advanced before the braced-up waters like a road crusher on a cosmic scale. The monstropolous beast had left his bed. The two hundred miles an hour wind had loosed his chains. He seized hold of his dikes and ran forward until he met the quarters; uprooted them like grass and rushed on after his supposed-to-be conquerors, rolling the dikes, rolling the houses, rolling the people in the houses along with other timbers. The sea was walking the earth with a heavy heel.

'De lake is comin'!' Tea Cake gasped.

'De lake!' In amazed horror from Motor Boat, 'De lake!'

'It's comin' behind us!' Janie shuddered. 'Us can't fly.'

'But we still kin run,' Tea Cake shouted and they ran. The gushing water ran faster. The great body was held back, but rivers spouted through fissures in the rolling wall and broke like day. The three fugitives ran past another line of shanties that topped a slight rise and gained a little. They cried out as best they could, 'De lake is comin'!' and barred doors flew open and others joined them in flight crying the same as they went. 'De lake is comin'!' and the pursuing waters growled and shouted ahead, 'Yes, Ah'm comin'!', and those who could fled on.

They made it to a tall house on a hump of ground and Janie said, 'Less stop heah. Ah can't make it no further. Ah'm done give out.'

'All of us is done give out,' Tea Cake corrected. 'We's goin' inside out dis weather, kill or cure.' He knocked with the handle of his knife, while they leaned their faces and shoulders against the wall. He knocked once more then he and Motor Boat went round to the back and forced a door. Nobody there.

'Dese people had mo' sense than Ah did,' Tea Cake said as they dropped to the floor and lay there panting. 'Us oughta went on wid 'Lias lak he ast me.'

'You didn't know,' Janie contended. 'And when yuh don't know, yuh just don't know. De storms might not of come sho nuff.'

They went to sleep promptly but Janie woke up first. She heard the sound of rushing water and sat up.

'Tea Cake! Motor Boat! De lake is comin'!'

The lake *was* coming on. Slower and wider, but coming. It had trampled on most of its supporting wall and lowered its front by spreading. But it came muttering and grumbling onward like a tired mammoth just the same.

'Dis is uh high tall house. Maybe it won't reach heah at all,' Janie counselled. 'And if it do, maybe it won't reach tuh de upstairs part.'

'Janie, Lake Okechobee is forty miles wide and sixty miles long. Dat's uh whole heap uh water. If dis wind is shovin' dat whole lake disa way, dis house ain't nothin' tuh swaller. Us better go. Motor Boat!'

'Whut you want, man?'

'De lake is comin'!'

'Aw, naw it 'tain't.'

'Yes, it is *so* comin'! Listen! You kin hear it way off.'

'It kin jus' come on. Ah'll wait right here.'

'Aw, get up, Motor Boat! Less make it tuh de Palm Beach road. Dat's on uh fill. We'se pretty safe dere.'

'Ah'm safe here, man. Go ahead if yuh wants to. Ah'm sleepy.'

'Whut you gointuh do if de lake reach heah?'

'Go upstairs.'

'S'posing it come up dere?'

'Swim, man. Dat's all.'

'Well, uh, Good bye, Motor Boat. Everything is pretty bad, yuh know. Us might git missed of one 'nother. You sho is a grand friend fuh uh man tuh have.'

'Good bye, Tea Cake. Y'all oughta stay here and sleep, man. No use in goin' off and leavin' me lak dis.'

'We don't wanta. Come on wid us. It might be night time when de water hem you up in heah. Dat's how come Ah won't stay. Come on, man.'

'Tea Cake Ah got tuh have mah sleep. Definitely.'

'Good bye, then, Motor. Ah wish you all de luck. Goin' over tuh Nassau fuh dat visit widja when all dis is over.'

'Definitely, Tea Cake. Mah mama's house is yours.'

Tea Cake and Janie were some distance from the house before they struck serious water. Then they had to swim a distance, and Janie could not hold up more than a few strokes at a time, so Tea Cake bore her up till finally they hit a ridge that led on towards the fill. It seemed to him the wind was weakening a little so he kept looking for a place to rest and catch his breath. His wind was gone. Janie was tired and limping, but she had not had to do that hard swimming in the turbulent waters, so Tea Cake was much worse off. But they couldn't stop. Gaining the fill was something but it was no guarantee. The lake was coming. They had to reach the six-mile bridge. It was high and safe perhaps.

Everybody was walking the fill. Hurrying, dragging, falling, crying, calling out names hopefully and hopelessly. Wind and rain beating on old folks and beating on babies. Tea Cake stumbled once or twice in his weariness and Janie held him up. So they reached the bridge at Six Mile Bend and thought to rest.

But it was crowded. White people had preempted that point of elevation and there was no more room. They could climb up one of its high sides and down the other, that was all. Miles further on, still no rest.

They passed a dead man in a sitting position on a hummock, entirely surrounded by wild animals and snakes. Common danger made common friends. Nothing sought a conquest over the other.

Another man clung to a cypress tree on a tiny island. A tin roof of a building hung from the branches by electric wires and the wind swung it back and forth like a mighty ax. The man dared not move a step to his right lest this crushing blade split him open. He dared not step left for a large rattlesnake was stretched full length with his head in the wind. There was a strip of water between the island and the fill, and the man clung to the tree and cried for help.

'De snake won't bite yuh,' Tea Cake yelled to him. 'He skeered tuh go intuh uh coil. Skeered he'll be blowed away. Step round dat side and swim off!'

Soon after that Tea Cake felt he couldn't walk anymore.

Not right away. So he stretched long side of the road to rest. Janie spread herself between him and the wind and he closed his eyes and let the tiredness seep out of his limbs. On each side of the fill was a great expanse of water like lakes – water full of things living and dead. Things that didn't belong in water. As far as the eye could reach, water and wind playing upon it in fury. A large piece of tar-paper roofing sailed through the air and scudded along the fill until it hung against a tree. Janie saw it with joy. That was the very thing to cover Tea Cake with. She could lean against it and hold it down. The wind wasn't quite so bad as it was anyway. The very thing. Poor Tea Cake!

She crept on hands and knees to the piece of roofing and caught hold of it by either side. Immediately the wind lifted both of them and she saw herself sailing off the fill to the right, out and out over the lashing water. She screamed terribly and released the roofing which sailed away as she plunged downward into the water.

'Tea Cake!' He heard her and sprang up. Janie was trying to swim but fighting water too hard. He saw a cow swimming slowly towards the fill in an oblique line. A massive built dog was sitting on her shoulders and shivering and growling. The cow was approaching Janie. A few strokes would bring her there.

'Make it tuh de cow and grab hold of her tail! Don't use yo' feet. Jus' yo' hands is enough. Dat's right, come on!'

Janie achieved the tail of the cow and lifted her head up along the cow's rump, as far as she could above water. The cow sunk a little with the added load and thrashed a moment in terror. Thought she was being pulled down by a gator. Then she continued on. The dog stood up and growled like a lion, stiff-standing hackles, stiff muscles, teeth uncovered as he lashed up his fury for the charge. Tea Cake split the water like an otter, opening his knife as he dived. The dog raced down the back-bone of the cow to the attack and Janie screamed and slipped far back on the tail of the cow, just out of reach of the dog's angry jaws. He wanted to plunge in after her but dreaded the water, somehow. Tea Cake rose out of the water at the cow's rump and seized the dog by the neck. But he was a powerful dog and Tea Cake was over-tired. So he didn't kill the dog with one stroke as he had intended. But the dog couldn't free himself either. They fought and somehow he managed to bite Tea Cake high up on his cheek-bone once. Then Tea Cake finished him and sent him to the bottom to stay there. The cow relieved of a great weight was landing on the fill with Janie before Tea Cake stroked in and crawled weakly upon the fill again.

Janie began to fuss around his face where the dog had bitten him but he said it didn't amount to anything. 'He'd uh raised hell though if he had uh grabbed me uh inch higher and bit me in mah eye. Yuh can't buy eyes in de store, yuh know.' He flopped to the edge of the fill as if the storm wasn't going on at all. 'Lemme rest awhile, then us got tuh make it on intuh town somehow.'

It was next day by the sun and the clock when they reached Palm Beach. It was years later by their bodies. Winters and winters of hardship and suffering. The wheel kept turning round and round. Hope, hopelessness and despair. But the storm blew itself out as they approached the city of refuge.

Havoc was there with her mouth wide open. Back in the Everglades the wind had romped among lakes and trees. In the city it had raged among houses and men. Tea Cake and Janie stood on the edge of things and looked over the desolation.

'How kin Ah find uh doctor fuh yo' face in all dis mess?' Janie wailed.

'Ain't got de damn doctor tuh study 'bout. Us needs uh place tuh rest.'

A great deal of their money and perseverance and they found a place to sleep. It was just that. No place to live at all. Just sleep. Tea Cake looked all around and sat heavily on the side of the bed.

'Well,' he said humbly, 'reckon you never 'spected tuh come tuh dis when you took up wid me, didja?'

'Once upon uh time, Ah never 'spected nothin' Tea Cake but bein' dead from the standin' still and tryin' tuh laugh. But you come 'long and made somethin' outa me. So Ah'm thankful fuh anything we come through together.'

'Thanky, Ma'am.'

'You was twice noble tuh save me from dat dawg. Tea Cake, Ah don't speck you seen his eyes lak Ah did. He didn't aim tuh jus' bite me, Tea Cake. He aimed tuh kill me stone dead. Ah'm never tuh fuhgit dem eyes. He wuzn't nothin' all over but pure hate. Wonder where he come from?'

'Yeah, Ah did see 'im too. It wuz frightenin'. Ah didn't mean tuh take his hate neither. He had tuh die uh me one. Mah switch blade said it wuz him.'

'Po' me, he'd tore me tuh pieces, if it wuzn't fuh you, honey.'

'You don't have tuh say, if it wuzn't fuh me, baby, cause Ah'm *heah*, and then Ah want yuh tuh know it's uh man heah.'

19

And then again Him-with-the-square-toes had gone back to his house. He stood once more and again in his high flat house without sides to it and without a roof with his soulless sword standing upright in his hand. His pale white horse had galloped over waters, and thundered over land. The time of dying was over. It was time to bury the dead.

'Janie, us been in dis dirty, slouchy place two days now, and dat's too much. Us got tuh git outa dis house and outa dis man's town. Ah never did lak round heah.'

'Where we goin', Tea Cake? Dat we don't know.'

'Maybe, we could go back up de state, if yuh want tuh go.'

'Ah didn't say dat, but if dat is whut you—'

'Naw, Ah ain't said nothin' uh de kind. Ah wuz tryin' not tuh keep you outa yo' comfortable no longer'n you wanted tuh stay.'

'If Ah'm in yo' way—'

'Will you lissen at dis woman? Me 'bout tuh bust mah britches tryin' tuh stay wid her and she heah – she oughta be shot wid tacks!'

'All right then, you name somethin' and we'll do it. We kin give it uh poor man's trial anyhow.'

'Anyhow Ah done got rested up and de bed bugs is done got too bold round heah. Ah didn't notice when mah rest wuz broke. Ah'm goin' out and look around and see whut we kin do. Ah'll give *anything* uh common trial.'

'You better stay inside dis house and git some rest. 'Tain't nothin' tuh find out dere nohow.'

'But Ah wants tuh look and see, Janie. Maybe it's some kinda work fuh me tuh help do.'

'Whut dey want you tuh help do, you ain't gointuh like it. Dey's grabbin' all de menfolks dey kin git dey hands on and makin' 'em help bury de dead. Dey claims dey's after de unemployed, but dey ain't bein' too particular about whether you'se employed or not. You stay in dis house. De Red Cross is doin' all dat kin be done otherwise fuh de sick and de 'fflicted.'

'Ah got money on me, Janie. Dey can't bother me. Anyhow Ah wants tuh go see how things is sho nuff. Ah wants tuh see if Ah kin hear anything 'bout de boys from de 'Glades. Maybe dey all come through all right. Maybe not.'

Tea Cake went out and wandered around. Saw the hand of horror on everything. Houses without roofs, and roofs without houses. Steel and stone all crushed and crumbled like wood. The mother of malice had trifled with men.

While Tea Cake was standing and looking he saw two men coming towards him with rifles on their shoulders. Two white men, so he thought about what Janie had told him and flexed his knees to run. But in a moment he saw that wouldn't do him any good. They had already seen him and they were too close to miss him if they shot. Maybe they would pass on by. Maybe when they saw he had money they would realize he was not a tramp.

'Hello, there, Jim,' the tallest one called out. 'We been lookin' fuh you.'

'Mah name ain't no Jim,' Tea Cake said watchfully. 'Whut you been lookin' fuh *me* fuh? Ah ain't done nothin'.'

'Dat's whut we want yuh fuh – not doin' nothin'. Come on less go bury some uh dese heah dead folks. Dey ain't gittin' buried fast enough.'

Tea Cake hung back defensively. 'Whut Ah got tuh do wid dat? Ah'm uh workin' man wid money in mah pocket. Jus' got blowed outa de 'Glades by de storm.'

The short man made a quick move with his rifle. 'Git on down de road dere, suh! Don't look out somebody'll be buryin' *you*! G'wan in front uh me, suh!'

Tea Cake found that he was part of a small army that had been pressed into service to clear the wreckage in public places and bury the dead. Bodies had to be searched out, carried to certain gathering places and buried. Corpses were not just found in wrecked houses. They were under houses, tangled in shrubbery, floating in water, hanging in trees, drifting under wreckage.

Trucks lined with drag kept rolling in from the 'Glades and other outlying parts, each with its load of twenty-five bodies. Some bodies fully dressed, some naked and some in all degrees of dishevelment. Some bodies with calm faces and satisfied hands. Some dead with fighting faces and eyes flung wide open in wonder. Death had found them watching, trying to see beyond seeing.

Miserable, sullen men, black and white under guard had to keep on searching for bodies and digging graves. A huge ditch was dug across the white cemetery and a big ditch was opened across the black graveyard. Plenty quick-lime on hand to throw over the bodies as soon as they were received. They had already been unburied too long. The men were making every effort to get them covered up as quickly as possible. But the guards stopped them. They had received orders to be carried out.

'Hey, dere, y'all! Don't dump dem bodies in de hole lak dat! Examine every last one of 'em and find out if they's white or black.'

'Us got tuh handle 'em slow lak dat? God have mussy! In de condition they's in got tuh examine 'em? Whut difference do it make 'bout de color? Dey all needs buryin' in uh hurry.'

'Got orders from headquarters. They makin' coffins fuh all de white folks. 'Tain't nothin' but cheap pine, but dat's better'n nothin'. Don't dump no white folks in de hole jus' so.'

'Whut tuh do 'bout de colored folks? Got boxes fuh dem too?'

'Nope. They cain't find enough of 'em tuh go 'round. Jus' sprinkle plenty quick-lime over 'em and cover 'em up.'

'Shucks! Nobody can't tell nothin' 'bout some uh dese bodies, de shape dey's in. Can't tell whether dey's white or black.'

The guards had a long conference over that. After a while they came back and told the men, 'Look at they hair, when you cain't tell no other way. And don't lemme ketch none uh y'all dumpin' white folks, and don't be wastin' no boxes on colored. They's too hard tuh git holt of right now.'

'They's mighty particular how dese dead folks goes tuh judgment,' Tea Cake observed to the man working next to him. 'Look lak dey think God don't know nothin' 'bout de Jim Crow law.'

Tea Cake had been working several hours when the thought of Janie worrying about him made him desperate. So when a truck drove up to be unloaded he bolted and ran. He was ordered to halt on pain of being shot at, but he kept right on and got away. He found Janie sad and crying just as he had thought. They calmed each other about his absence then Tea Cake brought up another matter.

'Janie, us got tuh git outa dis house and outa dis man's town. Ah don't mean tuh work lak dat no mo'.'

'Naw, naw, Tea Cake. Less stay right in heah until it's all over. If dey can't see yuh, dey can't bother yuh.'

'Aw naw. S'posin' dey come round searchin'? Less git outa heah tuhnight.'

'Where us goin', Tea Cake?'

'De quickest place is de 'Glades. Less make it on back down dere. Dis town is full uh trouble and compellment.'

'But, Tea Cake, de hurricane wuz down in de 'Glades too. It'll be dead folks tuh be buried down dere too.'

'Yeah, Ah know, Janie, but it couldn't never be lak it 'tis heah. In de first place dey been bringin' bodies outa dere all day so it can't be but so many mo' tuh find. And then again it never wuz as many dere as it wuz heah. And then too, Janie,

de white folks down dere knows us. It's bad bein' strange niggers wid white folks. Everybody is against yuh.'

'Dat sho is de truth. De ones de white man know is nice
colored folks. De ones he don't know is bad niggers.' Janie said
this and laughed and Tea Cake laughed with her.

'Janie, Ah done watched it time and time again; each and
every white man think he know all de GOOD darkies already.
He don't need tuh know no mo.' So far as he's concerned, all
dem he don't know oughta be tried and sentenced tuh six
months behind de United States privy house at hard
smellin'.'

'How come de United States privy house, Tea Cake?'

'Well, you know Old Uncle Sam always do have de biggest
and de best uh everything. So de white man figger dat anything less than de Uncle Sam's consolidated water closet
would be too easy. So Ah means tuh go where de white folks
know me. Ah feels lak uh motherless chile round heah.'

They got things together and stole out of the house and
away. The next morning they were back on the muck. They
worked hard all day fixing up a house to live in so that Tea
Cake could go out looking for something to do the next day.
He got out soon next morning more out of curiosity than
eagerness to work. Stayed off all day. That night he came in
beaming out with light.

'Who you reckon Ah seen, Janie? Bet you can't guess.'

'Ah'll betcha uh fat man you seen Sop-de-Bottom.'

'Yeah Ah seen him and Stew Beef and Dockery and Lias,
and Coodemay and Bootyny. Guess who else!'

'Lawd knows. Is it Sterrett?'

'Naw, he got caught in the rush. 'Lias help bury him in Palm Beach. Guess who else?'

'Ah g'wan tell me, Tea Cake. Ah don't know. It can't be Motor Boat.'

'Dat's jus' who it is. Ole Motor! De son of a gun laid up in dat house and slept and de lake come moved de house way off somewhere and Motor didn't know nothin' 'bout it till de storm wuz 'bout over.'

'Naw!'

'Yeah man. Heah we nelly kill our fool selves runnin' way from danger and him lay up dere and sleep and float on off!'

'Well, you know dey say luck is uh fortune.'

'Dat's right too. Look, Ah got uh job uh work. Help clearin' up things in general, and then dey goin' build dat dike sho nuff. Dat ground got to be cleared off too. Plenty work. Dey needs mo' men even.'

So Tea Cake made three hearty weeks. He bought another rifle and a pistol and he and Janie bucked each other as to who was the best shot with Janie ranking him always with the rifle. She could knock the head off of a chicken-hawk sitting up a pine tree. Tea Cake was a little jealous, but proud of his pupil.

About the middle of the fourth week Tea Cake came home early one afternoon complaining of his head. Sick headache that made him lie down for awhile. He woke up hungry. Janie had his supper ready but by the time he walked from the bedroom to the table, he said he didn't b'lieve he wanted a thing.

'Thought you tole me you wuz hongry!' Janie wailed.

'Ah thought so too,' Tea Cake said very quietly and dropped his head in his hands.

'But Ah done baked yuh uh pan uh beans.'

'Ah knows dey's good all right but Ah don't choose nothin' now, Ah thank yuh, Janie.'

He went back to bed. Way in the midnight he woke Janie up in his nightmarish struggle with an enemy that was at his throat. Janie struck a light and quieted him.

'Whut's de matter, honey?' She soothed and soothed. 'You got tuh tell me so Ah kin feel widja. Lemme bear de pain 'long widja, baby. Where hurt yuh, sugar?'

'Somethin' got after me in mah sleep, Janie.' He all but cried, 'Tried tuh choke me tuh death. Hadn't been fuh *you* Ah'd be dead.'

'You sho wuz strainin' wid it. But you'se all right, honey. Ah'm heah.'

He went on back to sleep, but there was no getting around it. He was sick in the morning. He tried to make it but Janie wouldn't hear of his going out at all.

'If Ah kin jus' make out de week,' Tea Cake said.

'Folks wuz makin' weeks befo' you wuz born and they goin-tuh be makin' 'em after you'se gone. Lay back down, Tea Cake. Ah'm goin' git de doctor tuh come see 'bout yuh.'

'Aw ain't dat bad, Janie. Looka heah! Ah kin walk all over de place.'

'But you'se too sick tuh play wid. Plenty fever round heah since de storm.'

'Gimme uh drink uh water befo' you leave, then.'

Janie dipped up a glass of water and brought it to the bed.

Tea Cake took it and filled his mouth then gagged horribly, disgorged that which was in his mouth and threw the glass upon the floor. Janie was frantic with alarm.

'Whut make you ack lak dat wid yo' drinkin' water, Tea Cake? You ast me tuh give it tuh yuh.'

'Dat water is somethin' wrong wid it. It nelly choke me tuh death. Ah tole yuh somethin' jumped on me heah last night and choked me. You come makin' out ah wuz dreamin'.'

'Maybe it wuz uh witch ridin' yuh, honey. Ah'll see can't Ah find some mustard seed whilst Ah's out. But Ah'm sho tuh fetch de doctor when Ah'm come.'

Tea Cake didn't say anything against it and Janie herself hurried off. This sickness to her was worse than the storm. As soon as she was well out of sight, Tea Cake got up and dumped the water bucket and washed it clean. Then he struggled to the irrigation pump and filled it again. He was not accusing Janie of malice and design. He was accusing her of carelessness. She ought to realize that water buckets needed washing like everything else. He'd tell her about it good and proper when she got back. What was she thinking about nohow? He found himself very angry about it. He eased the bucket on the table and sat down to rest before taking a drink.

Finally he dipped up a drink. It was so good and cool! Come to think about it, he hadn't had a drink since yesterday. That was what he needed to give him an appetite for his beans. He found himself wanting it very much, so he threw back his head as he rushed the glass to his lips. But the demon was there before him, strangling, killing him quickly. It was a great relief to expel the water from his mouth. He sprawled on the bed again and lay there shivering until Janie and the doctor arrived. The white doctor who had been around so long that he was part of the muck. Who told the workmen stories with brawny sweaty words in them. He came into the house quickly, hat sitting on the left back corner of his head.

'Hi there, Tea Cake. What de hell's de matter with *you*?'

'Wisht Ah knowed, Doctah Simmons. But Ah sho is sick.'

'Ah, naw Tea Cake. 'Tain't a thing wrong that a quart of coon-dick wouldn't cure. You haven't been gettin' yo' right likker lately, eh?' He slapped Tea Cake lustily across his back and Tea Cake tried to smile as he was expected to do. But it was hard. The doctor opened up his bag and went to work.

'You do look a little peaked, Tea Cake. You got a temperature and yo' pulse is kinda off. What you been doin' here lately?'

'Nothin' 'cept workin' and gamin' uh little, doctah. But look lak water done turn't aginst me.'

'Water? How do you mean?'

'Can't keep it on mah stomach, at all.'

'What else?'

Janie came around the bed full of concern.

'Doctah, Tea Cake ain't tellin' yuh everything lak he oughta. We wuz caught in dat hurricane out heah, and Tea Cake over-strained hisself swimmin' such uh long time and holdin' me up too, and walkin' all dem miles in de storm and then befo' he could git his rest he had tuh come git me out de water agin and fightin' wid dat big ole dawg and de dawg bitin' 'im in de face and everything. Ah been spectin' him tuh be sick befo' now.'

'Dawg bit 'im, did you say?'

'Aw twudn't nothin' much, doctah. It wuz all healed over in two three days,' Tea Cake said impatiently. 'Dat been over uh month ago, nohow. Dis is somethin' new, doctah. Ah figgers de water is yet bad. It's bound tuh be. Too many dead folks been in it fuh it tuh be good tuh drink fuh uh long time. Dat's de way Ah figgers it anyhow.'

'All right, Tea Cake. Ah'll send you some medicine and tell Janie how tuh take care of you. Anyhow, I want you in a bed by yo'self until you hear from me. Just you keep Janie out of yo' bed for awhile, hear? Come on out to the car with me, Janie. I want to send Tea Cake some pills to take right away.'

Outside he fumbled in his bag and gave Janie a tiny bottle with a few pellets inside.

'Give him one of these every hour to keep him quiet, Janie, and stay out of his way when he gets in one of his fits of gagging and choking.'

'How you know he's havin' 'em, doctah? Dat's jus' what Ah come out heah tuh tell yuh.'

'Janie, I'm pretty sure that was a mad dawg bit yo' husband. It's too late to get hold of de dawg's head. But de symptoms is all there. It's mighty bad dat it's gone on so long. Some shots right after it happened would have fixed him right up.'

'You mean he's liable tuh die, doctah?'

'Sho is. But de worst thing is he's liable tuh suffer somethin' awful befo' he goes.'

'Doctor, Ah loves him fit tuh kill. Tell me anything tuh do and Ah'll do it.'

''Bout de only thing you can do, Janie, is to put him in the

County Hospital where they can tie him down and look after him.'

'But he don't like no hospital at all. He'd think Ah wuz tired uh doin' fuh 'im, when God knows Ah ain't. Ah can't stand de idea us tyin' Tea Cake lak he wuz uh mad dawg.'

'It almost amounts to dat, Janie. He's got almost no chance to pull through and he's liable to bite somebody else, specially you, and then you'll be in the same fix he's in. It's mighty bad.'

'Can't nothin' be done fuh his case, doctah? Us got plenty money in de bank in Orlandah, doctah. See can't yuh do somethin' special tuh save him. Anything it cost, doctah, Ah don't keer, but please, doctah.'

'Do what I can. Ah'll phone into Palm Beach right away for the serum which he should have had three weeks ago. I'll do all I can to save him, Janie. But it looks too late. People in his condition can't swallow water, you know, and in other ways it's terrible.'

Janie fooled around outside awhile to try and think it wasn't so. If she didn't see the sickness in his face she could imagine it wasn't really happening. Well, she thought, that big old dawg with the hatred in his eyes had killed her after all. She wished she had slipped off that cow-tail and drowned then and there and been done. But to kill her through Tea Cake was too much to bear. Tea Cake, the son of Evening Sun, had to die for loving her. She looked hard at the sky for a long time. Somewhere up there beyond blue ether's bosom sat He. Was He noticing what was going on around here? He must be because He knew everything. Did He *mean* to do this thing to Tea Cake and her? It wasn't anything she could fight.

She could only ache and wait. Maybe it was some big tease and when He saw it had gone far enough He'd give her a sign. She looked hard for something up there to move for a sign. A star in the daytime, maybe, or the sun to shout, or even a mutter of thunder. Her arms went up in a desperate supplication for a minute. It wasn't exactly pleading, it was asking questions. The sky stayed hard looking and quiet so she went inside the house. God would do less than He had in His heart.

Tea Cake was lying with his eyes closed and Janie hoped he was asleep. He wasn't. A great fear had took hold of him. What was this thing that set his brains afire and grabbed at his throat with iron fingers? Where did it come from and why did it hang around him? He hoped it would stop before Janie noticed anything. He wanted to try to drink water again but he didn't want her to see him fail. As soon as she got out of the kitchen he meant to go to the bucket and drink right quick before anything had time to stop him. No need to worry Janie, until he couldn't help it. He heard her cleaning out the stove and saw her go out back to empty the ashes. He leaped at the bucket at once. But this time the sight of the water was enough. He was on the kitchen floor in great agony when she returned. She petted him, soothed him, and got him back to bed. She made up her mind to go see about that medicine from Palm Beach. Maybe she could find somebody to drive over there for it.

'Feel better now, Tea Cake, baby chile?'

'Uh huh, uh little.'

'Well, b'lieve Ah'll rake up de front yard. De mens is got cane chewin's and peanut hulls all over de place. Don't want de doctah tuh come back heah and find it still de same.'

'Don't take too long, Janie. Don't lak tuh be by mahself when Ah'm sick.'

She ran down the road just as fast as she could. Halfway to town she met Sop-de-Bottom and Dockery coming towards her.

'Hello, Janie, how's Tea Cake?'

'Pretty bad off. Ah'm gointuh see 'bout medicine fuh 'im right now.'

'Doctor told somebody he wuz sick so us come tuh see. Thought somethin' he never come tuh work.'

'Y'all set wid 'im till Ah git back. He need de company right long in heah.'

She fanned on down the road to town and found Dr Simmons. Yes, he had had an answer. They didn't have any serum but they had wired Miami to send it. She needn't worry. It would be there early the next morning if not before. People didn't fool around in a case like that. No, it wouldn't do for her to hire no car to go after it. Just go home and wait. That was all. When she reached home the visitors rose to go.

When they were alone Tea Cake wanted to put his head in Janie's lap and tell her how he felt and let her mama him in her sweet way. But something Sop had told him made his tongue lie cold and heavy like a dead lizard between his jaws. Mrs Turner's brother was back on the muck and now he had this mysterious sickness. People didn't just take sick like this for nothing.

'Janie, whut is dat Turner woman's brother doin' back on de muck?'

'Ah don't know, Tea Cake. Didn't even knowed he wuz back.'

'Accordin' tuh mah notion, you did. Whut you slip off from me just now for?'

'Tea Cake, Ah don't lak you astin' me no sich question. Dat shows how sick you is sho nuff. You'se jealous 'thout me givin' you cause.'

'Well, whut didja slip off from de house 'thout tellin' me you wuz goin'. You ain't never done dat befo'.'

'Dat wuz cause Ah wuz tryin' not tuh let yuh worry 'bout yo' condition. De doctah sent after some mo' medicine and Ah went tuh see if it come.'

Tea Cake began to cry and Janie hovered him in her arms like a child. She sat on the side of the bed and sort of rocked him back to peace.

'Tea Cake, 'tain't no use in you bein' jealous uh me. In de first place Ah couldn't love nobody but yuh. And in de second place, Ah jus' uh ole woman dat nobody don't want but you.'

'Naw, you ain't neither. You only sound ole when you tell folks when you wuz born, but wid de eye you'se young enough tuh suit most any man. Dat ain't no lie. Ah knows plenty mo' men would take yuh and work hard fuh de privilege. Ah done heard 'em talk.'

'Maybe so, Tea Cake, Ah ain't never tried tuh find out. Ah jus' know dat God snatched me out de fire through you. And Ah loves yuh and feel glad.'

'Thank yuh, ma'am, but don't say you'se ole. You'se uh lil girl baby all de time. God made it so you spent yo' ole age first wid somebody else, and saved up yo' young girl days to spend wid me.'

'Ah feel dat uh way too, Tea Cake and Ah thank yuh fuh sayin' it.'

"Tain't no trouble tuh say whut's already so. You'se uh pretty woman outside uh bein' nice.'

'Aw, Tea Cake.'

'Yeah you is too. Everytime Ah see uh patch uh roses uh somethin' over sportin' they selves makin' out they pretty, Ah tell 'em "Ah want yuh tuh see mah Janie sometime." You must let de flowers see yuh sometimes, heah, Janie?'

'You keep dat up, Tea Cake, Ah'll b'lieve yuh after while,' Janie said archly and fixed him back in bed. It was then she felt the pistol under the pillow. It gave her a quick ugly throb, but she didn't ask him about it since he didn't say. Never had Tea Cake slept with a pistol under his head before. 'Neb' mind 'bout all dat cleanin' round de front yard,' he told her as she straightened up from fixing the bed. 'You stay where Ah kin see yuh.'

'All right, Tea Cake, jus' as you say.'

'And if Mis' Turner's lap-legged brother come prowlin' by heah you kin tell 'im Ah got him stopped wid four wheel brakes. 'Tain't no need of him standin' round watchin' de job.'

'Ah won't be tellin' 'im nothin' 'cause Ah don't expect tuh see 'im.'

Tea Cake had two bad attacks that night. Janie saw a changing look come in his face. Tea Cake was gone. Something else was looking out of his face. She made up her mind to be off after the doctor with the first glow of day. So she was up and dressed when Tea Cake awoke from the fitful sleep that had come to him just before day. He almost snarled when he saw her dressed to go.

207

'Where are you goin', Janie?'

'After de doctor, Tea Cake. You'se too sick tuh be heah in dis house 'thout de doctah. Maybe we oughta git yuh tuh de hospital.'

'Ah ain't goin' tuh no hospital no where. Put dat in yo' pipe and smoke it. Guess you tired uh waitin' on me and doing fuh me. Dat ain't de way Ah been wid *you*. Ah never is been able tuh do enough fuh yuh.'

'Tea Cake, you'se sick. You'se takin' everything in de way Ah don't mean it. Ah couldn't never be tired uh waitin' on you. Ah'm just skeered you'se too sick fuh me tuh handle. Ah wants yuh tuh git well, honey. Dat's all.'

He gave her a look full of blank ferocity and gurgled in his throat. She saw him sitting up in bed and moving about so that he could watch her every move. And she was beginning to feel fear of this strange thing in Tea Cake's body. So when he went out to the outhouse she rushed to see if the pistol was loaded. It was a six shooter and three of the chambers were full. She started to unload it but she feared he might break it and find out she knew. That might urge his disordered mind to action. If that medicine would only come! She whirled the cylinder so that if he even did draw the gun on her it would snap three times before it would fire. She would at least have warning. She could either run or try to take it away before it was too late. Anyway Tea Cake wouldn't hurt *her*. He was jealous and wanted to scare her. She'd just be in the kitchen as usual and never let on. They'd laugh over it when he got well. She found the box of cartridges, however, and emptied it. Just as well to take the rifle from back of the head of the bed. She broke it and put the shell in her apron pocket and put it in a corner in the kitchen almost behind the stove where it was hard to see. She could outrun his knife if it came to that. Of course she was too fussy, but it did no harm to play safe. She ought not to let poor sick Tea Cake do something that would run him crazy when he found out what he had done.

She saw him coming from the outhouse with a queer loping gait, swinging his head from side to side and his jaws clenched in a funny way. This was too awful! Where was Dr Simmons with that medicine? She was glad she was here to look after him. Folks would do such mean things to her Tea Cake if they saw him in such a fix. Treat Tea Cake like he was some mad dog when nobody in the world had more kindness about them. All he needed was for the doctor to come on with that medicine. He came back into the house without speaking, in fact, he did not seem to notice she was there and fell heavily into the bed and slept. Janie was standing by the stove washing up the dishes when he spoke to her in a queer cold voice.

'Janie, how come you can't sleep in de same bed wid me no mo'?'

'De doctah told you tuh sleep by yo'self, Tea Cake. Don't yuh remember him tellin' you dat yistiddy?'

'How come you ruther sleep on uh pallet than tuh sleep in de bed wid me?' Janie saw then that he had the gun in his hand that was hanging to his side. 'Answer me when Ah speak.'

'Tea Cake, Tea Cake, honey! Go lay down! Ah'll be too glad tuh be in dere wid yuh de minute de doctor say so. Go lay back down. He'll be heah wid some new medicine right away.'

'Janie, Ah done went through everything tuh be good tuh you and it hurt me tuh mah heart tuh be ill treated lak Ah is.'

The gun came up unsteadily but quickly and levelled at Janie's breast. She noted that even in his delirium he took good aim. Maybe he would point to scare her, that was all.

The pistol snapped once. Instinctively Janie's hand flew behind her on the rifle and brought it around. Most likely this would scare him off. If only the doctor would come! If anybody at all would come! She broke the rifle deftly and shoved in the shell as the second click told her that Tea Cake's suffering brain was urging him on to kill.

'Tea Cake put down dat gun and go back tuh bed!' Janie yelled at him as the gun wavered weakly in his hand.

He steadied himself against the jamb of the door and Janie thought to run into him and grab his arm, but she saw the quick motion of taking aim and heard the click. Saw the ferocious look in his eyes and went mad with fear as she had done in the water that time. She threw up the barrel of the rifle in frenzied hope and fear. Hope that he'd see it and run, desperate fear for her life. But if Tea Cake could have counted costs he would not have been there with the pistol in his hands. No knowledge of fear nor rifles nor anything else was there. He paid no more attention to the pointing gun than if it were Janie's dog finger. She saw him stiffen himself all over as he levelled and took aim. The fiend in him must kill and Janie was the only thing living he saw.

The pistol and the rifle rang out almost together. The pistol just enough after the rifle to seem its echo. Tea Cake crumpled as his bullet buried itself in the joist over Janie's head. Janie saw the look on his face and leaped forward as he crashed forward in her arms. She was trying to hover him as he closed his teeth in the flesh of her forearm. They came down heavily like that. Janie struggled to a sitting position and pried the dead Tea Cake's teeth from her arm.

It was the meanest moment of eternity. A minute before she was just a scared human being fighting for its life. Now she was her sacrificing self with Tea Cake's head in her lap. She had wanted him to live so much and he was dead. No hour is ever eternity, but it has its right to weep. Janie held his head tightly to her breast and wept and thanked him wordlessly for giving her the chance for loving service. She had to hug him tight for soon he would be gone, and she had to tell him for the last time. Then the grief of outer darkness descended.

So that same day of Janie's great sorrow she was in jail. And when the doctor told the sheriff and the judge how it was, they all said she must be tried that same day. No need to punish her in jail by waiting. Three hours in jail and then they set the court for her case. The time was short and everything, but sufficient people were there. Plenty of white people came to look on this strangeness. And all the Negroes for miles around. Who was it didn't know about the love between Tea Cake and Janie?

The court set and Janie saw the judge who had put on a great robe to listen about her and Tea Cake. And twelve more white men had stopped whatever they were doing to listen and pass on what happened between Janie and Tea Cake Woods, and as to whether things were done right or not. That was funny too. Twelve strange men who didn't know a thing about people like Tea Cake and her were going to sit on the thing. Eight or ten white women had come to look at her too. They wore good clothes and had the pinky color that comes of good food. They were nobody's poor white folks. What need had *they* to leave their richness to come look on Janie in her overalls? But they didn't seem too mad, Janie thought. It would be nice if she could make *them* know how it was instead of those menfolks. Oh, and she hoped that undertaker was fixing Tea Cake up fine. They ought to let her go see about it. Yes, and there was Mr Prescott that she knew right well and he was going to tell the twelve men to kill her for shooting Tea Cake. And a strange man from Palm Beach who was going to ask them not to kill her, and none of them knew.

Then she saw all of the colored people standing up in the back of the courtroom. Packed tight like a case of celery, only much darker than that. They were all against her, she could see. So many were there against her that a light slap from each one of them would have beat her to death. She felt them pelting her with dirty thoughts. They were there with their tongues cocked and loaded, the only real weapon left to weak folks. The only killing tool they are allowed to use in the presence of white folks.

So it was all ready after a while and they wanted people to talk so that they could know what was right to do about Janie Woods the relic of Tea Cake's Janie. The white part of the room got calmer the more serious it got, but a tongue storm struck the Negroes like wind among palm trees. They talked all of a sudden and all together like a choir and the top parts of their bodies moved on the rhythm of it. They sent word by the bailiff to Mr Prescott they wanted to testify in the case. Tea Cake was a good boy. He had been good to that woman. No nigger woman ain't never been treated no better. Naw suh! He worked like a dog for her and nearly killed himself saving her in the storm, then soon as he got a little fever from the water, she had took up with another man. Sent for him to come there from way off. Hanging was too good. All they wanted was a chance to testify. The bailiff went up and the sheriff and the judge, and the police chief, and the lawyers all came together to listen for a few minutes, then they parted again and the sheriff took the stand and told how Janie had come to his house with the doctor and how he found things when he drove out to hers.

Then they called Dr Simmons and he told about Tea Cake's sickness and how dangerous it was to Janie and the whole town, and how he was scared for her and thought to have Tea Cake locked up in the jail, but seeing Janie's care he neglected to do it. And how he found Janie all bit in the arm, sitting on the floor and petting Tea Cake's head when he got there. And the pistol right by his hand on the floor. Then he stepped down.

'Any further evidence to present, Mr Prescott?' the judge asked.

'No, Your Honor. The State rests.'

The palm tree dance began again among the Negroes in the back. They had come to talk. The State couldn't rest until it heard.

'Mistah Prescott, Ah got somethin' tuh say,' Sop-de-Bottom spoke out anonymously from the anonymous herd.

The courtroom swung round on itself to look.

'If you know what's good for you, you better shut your mouth up until somebody calls you,' Mr Prescott told him coldly.

'Yassuh, Mr Prescott.'

'We are handling this case. Another word out of *you*; out of any of you niggers back there, and I'll bind you over to the big court.'

'Yassuh.'

The white women made a little applause and Mr Prescott glared at the back of the house and stepped down. Then the strange white man that was going to talk for her got up there. He whispered a little with the clerk and then called on Janie to take the stand and talk. After a few little questions he told her to tell just how it happened and to speak the truth, the whole truth and nothing but the truth. So help her God.

They all leaned over to listen while she talked. First thing she had to remember was she was not at home. She was in the courthouse fighting something and it wasn't death. It was worse than that. It was lying thoughts. She had to go way back to let them know how she and Tea Cake had been with one another so they could see she could never shoot Tea Cake out of malice.

She tried to make them see how terrible it was that things were fixed so that Tea Cake couldn't come back to himself until he had got rid of that mad dog that was in him and he couldn't get rid of the dog and live. He had to die to get rid of the dog. But she hadn't wanted to kill him. A man is up against a hard game when he must die to beat it. She made them see how she couldn't ever want to be rid of him. She didn't plead to anybody. She just sat there and told and when she was through she hushed. She had been through for some time before the judge and the lawyer and the rest seemed to know it. But she sat on in that trial chair until the lawyer told her she could come down.

'The defense rests,' her lawyer said. Then he and Prescott whispered together and both of them talked to the judge in secret up high there where he sat. Then they both sat down.

'Gentlemen of the jury, it is for you to decide whether the defendant has committed a cold blooded murder or whether she is a poor broken creature, a devoted wife trapped by unfortunate circumstances who really in firing a rifle bullet into the heart of her late husband did a great act of mercy. If you find her a wanton killer you must bring in a verdict of first degree murder. If the evidence does not justify that then you must set her free. There is no middle course.'

The jury filed out and the courtroom began to drone with talk, a few people got up and moved about. And Janie sat like a lump and waited. It was not death she feared. It was misunderstanding. If they made a verdict that she didn't want Tea Cake and wanted him dead, then that was a real sin and a shame. It was worse than murder. Then the jury was back again. Out five minutes by the courthouse clock.

'We find the death of Vergible Woods to be entirely accidental and justifiable, and that no blame should rest upon the defendant Janie Woods.'

So she was free and the judge and everybody up there smiled with her and shook her hand. And the white women cried and stood around her like a protecting wall and the Negroes, with heads hung down, shuffled out and away. The sun was almost down and Janie had seen the sun rise on her troubled love and then she had shot Tea Cake and had been in jail and had been tried for her life and now she was free. Nothing to do with the little that was left of the day but to visit the kind white friends who had realized her feelings and thank them. So the sun went down.

She took a room at the boarding house for the night and heard the men talking around the front.

'Aw you know dem white mens wuzn't gointuh do nothin' tuh no woman dat look lak her.'

'She didn't kill no white man, did she? Well, long as she don't shoot no white man she kin kill jus' as many niggers as she please.'

'Yeah, de nigger women kin kill up all de mens dey wants tuh, but you bet' not kill one uh dem. De white folks will sho hang yuh if yuh do.'

'Well, you know whut dey say "uh white man and uh nigger woman is de freest thing on earth." Dey do as dey please.'

Janie buried Tea Cake in Palm Beach. She knew he loved the 'Glades but it was too low for him to lie with water maybe washing over him with every heavy rain. Anyway, the 'Glades and its waters had killed him. She wanted him out of the way of storms, so she had a strong vault built in the cemetery at West Palm Beach. Janie had wired to Orlando for money to put him away. Tea Cake was the son of Evening Sun, and nothing was too good. The Undertaker did a handsome job and Tea Cake slept royally on his white silken couch among the roses she had bought. He looked almost ready to grin. Janie bought him a brand new guitar and put it in his hands. He would be thinking up new songs to play to her when she got there.

Sop and his friends had tried to hurt her but she knew it was because they loved Tea Cake and didn't understand. So she sent Sop word and to all the others through him. So the day of the funeral they came with shame and apology in their faces. They wanted her quick forgetfulness. So they filled up and overflowed the ten sedans that Janie had hired and added others to the line. Then the band played, and Tea Cake rode like a Pharaoh to his tomb. No expensive veils and robes for Janie this time. She went on in her overalls. She was too busy feeling grief to dress like grief.

20

Because they really loved Janie just a little less than they had loved Tea Cake, and because they wanted to think well of themselves, they wanted their hostile attitude forgotten. So they blamed it all on Mrs Turner's brother and ran him off the muck again. They'd show him about coming back there posing like he was good looking and putting himself where men's wives could look at him. Even if they didn't look it wasn't his fault, he had put himself in the way.

'Naw, Ah ain't mad wid Janie,' Sop went around explaining. 'Tea Cake had done gone crazy. You can't blame her for puhtectin' herself. She wuz crazy 'bout 'im. Look at de way she put him away. Ah ain't got anything in mah heart aginst her. And Ah never woulda thought uh thing, but de very first day dat lap-legged nigger come back heah makin' out he wuz lookin' fuh work, he come astin' me 'bout how wuz Mr and Mrs Woods makin' out. Dat goes tuh show yuh he wuz up tuh somethin'.

'So when Stew-Beef and Bootyny and some of de rest of

'em got behind 'im he come runnin' tuh me tuh save 'im. Ah told 'im, don't come tuh *me* wid yo' hair blowin' back, 'cause, Ah'm gointuh send yuh, and Ah sho did. De bitches' baby!' That was enough, they eased their feelings by beating him and running him off. Anyway, their anger against Janie had lasted two whole days and that was too long to keep remembering anything. Too much of a strain.

They had begged Janie to stay on with them and she had stayed a few weeks to keep them from feeling bad. But the muck meant Tea Cake and Tea Cake wasn't there. So it was just a great expanse of black mud. She had given away everything in their little house except a package of garden seed that Tea Cake had bought to plant. The planting never got done because he had been waiting for the right time of the moon when his sickness overtook him. The seeds reminded Janie of Tea Cake more than anything else because he was always planting things. She had noticed them on the kitchen shelf when she came home from the funeral and had put them in her breast pocket. Now that she was home, she meant to plant them for remembrance.

Janie stirred her strong feet in the pan of water. The tiredness was gone so she dried them off on the towel.

'Now, dat's how everything wuz, Pheoby, jus' lak Ah told yuh. So Ah'm back home again and Ah'm satisfied tuh be heah. Ah done been tuh de horizon and back and now Ah kin set heah in mah house and live by comparisons. Dis house ain't so absent of things lak it used tuh be befo' Tea Cake come along. It's full uh thoughts, 'specially dat bedroom.

'Ah know all dem sitters-and-talkers gointuh worry they guts into fiddle strings till dey find out whut we been talkin' 'bout. Dat's all right, Pheoby, tell 'em. Dey gointuh make 'miration 'cause mah love didn't work lak they love, if dey ever had any. Then you must tell 'em dat love ain't somethin' lak uh grindstone dat's de same thing everywhere and do de same thing tuh everything it touch. Love is lak de sea. It's uh movin' thing, but still and all, it takes its shape from de shore it meets, and it's different with every shore.'

'Lawd!' Pheoby breathed out heavily, 'Ah done growed ten feet higher from jus' listenin' tuh you, Janie. Ah ain't satisfied wid mahself no mo'. Ah means tuh make Sam take me fishin' wid him after this. Nobody better not criticize yuh in mah hearin'.'

'Now, Pheoby, don't feel too mean wid de rest of 'em 'cause dey's parched up from not knowin' things. Dem meatskins is *got* tuh rattle tuh make out they's alive. Let 'em consolate theyselves wid talk. 'Course, talkin' don't amount tuh uh hill uh beans when yuh can't do nothin' else. And listenin' tuh dat kind uh talk is jus' lak openin' yo' mouth and lettin' de moon shine down yo' throat. It's uh known fact, Pheoby, you got tuh *go* there tuh *know* there. Yo' papa and yo' mama and nobody else can't tell yuh and show yuh. Two things everybody's got tuh do fuh theyselves. They got tuh go tuh God, and they got tuh find out about livin' fuh theyselves.'

There was a finished silence after that so that for the first time they could hear the wind picking at the pine trees. It made Pheoby think of Sam waiting for her and getting fretful. It made Janie think about that room upstairs – her bedroom. Pheoby hugged Janie real hard and cut the darkness in flight.

Soon everything around downstairs was shut and fastened. Janie mounted the stairs with her lamp. The light in her hand was like a spark of sun-stuff washing her face in fire. Her shadow behind fell black and headlong down the stairs. Now, in her room, the place tasted fresh again. The wind through the open windows had broomed out all the fetid feeling of absence and nothingness. She closed in and sat down. Combing road-dust out of her hair. Thinking.

The day of the gun, and the bloody body, and the courthouse came and commenced to sing a sobbing sigh out of every corner in the room; out of each and every chair and thing. Commenced to sing, commenced to sob and sigh, singing and sobbing. Then Tea Cake came prancing around her where she was and the song of the sigh flew out of the window and lit in the top of the pine trees. Tea Cake, with the sun for a shawl. Of course he wasn't dead. He could never be dead until she herself had finished feeling and thinking. The kiss of his memory made pictures of love and light against the wall. Here was peace. She pulled in her horizon like a great fish-net. Pulled it from around the waist of the world and draped it over her shoulder. So much of life in its meshes! She called in her soul to come and see.

AFTERWORD

I first encountered Zora Neale Hurston in an Afro-American literature course I took in graduate school. She was one of numerous authors surveyed in the two-semester course, which began with Lucy Terry in 1746 and ended with the Black Arts writers of the sixties. Hurston's works were studied as a sort of holdover from the Harlem Renaissance, that period that coincided, at least in part, with the Jazz Age and witnessed the first concerted outpourings of formal artistic expression among Afro-Americans. The most important stylistic developments of the period were the attempt to use Afro-American folk culture as a basis for creating distinctive black contributions to serious or 'high' culture, and the attempt to repudiate the false and degrading stereotypes promulgated in Anglo-American popular (and high) culture by exploring the individual consciousness hidden behind the enveloping Sambo mask. *Their Eyes Were Watching God* was published in 1937, almost ten years after the stock market crash of 1929, the date most often given as the end of the

Harlem Renaissance.* The book's rural southern settings, the use of dialect and folkloric materials, even its romantic theme represent much that was distinctive and significant about this period.

It would have been difficult for most of the students in that class to prove these statements. We 'read at' Zora Neale in the same way we had read at most of the writers studied to that point (and quite a few that came after): in snatches. And although I'd never seen – much less read – an embarrassing number of the works discussed in the course, I felt lucky to be there. Afro-American literature was still an exotic subject then, rarely taught on any regular basis. Most of the works of the writers we studied had been out of print for a long time, and students relied on lectures, anthology selections (when available), what samplings could be garnered in a Saturday spent in a rare-book collection or an evening in the reserve book reading room, and Robert Bone's *The Negro Novel in America* for our impressions of William Wells Brown, Frances Harper, William Attaway, Jessie Fauset, and Zora Neale Hurston. We were fortunate to be in Washington, D.C., with its several large university and public libraries and the Library of Congress. But library holdings really couldn't make up for those out-of-print books. The few personal or library copies of this or that were shared around, but there were about forty students in the class. By the time a person got the book, it had

---

* Contemporary critics are less dogmatic about the dates; some consider the entire period between the world wars, 1919–39, as the Renaissance. See, for example, Eugene B. Redmond, *Drum-Voices* (New York: Doubleday, 1976).

usually been discussed at least four weeks prior, and the owner needed it back to write a paper. So, like many students in the class, out of sheer frustration I ended by concentrating on contemporary authors (i.e., Wright, Ellison, Baldwin), whose works were more readily available.

It did, however, finally become my turn to read *Their Eyes Were Watching God*, and I became Zora Neale's for life. In the speech of her characters I heard my own country voice and saw in the heroine something of my own country self. And this last was most wonderful because it was most rare. Black women had been portrayed as characters in numerous novels by blacks and non-blacks. But these portraits were limited by the stereotypical images of, on the one hand, the ham-fisted matriarch, strong and loyal in the defense of the white family she serves (but unable to control or protect her own family without the guidance of some white person), and, on the other, the amoral, instinctual slut. Between these two stereotypes stood the tragic mulatto: too refined and sensitive to live under the repressive conditions endured by ordinary blacks and too colored to enter the white world.

Even the few idealized portraits of black women evoked these negative stereotypes. The idealizations were morally uplifting and politically laudable, but their literary importance rests upon just that: the correctness of their moral and political stance. Their value lies in their illuminations of the society's workings and their insights into the ways oppression is institutionalized. They provide, however, few insights into character or consciousness. And when we (to use Alice Walker's lovely phrase) go in search of our mother's gardens, it's not really to learn who trampled on them or how or even why – we usually know that already. Rather, it's to learn what our mothers planted there, what they thought as they sowed, and how they survived the blighting of so many fruits. Zora Hurston's life and work present us with insights into just these concerns.

The date of her birth, like many of the facts of her life, is a matter of uncertainty. Robert E. Hemenway, in a first and much-needed biography, *Zora Neale Hurston* (Urbana: University of Illinois Press, 1977), cites January 7, 1901, as the date that makes the most sense.* Eatonville, Florida, the small, all-black town where Zora was born, is the setting for two of her four published novels, *Jonah's Gourd Vine* (1934) and *Their Eyes Were Watching God*. The gatherings on the front porch of the town's general store came to symbolize for Hurston the richness of Afro-American oral culture, and she struggled for much of her career to give literary renderings of that oral richness and to portray the complex individuality of its unlettered, 'uncultured' *folk* creators. Hurston studied cultural anthropology under Franz Boas, first as a student at Barnard College and later at Columbia University. In 1927 she returned to the South, where she lived off and on for the rest of her life, collecting examples of and participating in the dynamic culture created in the saw mills, turpentine camps, and small-town jook joints and cafés. She had at her command a large store of

* The point is not so much Zora's actual age, but rather, that the contradictory dates indicate how closely the gregarious Zora guarded her private life. Hemenway's book is a gold mine on Zora, her work, and the Renaissance.

stories, songs, incidents, idiomatic phrases, and metaphors; her ear for speech rhythms must have been remarkable. Most importantly, she had the literary intelligence and developed the literary skill to convey the power and beauty of this heard speech and lived experience on the printed page.

Hurston's evocations of the lifestyles of rural blacks have not been equaled; but to stress the ruralness of Hurston's settings or to characterize her diction solely in terms of exotic 'dialect' spellings is to miss her deftness with language. In the speech of her characters, black voices – whether rural or urban, northern or southern – come alive. Her fidelity to diction, metaphor, and syntax – whether in direct quotations or in paraphrases of characters' thoughts – rings, even across forty years, with an aching familiarity that is a testament to Hurston's skill and to the durability of black speech. Yet Zora's personality and actions were so controversial that for a long time she was remembered more as a *character* of the Renaissance than as one of the most serious and gifted artists to emerge during this period. She was a notable tale-teller, mimic, and wit, confident to the point of brashness (some might even say beyond), who refused to conform to conventional notions of ladylike behavior and middle-class decorum. To one of her contemporaries, she was the first black nationalist; to another, a handkerchief-head Uncle Tom. Larry Neal, in his recent introduction to her autobiography, *Dust Tracks on a Road* (1942; reprinted, New York: J. B. Lippincott, 1971), calls her a 'kind of Pearl Bailey of the literary world . . . a conservative in her political outlook with a remarkable understanding of a blues aesthetic and its accompanying sensibility.' To Alice Walker and others of our generation, Zora was a woman bent on discovering and defining herself, a woman who spoke and wrote her own mind.

Something of the questing quality that characterized Zora's own life informs the character of Janie – without, of course, the forcefulness of Hurston's own personality. In this and other instances, the character is more conventional than the author, for despite obvious idealizations, Janie operates in a 'real' world. Her actions, responses, and motivations are consistent with that reality and the growing assertiveness of her own self-definitions. Where Janie yearns, Zora was probably driven; where Janie submits, Zora would undoubtedly have rebelled. Author and character objectify their definitions of self in totally different ways. Zora was evidently unable to satisfactorily define herself in a continuing relationship with a man, whereas such definition is the essence of Janie's romantic vision and its ultimate fulfillment provides the plot of the novel. But in their desire and eventual insistence that their men accord them treatment due equals, they are one.

Janie is raised by her grandmother, Nanny, an ex-slave who has suffered most of the abuses heaped upon black women in slavery: hard physical labor, poor rations, whippings, the threat of being separated from children and mate, coerced sexual relations with the master, and vindictive treatment at the hands of the mistress. Nanny doesn't fare much better in freedom; her daughter, whom she'd hoped to make into a schoolteacher as the fulfillment of her own frustrated dreams, is raped by a local schoolteacher. Janie is the result of this brutal coupling. After Janie's birth, the mother runs away, leaving Janie in Nanny's care. Nanny sees in the baby girl another chance to fulfill her own dreams 'of whut a woman oughta be and to do.' Nanny works for a white family, and Janie is raised (as the saying goes) in the white folks' yard, elevated above the common run of black people and separated from the sustenance that the community provides. She is six before she even realizes that she is black. The revelation doesn't devastate Janie. Rather, it stands as both a symbol of Nanny's unrealistic attempts to shield the girl from life and a metaphor for Janie's lack of self-knowledge.

Janie is just entering young womanhood when Nanny, frightened by the advent of that maturity, tries to school Janie about the lot of black women: 'Honey, de white man is de ruler of everything as fur as Ah been able tuh find out . . . de white man throw down de load and tell de nigger man tuh pick it up. He pick it up because he have to, but he don't tote it. He hand it to his womenfolks. De nigger woman is de mule uh de world so fur as Ah can see.' The image of the black woman as the mule of the world becomes a metaphor for the roles that Janie repudiates in her quest for self-fulfillment and the belief against which the book implicitly argues. Love, for the old ex-slave, is 'de very prong all us black women gits hung on': that is, as Nanny goes on to explain, wanting a dressed-up dude who can't keep himself in shoe leather, much less provide for someone else; his women tote that burden for him. Love doesn't kill; it just makes a black woman sweat. Nanny dies believing that the only armor against this fate is money or the protection of good white people.

Janie holds onto her vision of a fulfilled and fulfilling love through two loveless marriages. Nanny arranges Janie's first marriage, to Logan Killicks, an older farmer whose sixty acres ought to provide Janie with the security Nanny has been able to achieve only through working for white families. Killicks, however, can't see any further than his plow, and Janie is stifled by his plodding nature. Realizing that Janie doesn't return his love, he tries to destroy her spirit by threatening to make her help with the back-breaking labor of the farm. Nanny's metaphor is almost actualized, but Janie rebels. She runs away with Joe Starks, an ambitious go-getter who pauses on his way to becoming 'a big voice' in the world (mayor and postmaster, principal landowner and businessman in Eatonville) to marry Janie. Joe stops making 'speeches with rhymes' to Janie almost as soon as the wedding ceremony is over. Instead of love talk, he buys her the best of everything.

Joe provides Janie with the 'front porch' existence of Nanny's dreams, but in doing so, he isolates her from direct participation in any life except his own. His stranglehold on her life and definition of self is symbolized in his prohibition against her participation in the tale-tellings, mock flirtations, and other comic activities that center around or emanate from the porch of his general store. Despite his own pleasure in these sessions, he charges that the people who gather at them are 'trashy,' and Janie is Mrs Mayor Starks. They don't even own their own houses, and a woman of Janie's respectability shouldn't want to pass the time of day with them. Thus, 'when Lige or Sam or Walter or some of the other big picture talkers were using a side of the world for a canvas, Joe would hustle her off inside the store to sell something.' The link between selling and Joe's attempt to isolate Janie from authentic membership in the community is striking and deliberate: Janie is Joe's personal possession, 'de mayor's wife.' It is an image that, as Hurston says of their marriage, is soon deserted by the spirit. But it is not only class that Joe uses as a means of browbeating Janie into submission. She is a woman; her place is in the home (or wherever he tells her to be, like the store, where he forces her to clerk because her many mistakes give him another opportunity to belittle her intelligence). Someone has to think for women, children, chickens, and cows. The instances of Joe's chauvinism are obvious and many. The metaphor of the mule is further reified in Joe's insistence that Janie tote his narrow, stultifying notions of what behavior is appropriate to her class and sex. Rooted at first only in the specificity of the Afro-American female experience, the metaphor has been transformed into one for the female condition; Janie's individual quest for fulfillment becomes any woman's tale.

Joe dies of a kidney ailment after some years of marriage. Janie, now a widow with property and still a very attractive woman, meets and marries Vergible 'Tea Cake' Woods, an itinerant laborer and gambler much younger than herself. Tea Cake is love and laughter and talking in rhymes. However, he fulfills Janie's dreams because he requires only that she be herself. At home with himself, he has no need to dominate Janie or curb her self-expression in order to prove his masculinity. In contrast to the social status that her previous marriages gave her (and the book is filled with contrasts), Janie's place in her relationship with Tea Cake is on the muck, a booming farming area, picking beans at his side. Janie has come *down*, that paradoxical place in Afro-American literature that is both a physical bottom and the setting for the character's attainment of a penultimate self-knowledge (think of Ellison's Invisible Man in his basement room or the hero of Baraka's *The System of Dante's Hell* in the Bottoms). Down on the muck, Janie's horizons are expanded by the love and respect she shares with Tea Cake. She becomes a participant in the life that Nanny, Logan, Joe, and other friends and advisors would have her believe is beneath her. 'The men held big arguments here like they used to do on the store porch. Only here, she could listen and laugh and even talk some herself if she wanted to. She got so she could tell big stories herself from listening to the rest.' Janie comes at last into her own, at home with herself, her man, and her world. This unity is symbolized in a final play on the black-woman-as-mule image. Tea Cake asks and Janie consents to work in the fields with him, because neither wants to be parted from the other even during the working day. Their love for each other makes the stoop labor of bean picking seem almost play. The differences between the image and the reversal of that image are obvious: Tea Cake has asked, not commanded; his request stems from a desire to be with Janie, to share every aspect of his life with her, rather than from a desire to coerce her into some mindless submission. It isn't the white man's burden that Janie carries; it is the gift of her own love.

Sherley Anne Williams

1978–2018

40 YEARS OF
VIRAGO MODERN CLASSICS

The first Virago Modern Classic, *Frost in May* by Antonia White, was published in 1978. It launched a list dedicated to the celebration of women writers and to the rediscovery and reprinting of their works. Its aim was, and is, to demonstrate the existence of a female tradition in literature, and to broaden the sometimes narrow definition of a 'classic'. Published with new introductions by some of today's best writers, the books are chosen for many reasons: they may be great works of literature; they may be wonderful period pieces; they may reveal particular aspects of women's lives; they may be classics of comedy, storytelling, letter-writing or autobiography.

'The Virago Modern Classics list contains some of the greatest fiction and non-fiction of the modern age, by authors whose lives were frequently as significant as their writing. Still captivating, still memorable, still utterly essential reading' SARAH WATERS

'The Virago Modern Classics list is wonderful. It's quite simply one of the best and most essential things that has happened in publishing in our time. I hate to think where we'd be without it' ALI SMITH

'The Virago Modern Classics have reshaped literary history and enriched the reading of us all. No library is complete without them' MARGARET DRABBLE

'The writers are formidable, the production handsome. The whole enterprise is thoroughly grand' LOUISE ERDRICH

'Good news for everyone writing and reading today'
HILARY MANTEL

VIRAGO MODERN CLASSICS

AUTHORS INCLUDE:

Elizabeth von Arnim, Beryl Bainbridge,
Pat Barker, Nina Bawden, Vera Brittain, Angela Carter,
Willa Cather, Barbara Comyns, E. M. Delafield, Polly Devlin,
Monica Dickens, Elaine Dundy, Nell Dunn, Nora Ephron,
Janet Flanner, Janet Frame, Miles Franklin, Marilyn French,
Stella Gibbons, Charlotte Perkins Gilman, Rumer Godden,
Radclyffe Hall, Helene Hanff, Josephine Hart, Shirley Hazzard,
Bessie Head, Patricia Highsmith, Winifred Holtby, Zora Neale
Hurston, Elizabeth Jenkins, Molly Keane, Rosamond Lehmann,
Anne Lister, Rose Macaulay, Shena Mackay, Beryl Markham,
Daphne du Maurier, Mary McCarthy, Kate O'Brien, Grace
Paley, Barbara Pym, Mary Renault, Stevie Smith, Muriel Spark,
Elizabeth Taylor, Angela Thirkell, Sylvia Townsend Warner,
Mary Webb, Eudora Welty, Rebecca West,
Edith Wharton, Antonia White

CHILDREN'S CLASSICS INCLUDE:

Joan Aiken, Nina Bawden, Frances Hodgson Burnett,
Susan Coolidge, Rumer Godden, L. M. Montgomery,
Edith Nesbit, Noel Streatfeild, P. L. Travers

THE VIRAGO MODERN CLASSICS
40TH ANNIVERSARY SERIES

Frost in May

ANTONIA WHITE

Introduced by Tessa Hadley

'Intense, troubling, semi-miraculous ...
It is not the only school story to be a
classic; but I can think of no other that
is a work of art' ELIZABETH BOWEN

A View of the Harbour

ELIZABETH TAYLOR

Introduced by Sarah Waters

'Every one of her books is a treat
and this is my favourite, because of
its wonderful cast of characters, and
because of the deftness with which
Taylor's narrative moves between
them ... A wonderful writer'
SARAH WATERS